THE NIGHT OF THE
SLEEPOVER

BOOKS BY KERRY WILKINSON

Truly, Madly, Amy

THE NIGHT OF THE
SLEEPOVER

KERRY WILKINSON

bookouture

Published by Bookouture in 2023

An imprint of Storyfire Ltd.
Carmelite House
50 Victoria Embankment
London EC4Y 0DZ

www.bookouture.com

ISBN: 978-1-83525-023-5
eBook ISBN: 978-1-83525-022-8

ONE

ONE DAY AFTER THE SLEEPOVER

SUNDAY 19 DECEMBER 1999

It was always Sunday mornings when the birds went mental. Every other day, when Leah had to be up for school, she wouldn't notice them. They'd be quietly keeping to themselves, not bothering anyone, and certainly not waking her up. Sunday would then roll around, when the opportunity to sleep in late presented itself, and the birds would be outside doing their nut from the second the sun came up.

Leah eased open her eyes and the birds were instantly an afterthought. Swirling green and pink stars replaced the sleepy grey behind her eyes, and it took a moment to remember she wasn't in her own bed.

Only a moment.

If she'd dreamt, it had been instantly forgotten. The floor of Vicky's living room was far more solid than Leah's mattress at home, not that it made much difference. Leah always slept solidly once she got off. She'd slept through a car crash once, having woken up to see the neighbour's wall demolished. Leah had found out about it the next day, once the car had already been towed.

It wasn't only car crashes, it was the arguments, too. Sleeping through those was Leah's real talent, but – somehow – chirping birds crept through her defences.

Leah had certainly slept solidly the night before and, if not for the birds having their weekly Sunday morning party, she would still be out of it.

The swirling stars were clearing as Leah blinked and tried to roll herself into a sitting position. It would have been easier if she wasn't cocooned in her sleeping bag. She kicked her legs, fighting against the material, until she caterpillared herself upwards.

And... yawn.

Oh, yeah.

There it was.

There had been all those drinks, mainly that vodka Vicky had found, which explained why Leah's stomach was gurgling.

The vodka.

Leah remembered now.

Not only the vodka, all that pizza. It was all or nothing for Leah when it came to food. Literal feast or famine.

She blinked and took in the room properly, scanning the other sleeping bags. There were three more, one for each of the other girls who'd been at the sleepover. Three more pillows, too.

Except none of them were occupied.

It took Leah a few more moments to fully grasp that she was the only person in the living room.

She wrestled her way out of her sleeping bag and stood, as the bristles of the carpet scratched her bare feet. The sofa was empty, and so was the armchair. The *Titanic* VHS case was splayed on the floor, next to the video player: the tape probably still in the machine. There was a fake Christmas tree at the back of the room, taking up space.

Leah crept to the back of the room and opened the curtains. It was a bright morning, and she was temporarily dazzled by the white. In the garden, the barbecue cover had blown off, and was joined on the ground by a bin lid. The grass was speckled by brown mounds of soil.

No people, though.

Into the kitchen, and there was little to see other than a letter from the school that was attached to the fridge with a magnetic letter 'V'. It was about the end-of-term school trip and Leah had been given the same letter to take home. She hadn't bothered giving it to her mum, and it wasn't as if they could afford it. It had not made it to Leah's house, having been dispatched into the bin outside the paper shop.

Leah returned to the living room and stared at the empty sleeping bags. They were more or less in a row, with the coffee table shunted to the side to make space. She'd helped Vicky move that table hours before. Leah remembered the vodka bottle, the glasses in the kitchen, the pizza, and then... what?

Where was everybody?

TWO

NOW

THURSDAY

Leah scanned the letter from school that was attached to the fridge. She hesitated, falling through time to another place in which there had been a different letter on a different fridge. It took her a second to focus on the actual words, before she turned to the woman behind her.

'Is Cody going on this?' Leah asked.

Fiona was sitting at the dining table in a cramped kitchen, wedged in by a drying rail laden with damp children's clothes. She squinted and started to nod. 'The school reckoned they'll find a way to cover the money. He's been doing really well with his reading, and everyone else in his class is going.'

Leah re-read the top few lines, about a class trip to the theatre. It was the sort of thing which Leah always missed out on when she was young. Her mum wasn't the type to get onto the school and ask about a contingency fund for poorer students. That's if one had existed back then.

'Did he get off to school on time today?' Leah asked.

'He's not been late for three weeks. I walk him to the corner but he doesn't like me to go to the gates with him.'

'And his teacher's happy?'

'She said it's been a total turnaround.' Fiona laughed to herself. 'Asked me if he's got a twin, because he's suddenly putting up his hand when he knows the answer.' A pause. 'He goes up to big school next year. Can you believe it? He's going to be so small among the big boys.'

Leah found herself smiling as she nodded along. The draining board was clear, the sink empty, clothes washed and drying. There was a small cluttered pile of mail on the kitchen table but that wasn't a big deal. It wasn't only Cody who'd turned things around.

Except, there was a question Leah still had to ask: 'What about Kevin?'

Fiona's features clouded as she shook her head slightly. She glanced across to the wall, distracted and distant. 'Not heard from him in about six weeks. The DSS are chasing him 'cos he hasn't paid maintenance in four months. I heard he's got a new woman down Whitecliff way.'

Leah pondered the next question. In her role as community support worker, she checked in on various people who'd undergone upheaval in their lives. Their relationships were technically none of her business, except, in reality, it was usually the thing that had led them to where they were.

'Are you OK with that?' she asked.

Fiona's 'She's welcome to him' took half a second too long to come.

It was like a person trying to convince themselves one biscuit would be enough. Leah saw it over and over, as people welcomed destructive forces back into their lives. Still, only so much she could do. For now, the house was in a good state, so was Fiona, and so was Cody.

Leah edged around the kitchen, peering through the back

window towards the small yard. The pile of filled black bin bags that had been there a week ago had been cleared.

'What about your mum?' Leah asked.

Fiona's attention had drifted since the mention of Kevin. Her voice was quieter: 'I've stopped Cody visiting. Don't want him to see her like that. The doctor says she's only got a month left. Maybe not even that...' She blinked and then moved on instantly, nodding towards the back. 'Someone out there had a party Saturday night. Music was on 'til about three. I think the police came...'

Leah looked through the window, towards the direction indicated, though she couldn't see much past the back fence. There wasn't a lot to add. The change of subject had been abrupt, deliberate, and understandable.

She should probably get back to the office anyway.

Before she could move, there was a bang of the letterbox that made both women jump. Fiona was quickly on her feet, shuffling around the drying clothes, and heading into the hall. She was muttering about expecting a parcel but reappeared moments later with the free local newspaper in her hand.

'I told them to stop delivering it,' she said. 'It's all adverts anyway.'

She was angling towards the bin but stopped at the last moment to unfold the paper. As Fiona held it out to take it in, Leah saw it too.

MISSING GIRLS TV DOC CREW IN TOWN

Fiona froze, looking between the paper and Leah, before fumbling an 'Oh...' and then: 'Sorry.'

She offered the paper, and Leah took it without thinking. It felt like the polite thing to do. She stared at the headline, which was topped and tailed by adverts for second-hand cars and someone's gardening services.

'Did you know?' Fiona asked.

Leah was nodding, still staring at the headline. It took her a second to blink back into the room and she put down the paper on the side. She *had* known but it felt more real when there were actual words saying so.

'I'm talking to them tomorrow,' Leah replied, before correcting herself. 'No, later. I think it's later?'

She said it like a question, and suddenly wasn't sure herself. Fiona was only half listening, anyway. Like so many people that knew about Leah's past, which included a *lot* of people in town, they wanted to talk about their own way of experiencing what had happened.

'It was awful, wasn't it?' Fiona said. 'Those girls just... disappeared. And poor you, right there when it happened.'

Leah nodded, though she was blank. She'd heard something similar many times since waking up on Vicky's living-room floor. The facts were simple: four girls had gone to sleep in that house; only one was there the next morning.

Fiona picked up the paper and flipped inside. She was speaking without looking up. 'Do you think this TV lot will find out what happened? You must want to know?'

Leah almost laughed, because it was the understatement to end them all.

Fiona was still speaking, though, this time, she glanced up to catch Leah's eye. 'It's twenty-five years next year?!' She sounded amazed. 'I can't believe how fast it's gone. I was only five or six and after that Mum wouldn't let me have sleepovers when I was growing up. She said she didn't want to be responsible for any girls other than me.'

It was another thing Leah had heard before. There was a generation of the town's kids banned from having their friends stay overnight. What parent would want to have the same thing happen to them as had happened to Vicky's dad? Who craved that responsibility?

Fiona had put down the paper and was counting on her fingers. 'I guess they'd be, thirty-five, six...'

'Thirty-nine,' Leah replied. 'We'd all be thirty-nine, about to turn forty.'

Fiona's eyes widened for a moment. 'Sorry...'

'It's OK.'

The paper was on the side again and Leah watched Fiona's gaze wander towards it momentarily.

'I should get off,' Leah said, angling for her bag. 'I'll be back next week but then we can probably drop down to every two, if that works for you...?'

Fiona wasn't listening and mumbled a vague 'yeah'. She'd come a long way since Leah's first visit, especially considering everything still going on in her life. And then, a moment after the 'yeah', she realised what Leah had said. 'You can still come every week if you want, though? For a cup of tea, or whatever? I can get some Hobnobs in?'

There was a tinge of desperation there, a reminder that Leah's job blurred those lines between professional and friend-ship. It had to.

'I can come over for tea,' Leah replied, assuring the other woman, as she gave the newspaper a final glance. 'And don't worry about the biscuits. I'll bring those.'

THREE

Leah wasn't sure how she'd messed up her days. For some reason, she'd woken up thinking she was meeting the documentary crew tomorrow. If it hadn't been for the newspaper at Fiona's house, she'd have turned up for an afternoon at work, with a boss querying why she was there.

As it was, she was standing on a street that lived in her dreams. There was a steady smattering of detached and semi-detached houses along each side, plus cars on both sides. A sort of leafy nothing street that existed in every town up and down the land. Nobody loved the area but nobody hated it either. There'd be Facebook groups, cluttered with posts asking if anyone had heard the noisy motorcycle the night before, or complaining about rumours of a bike lane going in.

Off to the side, a navy van was parked with the back doors open. Two men were sitting on the tailgate, chatting to each other, as a third stood on the pavement, smoking and typing one-handed into his phone.

The last time Leah had seen Owen, he'd been short and dumpy in clothes that were far too big. A stereotypical annoying younger brother, into geeky videogames, who only wore black. He'd grown into his body and was now six foot and a bit, with a sinewy runner's build, wearing jeans with a smart close-fitting shirt. The sort who took one stride when everyone else needed two and carried a designer satchel that he didn't mind calling a manbag.

As soon as Owen spotted Leah, he dropped his cigarette to the ground and stubbed it out with a brown brogue.

'Lee,' he said, as she approached. He held his arms to the side, though not too wide. A silent offer of a hug hello but no obligation. #Metoo and all that.

The other two men stood from the tailgate of the van and hovered awkwardly, awaiting introduction.

'How long's it been?' Owen added. 'It's gotta be twenty years?'

Leah didn't give much of an answer, though she gave him his hug hello. They barely touched, chests in, arses out, gentle pat on the back, and relax. He looked her up and down; though, in fairness, she did the same to him.

Jasmine had been one of the girls asleep in Vicky's living room twenty-four years before. Owen was her younger brother and, for the most part, an irrelevance in their lives. Leah and her friends had been invested in themselves, their own world, and he just happened to be the annoying kid who had the bedroom next door to Jazz's. Leah could still picture the football posters on his wall, and the steady, hypnotic music that came from his games console.

Owen hadn't seen his sister for twenty-four years. What had it been like for him?

Leah and Owen had been in contact via email over the past couple of months but it had been a long time since she'd seen him in person. If Leah was nearly forty, he was close to thirty-five, though he looked younger.

Owen was wearing a pair of thick-rimmed glasses and, as he

moved them up his nose, Leah remembered that Jazz used to wear glasses as well.

'I think I saw you in town a few times,' Leah said, which felt like it was true. She'd have been twenty-something when he was a teenager. They'd have been in the same pub or club, standing at the same bar, nodding in acknowledgement. Probably.

In truth, she didn't remember when she'd last seen him, and he wasn't listening anyway. He introduced her to a man who had picked up a boom mic, and the other who was now holding a camera. Leah instantly forgot their names, though they went through the rigmarole of 'nice to meet you' and the like. Yes, it was good that the rain had held off.

'I should probably say thanks for agreeing to do this,' Owen added at some point. It didn't feel as if any of them were listening to anybody else. Everybody breezily having their own conversations.

Leah was trying to remember the thing she'd told herself she had to say to him. There was something she wanted to bring up. Something that might make him like her.

And then: 'I watched your film,' she said. It blustered out with unhidden relief that she'd remembered.

Owen blinked, apparently surprised.

'It was on the Channel Four player thing,' Leah added, speaking too quickly. 'It used to be 4OD, then they renamed it about five times. I needed to update the app but it was on there.'

'Oh,' Owen replied, and then: 'What did you think?'

Leah hadn't managed to slow down. 'Good. I work with vulnerable people in the community, and most of them are women. It's nice for people to get a voice, without having to be the victim. You did that really well.'

Yes! That was the line. She'd thought it over the day before while watching Owen's film. She wasn't sure why she wanted him to like her, except that he was Jazz's brother and there had been a time in which she hadn't liked him. It was probably guilt for that.

Owen was nodding along, though not replying. She wondered if he believed her that she'd seen his film. She really had, though she couldn't repeat herself, else it would make it sound like she hadn't.

Instead, Leah nodded past him, towards the street beyond. 'Is this your next film?'

There was more nodding. 'I got a bit of funding from the Lottery and Arts Council,' Owen said. 'I made a big thing of it being the twenty-fifth anniversary next year, which meant everything had to happen now to be ready in time.'

Until his first email had arrived, Leah had managed to blank out this particular anniversary. It would have come up, of course, it always did. The first year had been a big one, mainly because at least some people assumed the three girls were still out there. They were still doing searches of the woods each weekend. There was the local newspaper interest, of course, back when they mattered. The local TV and radio news, as well, plus someone from the *Sun* and the *Mirror* had been in town. In Leah's own world, there had been a big school assembly that she had been allowed to miss.

There might have been something for the second, though Leah didn't remember. After that, it was just numbers. Five years got some attention, then things had really ramped up for the tenth anniversary. One of the Sunday papers had done an E-fit thing, where they had created images of what the missing trio might look like, and then put it on the front page. Someone had knocked on Leah's door, and there had been some *Crime-watch* thing, in which they re-enacted everyone's last-known movements. Leah had watched, even though she'd told herself she wouldn't. Some child actress ended up playing her, though the girl's hair was too short and too blonde. Plus there was some-thing about her accent, probably a bit too posh. Leah had recorded it anyway and watched it over and over, apparently unable to stop herself until, at some point, she had.

The twentieth had been a bit like the tenth – including a new set of E-fits – except everything was a bit fuzzier in people's minds. The missing girls felt like a dream, perhaps a nightmare, as opposed to something that had happened. There had still been a front page in the paper, a few things on various websites, plus four or five minutes on the local news. The big papers and TV channels had forgotten, though.

And now, four years on, they were a little over a year away from the next big date. Except this anniversary was going to come with a full-on documentary, made by the grown-up brother of one of the missing girls.

That would start everything up again. Then they'd be full march onto the thirtieth anniversary, and beyond. It would never stop.

Leah was daydreaming, as one of the other crew members said something about the light, or maybe the time. Owen replied to him as Leah drifted back onto the pavement.

'How's your mum and dad?' she asked. She hadn't seen Jazz's parents in years. When they were teenagers, Jazz's mum used to wear perfume so strong, it made Leah's skin tingle. Leah had never really liked Jazz's mum, mainly because she was convinced Jazz's mum didn't like her. Her dad worked at a bank or something, that sort of place, and rarely seemed to be home.

Owen turned to her as Leah realised he'd been halfway through a sentence about something else. He stumbled for a second. 'They're OK,' he said. 'Moved to France about fifteen years ago. They co-own a vineyard, so Dad talks about grapes all the time.'

Leah nodded along, not really interested, unsure why she'd asked.

'Jazz would have loved it,' he added. 'She always wanted to be a dancer and they're only an hour from Paris on the train.'

Leah was still nodding, unable to stop herself. Had Jazz wanted to be a dancer? It felt like something that could be true, though, if it was, Leah had forgotten. She wondered if there was more she had overlooked about the three girls. Could she even remember their faces without looking at a photo?

Owen was back talking to his crew as Leah tried to listen to what they were saying. She was stuck attempting to picture Jazz. She definitely had long black hair and glasses but then... what?

It took Leah a moment to realise Owen had asked her something. She didn't want to seem distant, so blurted out a: 'Yeah, yeah, that's fine', even though she had no idea to what she had agreed.

It turned out Owen was talking about a series of set-up shots. He wanted her to walk along the road as they filmed her from behind, and then again from the front. Leah was suddenly conscious that she had shown up in her just-come-from-work clothes. She should have probably found a top that was ironed, maybe tidied up her hair a bit? In the rush of mixing up the days, and then trying to remember to tell Owen she liked his film, Leah had somehow forgotten she actually had to be filmed.

She suggested going home to get changed but Owen insisted everything was fine. There was another bit of talk about the light, and then Leah was doing as they'd asked. She walked every day – right foot, left foot – hardly a challenge, except she was suddenly all-too conscious about possibly leaning to the right a bit. Did she have one leg shorter than the other? If so, this was the first time she'd noticed. Then there was a flappy bit of hair that wouldn't stay down, plus the fluttering of a curtain or two as neighbours cottoned on.

Leah felt underprepared and annoyed with herself. This wasn't like her. She was *never* the sort to mix up days. Something about Owen and his emails had thrown her. If it had been anyone else who'd asked, she'd have said 'no' automatically. The director being Jazz's brother had changed everything. Or maybe it wasn't him, and simply the idea of a documentary being made.

Before Leah knew it, she was in front of Vicky's old house. The crew filmed her heading onto the path, although the gate itself was much newer than the old iron one that used to be there. The house itself had new windows, with black frames; there was gravel instead of lawn, cleaner numbers on the wall – and probably dozens of things that had changed.

Except it wasn't *really* different. It was the same house, in the same place.

As they filmed her walking along the path towards the front door, Leah wondered if she'd actually agreed to be interviewed. She must have done, else she wouldn't be there, though she couldn't remember typing the words back to Owen. It felt like something inevitable had happened. Like being invited to the evening do of some distant relative. Everyone wanted to say 'no', but ended up going anyway.

Leah hadn't been back to Vicky's house since she was fifteen. She'd driven past now and then, probably walked past once or twice, but, with the house now in front of her, those memories long gone felt close again.

When she turned, the camera was closer than she realised and she almost bumped into it. The man clasping it held his ground, making Leah step away.

'Are we allowed to be here?' she asked, suddenly realising the implication of where they were. 'Did Tom say it was OK?'

Leah had always thought it strange that Vicky's dad had held onto the house, instead of selling up. Not that Leah herself had moved. She had never quite managed to escape her hometown and, perhaps, it was the same for him. Either that, or nobody wanted to buy the house from which the girls had gone missing.

There was a hint of something detached about Owen. 'He's in a nursing home,' he replied, as he picked at a fingernail.

'Tom?'

Leah pictured Vicky's dad as he'd been back then, with his hairy arms, dark eyes and darker stubbly beard. It had seemed all right to fancy her friend's dad at the time, now it felt weird and distant. The last time she'd seen Tom, he'd lost his hair, was wearing shorts in January, and cradling a pint by himself outside the Wetherspoon's in town. She hadn't even said hello. This was the first she'd heard of him being in a nursing home. What did that mean? Was he ill? Dying?

'Esther signed the releases,' Owen said, as he reached into his back pocket to pull out a Yale key, that he held up for her to see.

'How long has Tom been in a nursing home?' Leah asked.

'I don't know. Esther's been my go-between.'

Owen stepped around her, towards the front door of the house Leah assumed she would never again enter. It felt so matter-of-fact now.

Leah was busy picturing another face: Vicky's older sister, Esther. Somebody else who had never quite left town. Leah was about to ask how Esther was, largely through politeness, when her phone buzzed. She thought she'd put it on silent but the device seemed to have a mind of its own.

Owen pushed open the front door and stood aside, leaving it clear for Leah to enter. She needed a moment, probably more – and, better yet, an excuse to not go in at all.

'Let me just check my phone,' Leah said, hoping the extra few seconds would give her an out. Any luck and there would be an emergency at work. Perhaps Naomi had overdone the peroxide and burned her scalp again? Leah would tell Owen she had to go, and that would be that.

As the cameraman shuffled past her into the house, Leah fumbled her phone from her bag and unlocked the screen. She was meticulous about reading and deleting emails, mainly to stop that little red flag appearing. Leah had never understood people who would proudly have ten-thousand unread emails in their inboxes. It made her shiver thinking about it.

There was only one in hers, something that had just arrived. The sender's name was immediately a curiosity, reading simply 'A Friend'. Leah tried to remember if she knew someone with that last name. Amy Friend? Andy Friend? Something like that?

The subject was 'Read me', and Leah pressed into the email to see the rest. There were only two further words.

Stop them.

FOUR

ONE DAY AFTER THE SLEEPOVER

SUNDAY 19 DECEMBER 1999

Leah had met more than one police officer. They sometimes came to the house if the neighbours called to say they'd heard shouting, or something smashing. By the time that happened, Leah's dad was often long gone, leaving her mum to open the door and insist that everything was fine. Officers would come into the house anyway and sit with Leah in her bedroom, asking if everything really was OK. Those officers always forced their smiles and dropped their tones an octave or two.

This officer was different and it had taken Leah a few minutes to realise what it was. Although the forced smile was consistent, there was something new.

Fear.

The woman sat with her knees together, leaning in, trying to make eye contact, even as her gaze kept flickering to the empty sleeping bags. Nobody had moved them.

'Can you tell me what happened last night, Leah?' she asked. There was the gentlest of quivers to her voice, as her eyes again shifted to the sleeping bags and back.

Leah was sitting on the sofa, with the officer on a chair that had been dragged through from the kitchen.

'Nothing really,' Leah said.

'You must have done something?'

'We watched *Titanic*.' Leah nodded towards the case, which remained open and on the floor, next to the video player.

'Is that all?'

'When it finished, we started watching it again. It's Jazz's favourite film.'

The officer wrote something in her notebook. 'Did you do anything else?'

'Just kind of... talked.'

'What about?'

'Nothing really, just... stuff.'

The officer made another note, which Leah assumed read 'stuff', and then the real question came. 'Did you have anything to drink?'

Leah knew it would come up and she found herself staring at the empty plug socket on the wall. It looked a bit like a face.

'You won't be in trouble,' the officer added.

Leah licked her lips and considered her reply. She continued staring at the socket as she croaked her reply. 'Vicky found some vodka in the cupboard,' she said.

'And you drank that?'

It didn't sound as if there was judgement there.

'Yeah.'

'How much did you drink?'

'I dunno.'

'Have you had vodka before?'

Leah took a breath, still focusing on the plug socket. The officer had said she wasn't going to be in trouble, but it felt like someone would be. 'We stayed here for Halloween,' Leah said. 'We had a bit then, too.'

Something more got scratched into the notebook. 'Did Vicky's dad say it was OK?'

This felt like a big question, too. A loaded one. 'He, er, said it was better if we drank here than outside.'

'Right.'

Those incriminating words were put into the officer's notebook, leaving Leah feeling particularly guilty about dropping him in it.

'He didn't *give* us the vodka,' Leah added, wondering if it might help. 'We still found it.'

'Uh-huh.'

That wasn't written into the notebook.

'Was Vicky's dad here last night?' the officer asked. It felt as if she already knew.

'He was at something to do with football,' Leah replied. 'Some sort of dinner? Or awards?'

'Did he come back last night?'

'I don't remember.'

'So you went to sleep before he got home?'

'I think so.'

Something else was written into the book, and then: 'Did you all go to sleep together?'

'I don't know. I was tired.'

'You fell asleep first?'

'I think so.'

'Do you remember what time you went to sleep?'

Leah finally looked away from the socket, allowing herself a glance across the sleeping bags, past the *Titanic* case, and towards the table at the other end of the room. There was still a plate there, dotted with pizza crumbs.

'I don't know.'

The officer noted something more and then fidgeted in the seat. She scratched her nose and then shifted again. Leah understood why. It didn't feel right being in this room and the only reason they hadn't moved was because it was raining outside, and Vicky's dad was upstairs with a different officer. Some older bloke, who looked a bit more serious than the person downstairs. Leah wondered what was happening to him.

'Do you have any idea at all?' the officer tried again. 'If you started the film at about seven, it's three hours long, so that's ten. Then you said you restarted it...'

Leah wasn't sure if that was a question. It sounded like one but adults had a habit of not saying what they actually meant.

'There's no clock in here,' Leah said. 'I don't have a watch. I don't remember.'

The officer paused for a moment and Leah sensed her frustration. Still that hint of fear there, too. An idea that something awful had happened, that things would never quite be the same again. Leah felt it, too.

'Do you remember anybody saying anything about leaving to go somewhere else?'

'No.' Leah thought for a second and then added: 'Did you go to their houses?'

That got the merest of nods. 'Officers are round there now. Nobody has seen the girls.'

The final two words sat between them as Leah wondered if that's what the police were calling her friends. Not three individuals, already 'the girls'.

'Is there somewhere you used to go as a group?' the officer added, beginning to sound more desperate. 'Some sort of secret place. You can tell me and I don't have to tell anyone you don't want to know.'

'It wasn't like that,' Leah replied. 'We came here a lot.'

Something more was added to the officer's pad. She scratched her head and then glanced to the sleeping bags. There was a bump from upstairs and Leah wondered what was going on with Vicky's dad. Was he going to be in trouble for going to his football thing? They were all fifteen, and it's not like they needed constant supervision.

'How long have you been friends?' the officer asked.

Leah shrugged instinctively, before trying to figure it out. 'Ages,' she said. 'Since primary school, so ten years? Something like that?'

'All four of you?'

'We've always been in the same class.'

'Do you ever fall out?'

'No.'

Leah had answered too quickly, and realised it when the officer looked up from her pad and caught her eye. Leah hadn't been able to return her stare to the plug socket in time.

'Sometimes, I guess,' she added.

'Recently?'

'No.'

The officer paused for a moment, perhaps wondering if there was more to come. It felt as if there was going to be a follow-up question, though it never arrived.

'We've been trying to get hold of your parents,' she said. 'Nobody's answering the door. Are they away?'

Leah made eye contact with the officer. She'd learned a long while back that people tended to believe you more when you did that. 'Mum should be in – but she goes for walks sometimes.'

The officer turned away to add something new to her pad. 'What about your dad?'

'He's in prison.'

The pen stopped mid-word and wobbled in the officer's hand, before she strengthened her grip. 'Prison...?'

She didn't get a chance to ask anything more because there was the sound of voices from somewhere at the front of the house. A man and a woman were talking over each other and, before anyone could stop her, Leah stood and crossed to the front window. She moved into the hall and then opened the front door, standing on the step as a young woman tried to manoeuvre around a uniformed officer. He had his hands wide, trying to block her.

'I live here!' the woman insisted. She was blinking, bleary-eyed, barefooted, and carrying a pair of heels. 'Tell him,' she added, talking to Leah. 'Where's Vick? And Dad?'

'She lives here,' Leah said, partially talking to the first officer, who was standing behind her. 'That's Esther. She's Vicky's sister.'

FIVE

NOW

Leah looked up from the email on her phone and there was a moment in which the house zoomed towards her and then away again. Owen and his crew had gone inside, leaving Leah by herself as she realised she was in the exact spot Esther had once stood, holding those heels. The memory had been gone for so many years and, now, in a blink, Leah could see the young woman as if she was actually there.

'Are you OK?'

It was Owen who brought Leah back to the present. She rubbed her eyes and took him in, as he stood over her on the step and nodded to her phone.

'Yeah, just, uh... work stuff.'

Leah glimpsed down to read 'Stop them' again, and then locked the screen. She needed to be by herself to have a proper look at who'd sent it. Stop who? Was it some sort of viral marketing campaign? You couldn't buy anything, even in a shop, without some idiot wanting your email address.

'The lads are setting up inside,' Owen said. 'It'll take them a few minutes. When was the last time you were here?'

It was an innocent question, probably the obvious one, and yet it felt like such a stupid enquiry.

'Never,' Leah replied. 'I mean, not since the morning after. This is the first time.'

Owen opened his mouth as if to say something but then he bit his lip. 'Do you ever see anyone from back then?' It sounded as if he knew the answer.

'I see Esther around town,' Leah replied. 'Used to see Tom now and then, but not for ages.' She left out the bit about seeing the sad, bald man outside the 'Spoons in the middle of winter. 'I'm quite friendly with Harriet's mum and dad.'

Victoria, Jasmine, Harriet.

The Girls.

The Missing Girls.

Owen took a breath and it again seemed as if he was stopping himself from adding something.

One of the crew called through the house and Owen turned and headed inside, leaving Leah alone on the step. It was impossible not to feel the pull to the previous century. Esther in her bare feet, heels in her hands, because she'd slept at her boyfriend's on the Saturday and walked home the next morning. It must have been quite the shock for the hungover eighteen-year-old to arrive home and find police cars outside.

Leah barely had time to dwell, let alone check that email, because Owen was almost immediately back in the doorway. 'We're ready when you are,' he said, holding the door wide for her.

Leah tried to think of an excuse for why she couldn't go inside, and still couldn't remember agreeing to all this. She would have said she'd meet Owen but did she really say she'd be interviewed? In this house of all places?

Except she was somehow stepping past Owen, into the hallway. It had once been a dusty light brown, but was now a beigey grey. The passage to the kitchen which was once lined with photos was now bare, except for a large mirror.

And then Leah was in the living room, where the purply-maroon carpet was now hardwood. The fat-backed television and video player were nowhere to be seen, replaced by a flatscreen pinned to the wall at the opposite end of the room. The plastic Christmas tree at the back was long gone, even though the room didn't feel right without it.

A single chair was angled towards the bay window, faced by a camera on a tripod. There were white screens hanging from the ceiling, reflecting light for the shot, while one of the crew members hovered a boom mic towards the seat.

He was standing in the place where Leah's sleeping bag had been.

Leah waited next to the chair, not on it, trying to push away the ghosts of those sleeping bags. She could picture the four of them, in a line at her feet, as that officer asked what time they had gone to sleep.

'How long are you in town?'

It was Leah who'd spoken, though it was as if it was some-body else. She wanted to leave but couldn't think of a good way out.

'We've blocked out seven days for interviews and set-ups,' the guy with the mic said casually. 'We can stretch it to ten or eleven if need be.'

Leah wasn't listening properly and it took her a couple of seconds to realise what he'd said. 'Seven days? Who else are you talking to?'

The answer didn't come because Owen had appeared in the doorway, and was asking whether there was an echo.

And then they were ready.

Leah found herself sitting on the chair, facing Owen, who was a little to the side of the camera. He asked if she was comfortable, which she wasn't, although she said she was. The fluffy microphone hovered above her head and Leah felt the gaze of the camera, even though she wasn't looking directly at it.

Owen asked Leah her name and place of birth, as the trio talked about levels until they were set.

Owen's first proper question was something about what Leah remembered of the sleepover. Leah found herself drifting into the same familiar snippets she'd repeated across the years. To the police in the first place, but then friends, boyfriends, neighbours, journalists, plus strangers who knew her name. She'd even spoken about what happened in a job interview, when the woman hiring had recognised her. It was impossible not to repeat herself.

Leah had become so familiar with saying the same things over the years that it was hard to know what was a real memory. Like a playground game of whispers, where the original sentence became something entirely different by the time it reached the end of the line. Was it *Titanic* they watched? Was it pizza they ate? That's what she told everyone, and it was probably true, but she didn't think she actually remembered the film, more that she'd told everyone there was a film.

But the story came out as it always did. Vicky's dad was off at some football dinner, leaving the four girls in the house. They cooked frozen pizza in the oven; watched *Titanic*, then started it again; drank some vodka, and then they went to sleep. None of it was new.

'What was it like when you woke up the next morning?' Owen asked.

Another familiar question. How did you feel? What was it like? Always the same, as if she could conjure up those thoughts after twenty-four years. Could anyone really remember how they felt after such a long time?

Leah went with it anyway. It probably sounded practised, but it was, through literal decades of saying the same things.

She woke up and there was nobody around, so she went

upstairs, where she could hear Vicky's dad snoring. It was the only noise in an otherwise quiet house. She looked in Vicky's room, which was empty. There was nobody in the bathroom, garden, or kitchen – and Leah even checked the cupboard in which the coats were kept.

Leah waited a bit, wondering if her friends might have gone to the paper shop to get a magazine, or some chocolate, something like that. Then, after a while, maybe half an hour, Leah knocked on the bedroom door of Vicky's dad. It took about a minute for the snoring to stop, there was some shuffling, and then he opened the door. He was in a red dressing gown and yawning. He asked if Leah was OK and she asked if he knew where Vicky was. There was a bit of confusion, then a lot of confusion, then calls to the other parents, and then they called 999. When the police arrived, officers spoke to Vicky's dad upstairs and Leah downstairs.

Owen said very little as Leah spoke. None of it would have been new to him, with everything reported across numerous publications over the years. There was also the *Crimewatch* recreation, with the too-blonde actress waking with a cliched stretch and a yawn, before heading up the stairs to find Vicky's dad.

Leah had been in something close to a trance as she told the story. She could do it without thinking too much, like someone repeating a landline number they had as a child, or the number plate of their first car.

When she looked up properly, Leah realised Owen was focused on her, steel having appeared from nowhere in his features. The questions before had been standard stuff but there was a punch to his next that made it sound like this was the real reason for them being back in the house.

'What do you say to those who insist you know more than you've ever let on?'

Leah had to force her gaze away from Owen's locked

expression that was burning into her soul. She managed to glance sideways to the man with the boom mic, who was staring past her towards the window. The other man was partially out of sight behind the camera. Neither had reacted.

'Um,' Leah said. 'I mean, I guess I don't...'

'Let me read you this,' Owen said. He was looking at a phone which had materialised out of nowhere. 'This is from a comment piece in the *Mail* from the ten-year anniversary. "There are, of course, those who find it hard to believe a girl slept through three of her friends disappearing into thin air."'

Owen looked away from the device but Leah knew the quote. Before the days of cancel culture and tweeted apologies, there had been a muted outrage over the column. Not that anything had happened to the bloke who wrote it. He was still faking outrage over British politics, while stealing a living from his villa in Florida.

Leah was stumbling. 'Sorry, I er, didn't know it was this sort of interview. I thought, um—'

Owen wasn't done. He was a different person to the one he'd been outside. 'Your husband says you once told him you thought you saw the girls being carried out of the living room.'

SIX

Leah's mouth bobbed open, a fish gasping for life. 'What?'

'That's what your husband told us.'

'Mark? You spoke to Mark?' Leah was trying to catch the eye of any of the crew members, though they were ignoring her. 'He's my *ex*-husband. My very *ex*-husband.'

Owen wasn't letting it go. 'Did you tell your *ex*-husband that you saw the girls being carried out of the living room?'

'No,' Leah replied, instinctively. Except it wasn't true. 'I mean, yes. But not really.' She sighed and pulled at her hair, then pinched her chin. 'I told him I had *a dream* about it afterwards. *Years* afterwards. I told him about my dream. I can't believe you've talked to him. I can't believe he said that.'

Leah's bag was behind the cameraman on the window ledge. She had to fight the urge to grab her phone from it and call her ex-husband to ask precisely what he was playing at.

'But memories blur,' Owen replied, which was all too true. 'Could it be that what you thought was a dream was actually real?'

This is why Leah and Mark were divorced. Well, not this *specifically*, but this sort of thing. Leah's husband – her *ex-*

husband – was an arsehole. She had told one person, and only one person about her dream – and now the whole world was going to know.

'It was a dream,' Leah reiterated, sounding as firm as she could. 'I told him about a dream.'

'Did you have the dream more than once?'

'I don't want to talk about it. It was years ago.'

Owen pressed into his chair a little further, as Leah wondered how far ahead this whole thing had been engineered. Bringing her here meant she was already thrown off, and then – bang! – they'd spoken to Mark, and – bang! – he'd told them about her dream. It felt like she'd been punched.

'Did you have any other dreams about what happened?'

'No. I mean…' Leah sighed. 'Maybe. I don't know.'

Leah half-expected another quote from her arsehole of an ex-husband. She tried to recall if there was anything else she might have told him, though she'd forgotten about the dream until Owen brought it up.

Owen's phone was back in front of him, as he started to read again. 'The day after the sleepover, you told an officer that the four of you hadn't fallen out recently. Then, three days after that, you admitted there had been an argument roughly a week before what happened.'

Leah stumbled over a reply of unconnected words. This was something else she'd forgotten. 'It wasn't a big argument,' she said. 'I suppose I didn't know what they meant by "falling out". I was only a kid… Vicky reckoned Jazz was showing off because she'd bought this bag, and nobody else could afford anything like that. It wasn't a fight, or anything like that. I just…' Leah sighed and again tried to catch the eye of the bloke with the boom mic. 'Can we stop? I didn't think this was what we were going to do.'

For a second, perhaps two, nobody moved. Leah had visions of storming past them, grabbing her bag, and dashing away –

but she knew how it would look to anyone watching the eventual film. They had really set her up, and everyone – including her – knew it.

Then the microphone swerved away from Leah's head and was pressed into the corner. The cameraman stood taller as he pressed a couple of buttons on the device, before saying he'd stopped filming. Owen had barely moved, other than angling his body slightly away from Leah.

'What was that?' Leah asked, as she found it impossible to hide the annoyance.

'What was what?'

'About Mark. When did you talk to him? You should have said something.'

'We just wanted the details before we spoke to you.'

'Details of what?'

Owen's friendliness from outside, not to mention his emails, was gone. He shrugged coldly. 'My sister and her friends haven't been seen in twenty-four years,' he said. 'That's why we're here. No other reason.'

Leah wanted to stare him down, except she knew she didn't have it in her. She wanted to be angry but knew she couldn't be, especially not while the camera was still in front of her. The operator had said he'd stopped filming but it wasn't as if there was a light.

'Do you have anything else you'd like to say?' Owen asked.

'Like what?'

'I don't know.'

'I can't believe you spoke to Mark. I can't believe he told you about my dream. Why didn't you say something in your emails?'

Leah knew the answer. Owen wanted to see how she'd react.

'I just want to find out what happened to my sister,' Owen said, matter-of-factly.

Leah stood and moved around the camera. She picked up

her bag from the window. 'I didn't think it would be like this,' she said, immediately regretting how weak she sounded.

'Don't you want to know what happened?' he asked.

'Of course – but I don't see what a dream has to do with anything.'

Owen didn't reply and he didn't stand. Leah ended up heading into the hall as nobody tried to change her mind. She supposed they had what they wanted.

Leah struggled to unlock her phone as she reached the outside, such was her anger. Mark probably wouldn't pick up but she would at least leave him a message to say what she thought of him. He already knew, of course, which is why they were divorced.

Except Leah didn't get as far as phoning her ex, because another email had arrived during the time in which she'd been getting interviewed. The name was the same as before – A Friend – with the subject line 'Please read'. There was a little more to the body text this time.

You need to stop this doc being made. Trust me.

Leah looked up from the phone. She had drifted onto the street outside Vicky's old house, and turned in a circle. There were still parked cars, still windows obscured by the glare, but nobody actually around. That didn't stop her from feeling watched.

'Trust me', the email read. But trust... who?

SEVEN

Leah was sitting in her car at the end of the street where Vicky used to live. Since leaving the house, there had been no movement of Owen or anybody else heading in or out. Despite that, Leah had sunk into the driver's seat, not wanting anyone to spot her.

The emailer was named 'A Friend', and the Gmail address had likely been set up specifically for this purpose. It was the town's name, then the word 'friend', then 123 before the @ symbol. The sort of email address more used to distributing the fictional wealth of fictional princes to unsuspecting souls.

Leah knew she should ignore both messages, except neither were the usual spam she'd receive. There was no link to click, no mentioning of a product. Both had been sent only to her, and the second specifically mentioned the documentary. It had to have come from someone who knew about it. For a moment, Leah thought it couldn't be many people, then she remembered it had been on the front page of the free paper. It would also be on their website, so that meant Facebook as well. Loads of people would know.

It took Leah a few attempts to settle on a simple reply that read: 'Who is this?' She didn't know whether she expected an answer.

After that, she scrolled through her older messages to find Owen's first email.

Hi Leah.

You might not remember me but my name is Owen Poole. I am Jasmine's younger brother and now a filmmaker.

I made a film two years ago about university students turning to sex work to fund their courses. It was screened around the European festivals and longlisted for a BAFTA.

My next project is about what happened to Jazz and her friends. I've been finalising funding and am hoping to begin filming in around three months. I was wondering if I could interview you? We could talk about specific times and places closer to the date but, as you likely realise, your version is key to everything else.

If you'd like to talk, my number is below, or email works if that's good for you.

I hope you're well.

Best,

Owen

Leah read the email twice, though it felt less friendly with each read. The phrase 'your version' suddenly felt like an accusation, as opposed to something factual. Even the 'Jazz and her friends' bit felt as if it deliberately left out Leah. The three girls were the ones who were missing, but it was Leah who was left answering questions for the next twenty-odd years.

As she read the email a third time, a tab slipped onto the screen to indicate a new email. Another from 'A Friend'.

I am a friend. You have to stop Owen and his doc.

It didn't take long to re-read that email. The sender hadn't said who they were, but at least Leah knew the email was referring to Owen's film – plus it was definitely meant for her. In many ways, that made it worse.

Leah glanced over the steering wheel, scanning the road for any movement. It was impossible not to feel watched, even though nobody was there.

If the past fifteen minutes hadn't have happened, there was a reasonable chance Leah would have shown the email to Owen. Somebody wanted to sabotage him – except it now felt as if someone was after her as well.

Leah tapped out 'Who are you?' once more, deleted it, then typed it again. The emailer had already ignored that question once, and gone out of their way to use a pseudonym. Instead, Leah deleted it a final time and wrote 'Why have I got to stop it?', thought for a bit more, then added 'How can I stop it?' and pressed send.

It was hard to know whether any attempt to stop the documentary was in her best interests, though it felt to Leah as if Owen might have a problem with her. She certainly didn't want to see the already filmed version of her showing up on a screen somewhere, so would wait to see what else came from her apparent friend.

Next up was Mark.

Leah was still boiling that her ex-husband had done an interview with Owen without either of them telling her. Then there was the fact Mark had brought up her dream. Leah was so annoyed that she almost pressed to dial one of the other Marks in her phone. After finding the correct one, his phone rang and rang – which wasn't a surprise. He never picked up. When they were together, he'd often glance at the screen and roll his eyes, regardless of who was calling. She could picture him doing the same now, so she called again. This time, it rang once before the screen went to black.

That was the thing with mobiles: people could hang up before they'd even answered.

Leah hammered out a message instead, asking what he'd told Owen, and why he'd spoken to him at all. She was a skin's width away from sending it before she stopped herself and scrolled up instead. Perhaps there *was* a message, buried among the mundanity. Maybe he *had* asked her permission but it had got lost in among their passive-aggressive back and forths about custody times, drop-offs, and pickups.

There wasn't, of course. Leah knew there wouldn't be. She scanned months and months of dull messages about being 'five minutes late', or Mark telling her that he'd not had time to feed their son as he wondered if she could do something.

Leah sent her message and waited to see if he'd fire back. That was Mark's way: either an instant reply, or something that might arrive in the dying days before the sun swallowed the earth. Little in between.

No reply came.

Leah shuffled up in her seat and drove across town. Roads blurred into roads, roundabouts into roundabouts. She was on autopilot, too busy thinking about Mark's latest betrayal, Owen's possible motives for ambushing her, and the mystery emailer. It was a lot for one day.

The leafy estates gave way to the A-road out of town, then the giant Asda. Cars were queuing for petrol as Leah followed the route around the store onto a bumpy, pothole-ridden lane, until she bounced her way to a stop outside a small cottage.

She parked and crunched across the gravel, before knocking on the front door. There was no point in waiting for an answer, plus it was always open anyway, so Leah headed inside, calling a cheery 'Hello!' as she did.

The hall was the usual clutter of coats and shoes as the

smell of something meaty drifted. The older woman in the kitchen had never quite escaped the matriarchal role, not that she appeared to mind. Most of Leah's conversations with her happened in, or around, a kitchen.

Deborah Carpenter was hunched over a baking dish as she scattered grated cheese over the top. She stopped and turned to take in Leah. 'You all right, love? I didn't hear you come in.'

They cheek-kissed, because they always did. Leah couldn't remember when it had started but it was now their thing.

'What are you making?' Leah asked.

'Lasagne. The meat and pasta is already cooked, so it's just melting it all together.'

Deborah opened the steaming oven, gasped an 'ooh' at the heat, and then placed the tray inside before closing the door. When she stood, her face was flushed. She fanned herself as sweat formed on her hairline. She was in her sixties, yet had looked ten to fifteen years older than her actual age for a long time.

Not a surprise, really. That's what happened when your daughter disappeared from somebody else's living room.

Harriet Carpenter's mother had lost her only child twenty-four years before, yet, in one way, she'd found another.

'Has he been OK?' Leah asked.

'Good as gold, like always. He's in the living room with his Nintendo thing.' Deborah mimed playing a video game and grinned. The wrinkles around her mouth melted into the ones near her eyes.

It wasn't only Leah who'd ended up being a surrogate daughter for Deborah. Leah's son, Zac, had become something of a surrogate grandson. In the weeks after Leah and Mark had split, when work and childcare was too difficult to juggle, Deborah had been there.

Zac had been going to Deborah's after school for years, even though he was now fourteen, and capable of heading to his actual home by himself. Not only did she see him as a grandson, but he seemingly saw her as a grandmother. Part of that was probably because she would happily cook whatever he wanted, and never give him grief over homework that wasn't complete.

'You staying for tea?' Deborah asked, and Leah knew she should say 'no'. She already leaned too much on parents that weren't hers. It wasn't that they minded, quite the opposite, and yet Leah was always aware of how it looked to anyone outside their circle. She'd heard the whispers here and there. Deborah and her husband had lost one daughter – and then moved onto mothering the only girl left.

It wasn't like that, not really, but it *looked* like that.

'I should probably get Zac home,' Leah replied.

'There's plenty here. I can put it in tubs for your freezer?'

Leah didn't have the heart to tell the other woman that there were still *lots* of containers of frozen food in her freezer. It wasn't that she and Zac failed to eat what Deborah cooked, more that there was an endless supply of it.

'I'll check with Zac,' Leah said.

Before she could make a movement towards the living room, Deborah was talking again. 'Have you seen the paper? I kept it for you.' She nodded across to the counter on the far side of the kitchen, where the local free paper was splayed. 'MISSING GIRLS TV DOC CREW IN TOWN' blared silently across the room.

'I saw it,' Leah replied.

'How was the interview?'

Leah almost laughed, seeing as Deborah had remembered the day, yet she hadn't. It was impossible not to sigh, which was an answer in itself.

'Oh,' Deborah said. She reached and touched Leah's shoulder in concern. 'I thought with it being Jasmine's brother...'

There wasn't quite a question there and Leah didn't want to get into details. It was going to come out, and, at some point, she was going to have to tell Deborah that she'd had a dream about Harriet and the other girls being taken from the living room. That wasn't a conversation for today.

'Is it tomorrow they're talking to you?' she asked.

Deborah didn't appear to notice the evasion. 'I've been tidying,' she said. 'They asked if I've got any photos from the time, so I've got all the albums out. There's one or two of you in there. I can't remember if I've ever shown you?'

She had, many times, but Leah found it hard to get excited about those pictures of herself as a teenager, smiling alongside friends who had vanished.

'It sounded like this Owen character really wants to help...?'

Leah took a breath, unsure what to say. It was, again, an answer of sorts.

'Did something happen?'

Leah wondered if she could explain that she'd felt ambushed by Owen and then bemused by an anonymous emailer. It felt too messy to share, at least for now. Besides, the more she thought about it, perhaps Owen's questions *were* fair. He had lost a sister, after all. He was only following up information he had.

'It's all fine,' Leah replied. 'I'm sure he'll be interested in your photos tomorrow. The house is looking great.'

Deborah was happy enough at that. As well as the compulsive cooking, she loved compliments on her spotless house.

'I was thinking they could film in here,' she said, indicating the kitchen around them. 'There's a really nice light in the morning. But then the living room has that peach wallpaper, so maybe they'll prefer that?'

Leah let the other woman talk as her thoughts drifted to the anonymous emailer. Who could want the documentary stopped? She could only think of people who enthusiastically *wanted* it to happen: Deborah included.

'...You going to the public forum thing on Sunday?'

Leah caught the second part of the sentence as she honed back into the kitchen. The smell of the lasagne was beginning to escape the oven, with the tang of melting cheese impossible to ignore.

'What forum thing?' Leah asked, wondering if she'd been told and forgotten.

Deborah crossed the kitchen and picked up the paper. She flicked a few pages inside and then held it up. 'There's a public meeting at the community centre,' she said. 'This Owen chap is going to answer questions from anyone who wants to go. He said he hopes for the support of the community.'

Leah shook her head as the paper was offered, and Deborah returned it to the side. The forum didn't sound like the sort of thing Leah would go to. Most of the community appeared to be in support of the documentary anyway and those that weren't would be full of questions about something that felt far too personal to Leah. Yes, three girls had disappeared – but she was left, and had answered more than enough questions over the years.

Deborah seemingly took Leah's lack of interest as an answer. 'Is tomorrow the day that...?'

She didn't finish the sentence, not that Leah needed her to. 'Yes.'

'Are you doing anything?'

'The usual.'

'If you need company...?'

Leah considered the offer for a moment. It was kind and, in a lot of ways, welcome. Except Deborah had given Leah so much over the years.

'I'll be OK,' Leah replied.

Deborah hovered, partway back towards the oven. The cheese was bubbling. 'Are you sure you don't want to stop for tea?'

EIGHT

ONE DAY AFTER THE SLEEPOVER

SUNDAY 19 DECEMBER 1999

Leah sat quietly at one end of Vicky's living room as Esther sat at the other. The officer who'd asked all the questions had her pad open again, this time talking to Esther. There were voices from above, too, as the apparent interrogation of Vicky's father continued.

Leah wasn't sure what to do, or where to go. Was she allowed to leave? Where would she go if she did?

'I was at my boyfriend's,' Esther croaked. She was glugging from a bottle of Coke that had been in the fridge, seemingly trying to force her eyes open wider. 'I only came back to change and get some shoes. I was going back out again.' She muttered something Leah didn't catch and then added a little louder: 'I'll have to call him.'

The landline was on the wall in the hall, not that Esther made a move for it. She looked from side to side and then checked over her shoulder, before having another drink from the bottle. It was only as she groaned that Leah realised the older girl was hungover. They were at the age where kids at school would talk about the headaches and the vomiting, not that Leah had ever drunk that much. There had been the vodka the night before but she hadn't been drunk and was fairly sure she wasn't hungover. It felt like something a person would know about.

'Should I stay here?' Esther asked the officer. 'I don't know what to do.'

Leah watched as the officer fidgeted, and she realised that the woman in the uniform didn't know what to do either. Adults should know, shouldn't they? Especially the police.

Before anyone could say anything else, there was a clump from the hall and the door opened. A male police officer was standing tall, his head almost touching the beam of the frame. The one who'd been upstairs, with Vicky's dad.

'You got a minute?' he asked, talking to his colleague.

The woman said something about being 'right back' and then disappeared into the hall, as the door was closed with a soft bump.

Leah and Esther were alone in the living room, the sleeping bags sitting on the floor between them. Esther had been watching the bags but looked up to take in Leah. It felt like she was going to say something but, instead, the officers' voices seeped through the door.

'He says he got in from the football dinner at half-twelve,' a man's voice said.

Esther locked eyes with Leah as they shared an acknowledgement of their ear-wigging.

'Ray Clemence was doing an after-dinner event and the dad reckons loads of people saw him leave in a taxi. He says he looked in on the girls, who were all asleep, then he went to bed.'

'What did the taxi company say?'

'Nothing official. We're trying to get hold of someone who was on duty last night but the dispatcher said they had five or six taxis shuttling back and forth at that time, so it'll probably check out.'

There was a pause and then the female officer spoke: 'The mum's not in the picture. Cancer.'

Leah glanced to Esther, and the two girls again locked eyes. One word, the C-word, and it felt brutal even to Leah. She couldn't imagine how Esther was taking it, regardless of the hangover. Her mum's existence trimmed to a single word.

'What d'you reckon?' the female officer asked.

'Sounds plausible. I dunno. The dad reckons the girls often have sleepovers here. He says he doesn't know how long until he fell asleep, but it wasn't long. Sounds like they went missing between about 12.45 and nine o'clock this morning.'

The voices went muffled for a moment, before returning.

'How can you get three girls out of a house with nobody noticing?' the male officer asked. 'They must be somewhere...'

There was another silence but this was different. When Leah looked across the room, Esther was watching her. She had the sense that the two officers on the other side of the door might be looking in her direction, too. That the question about her missing friends might not be entirely hypothetical, but something specifically directed at her.

Before anything else was said, shadows marched past the front window. There were muffled voices from outside and then the sound of the door opening.

Leah didn't bother waiting. The living room was stifling, the house itself claustrophobic. She headed into the hall, ducking under the arm of the male officer and poking her head outside to see who was there.

Harriet's mum and dad were standing a little along the path; two new officers between them and the house. Deborah had been in the middle of saying something when she spotted Leah and stopped.

'They're saying Harriet's missing?'

Her voice broke halfway through her daughter's name and Leah felt it as much as she heard it. She'd never sensed anything like it when either of her parents said her name.

It was love.

Leah felt her knees wobble a fraction as she ached for such a thing. Before she knew what she was doing, she'd stepped around another officer and was in Deborah's arms. Harriet's mum rubbed Leah's hair and pulled her in.

'I don't know,' Leah said. 'I woke up and she wasn't there.'

Deborah tensed but only momentarily. Leah felt the woman's chest rise and fall. 'What about Jazz? Victoria?'

'They're all gone.'

'Gone where?'

Leah pressed herself into the woman's side, craving the touch. 'I don't know.'

Deborah sighed and used her free hand to rub her own head. She might've been talking to Leah, but maybe it was her husband, or the officers. Perhaps it was nobody in particular, but everything and everyone in general?

'I don't understand,' she said. 'How can three girls just disappear?'

NINE

NOW

Leah's microwave hummed as the lasagne within fizzed. Deborah hadn't let her or Zac leave the house without taking food with them, which is what so often happened. Two portions had gone into the fridge, and would likely end up in the freezer. One of the remaining portions was on the side, as Zac's turned inside the microwave.

'Can I be in the film?' Zac asked.

He was sitting at the kitchen table, idly tapping his foot. He'd never been one for sitting still, something he got from his father.

His father who hadn't replied to Leah's text.

'What film?' Leah asked. Her son had barely said a word in the car on the way home. He was that age in which a good forty per cent of his communication happened via a series of grunts.

'Deb said you were filming for a movie today. She showed me it in the paper.'

Leah was sure she'd told Zac about it, yet she'd forgotten the day, so was no longer certain of anything.

'It's a documentary,' Leah replied. 'I'm not really *in* the film. They just interviewed me for it.'

'Maybe they could interview me? Ask me what it's like being your son?'

Zac sounded earnest, although Leah suspected it was likely more to do with getting onto TV, or the cinema, in an attempt to impress girls.

Hard to blame him for that.

'It's not that sort of film,' Leah said, although she was beginning to wonder exactly what type of film it was.

The microwave pinged and Zac pushed himself up. He oohed and aahed as he removed the tub and dropped it onto the counter. The oven gloves were *right there*, and so were the tea towels, though there was little point in telling him that again. Zac shunted the tub across onto the table and then opened the wrong drawer to find a fork, before settling on the right one. They'd lived in the same house his entire life, and the forks had never once moved, yet he still fumbled around like a stranger.

Leah stifled the smile as her son blew on a forkful and then shovelled it down. 'Hot!' he said, as he wafted a hand in front of his mouth. The same scene played out close to every day. He mushed around a bit of the lasagne, letting it cool, before clearing his throat. He didn't look up when he spoke. 'Do you think they'll find out what happened to your friends?' A short pause and then: 'Is that why they're making the film?'

Leah slipped her own lasagne into the microwave and fiddled with the buttons, giving herself a second. She wasn't sure how to answer. The mystery had hung over her entire life, but it had been his, too. Leah had never got out of the town and everybody knew she was the girl who was left. They also knew he was her son. At least two of his teachers used to teach Leah, Jazz, Victoria and Harriet. It was that sort of place.

'I don't know,' Leah replied. 'Maybe.'

The microwave started to hum and Zac risked another mouthful of lasagne. He had never shown much of an interest in what happened to her friends and didn't follow up her reply.

'Can I stay at Josh's tomorrow? He's got the new *Call of Duty*.' He paused, though only momentarily, anticipating the next question. 'His dad's gonna be there all night. He said you can call him if you're not sure.'

Leah forced herself not to smile. As ever, the groundwork had already been laid, permission sought, concerns dealt with – all before Zac presented his proposal. After all, if anyone might have a problem with a sleepover, it should be her.

Leah wasn't particularly tight with any of the other parents. She knew Josh's father, Ben, in the way most did when it came to a child's friends. Regardless of whether you liked one another, or had anything in common, you were forced into a series of pleasant enough interactions. She and Ben were in the class WhatsApp group, of course, so they had each other's numbers. They'd swapped the odd message about pickup, when Zac or Josh had been at one another's house, or out doing something. If anyone was to ask her what she thought about Ben, it would be a solid 'he's all right' – because he was.

Leah had been silent too long as she felt her son looking to her. The instinct was to say 'no'. He'd reached fourteen and had never really been allowed to sleep at someone else's house. Josh had slept over once, plus there had been a school trip on which Zac had been gone for three nights. One of the teachers had gone out of her way to check in with Leah each night. It was like they all felt she was an emotional mess, in constant fret of her son disappearing in the way her friends had. It wasn't true, not really, but maybe a little.

'I'll talk to Josh's dad,' Leah replied.

Zac grinned, taking that as a 'yes'.

'Have you got homework?' Leah asked.

'Done it.'

She narrowed her eyes, though he didn't back down.

He blew on another square of lasagne and then nodded upstairs. 'Can I take this up?'

He must have really wanted to go to Josh's, considering he rarely asked for permission to take his food into his room.

Leah told him it was fine and then she sat by herself in the empty kitchen, picking at the lasagne she felt guilty about accepting.

Zac would be fine at his friend's house overnight, she knew that. Her friends had disappeared more than twenty years ago. Times had changed.

Leah thumbed through the WhatsApp group, finding Ben's last message. He'd written that he was taking time off work to support the striking teachers and that, because it was a nice day, he was going to the park with Josh. Any parents were welcome to drop off their kids.

All their children were at the age where they didn't particularly need sitters, yet plenty had accepted the offer, leaving Ben to take charge of what sounded like a giant, hours-long football game.

Maybe he was a little above the 'all right' level.

Leah hard-pressed his name to start a call. There were a couple of rings and then a chirpy man's voice: 'Leah? Hi. How are you? Josh said you might call.'

Leah hadn't replied quickly enough, and Ben was still going: 'Josh has just got a new game and you know what they're like. He wanted Zac to come over. I didn't want to say "yes" without talking to you.'

'Sounds like they figured things out between themselves.'

Leah said it with a laugh and Ben joined in. 'I was the same at that age. I know why you might want to say no, so I wanted to assure you that I'll be in all night on Friday. I can even pick up and drop off Zac? Or he can come after school? Whatever's easier.'

She probably shouldn't have been surprised that everyone had appeared to think through the possible questions and outcomes before coming to her.

Leah still wanted to say no. It was safer if Zac was sleeping in the room next to her. She knew he was often out of her sight – when he was at school for starters, or when he had weekends at his dad's. Except there was something different about an overnight in this town. At least for her.

The hesitation had gone on too long. Much too long. 'I can make sure he calls you before bed,' Ben added. 'Or sends you a message?'

'No, uh...' Leah was stumbling. 'He doesn't have to do that. I mean, yeah... Maybe if you pick him up from school?'

Leah had said no to the potential call, even though she wanted it. She doubted Ben had missed the obvious reluctance in her voice.

They went through the motions of asking whether Zac had any allergies, that sort of thing. Then Leah found herself saying she'd take both boys on the Saturday, even though she had no idea where that had come from. There was more small talk, something about a concert at the school the next month, and maybe a bake sale, and then Ben was gone.

Leah had somehow ended up agreeing her son could have a sleepover, and then offering to take both boys somewhere the following day. The call couldn't have gone much worse.

Leah put down her phone, picked at her food, checked her phone again. There was nothing from either her ex-husband, or the mystery emailer – only the previous request.

You have to stop Owen and his doc.

Leah was beginning to come around to the idea that she *should* probably try to stop Owen if he was ambushing people in the way he had her. She also didn't want that footage of her ending up being shown to others. Somebody else clearly thought the same way and it was impossible for Leah not to wonder what they wanted to keep hidden. Or why they couldn't try to stop it themselves.

She found herself browsing the town's local Facebook page. It was always a baffling prospect; with a heady mix of people trying to sell their rust bucket of a car for eight grand, or some maniac threatening to wallop the next kid who skateboarded past his house. The latest war was about the prospect of wind turbines on the outskirts of town. One side was adamant it would destroy everyone's views, and lower the value of their homes; the other said it would save the planet and give cheaper electricity. There was no middle ground or nuance. Both sides thought the other was out to ruin the community.

It didn't take long for Leah to find the link to the local news article about the documentary. She didn't click that, instead diving into the sewer of the comments. A few were saying they were stunned it was almost twenty-five years since the girls went missing, others insisting it was time to move on. One person reckoned the film could bring a degree of closure for the town, with at least three claiming it would be good for tourism.

It always came down to that in the end. Sure, the film might open old wounds, divide a community, and put Leah and her teenage son in a spotlight they didn't want – but if there was a chance someone could make a bit of bunce from it, then full steam ahead.

Leah was considering whether to reply to any of the disaster capitalists when a different comment caught her attention.

The arsehole.

As Mark had been studiously avoiding her calls and messages, he'd been busy replying to a public Facebook thread.

I've already had my say. The truth will come out.

Leah stared. It couldn't be her Mark, could it? Except it was. Right there, with his name alongside that gormless picture of him hugging his hag of a girlfriend. The photo where they were both wearing tie-dye for some reason.

Definitely her Mark.

She called him. No answer. Called him again. And again. 'Pick up,' she told the empty kitchen. 'Pick up.'

He did on the fifth try, giving a cheery ''Ey up' instead of a hello. 'What's going on?' he added, with the smugness of a person who knew for certain what was going on.

'Why didn't you tell me you were talking to the film crew?' Leah said, a raging fire in her voice.

'What film crew?'

'How many crews do you know?'

That got a snidey chuckle. 'Oh, right. I thought you knew.'

'How would I know?'

He ignored the question, instead laughing an: 'I didn't tell them much.'

'You told them about my dream. That was between us.'

There was a huff from the other end, the sort that might usually come with a 'keep your hair on'. 'What does it matter?' he replied.

'Because they're acting like I know something about what happened!'

Mark left it a second and then: 'Do you?'

'Are you joking?'

There was more merriment. 'Are you still seriously expecting people to believe you slept through your friends disappearing?'

He was goading her, wanting the reaction – and Leah had fallen right into it. She took a breath.

'Why didn't you tell me you'd spoken to the documentary crew?'

'The director guy asked me not to.'

Leah had been about to say something about the Facebook comment but his reply threw her. 'Owen asked you not to?'

'Yeah.'

'Why didn't you say no?'

He cleared his throat and Leah suddenly knew why. She should have figured it out hours before.

'How much did he pay you?'

Of course it was about money. It always was with Mark. That was one of the issues between them. He would spend every penny he made and somehow end up with nothing to show for it. No wonder he'd blurted the details of her dream.

'You're breaking up,' Mark said, even though the line was as clear as the rest of the call.

Leah checked her screen anyway, where there was full reception. 'Don't you dare,' she said.

'I— it— when— now—Monday—'

And he was gone. She'd seen him fake bad reception in the past – and now he'd done it *to* her. The arsehole.

Leah clasped the phone hard, so furious, she almost threw it. It was only a new email that stopped her. She clicked into it, loading the latest message from her mystery friend.

To stop them finding out what you did.

TEN

TWO DAYS AFTER THE SLEEPOVER

MONDAY 20 DECEMBER 1999

Leah was sitting in her bedroom, staring through the window, out towards the treeline and the fields beyond. A line of people were stepping carefully across the muddy green. Some of them had slender white poles, with which they poked the earth. They were an arm's length apart, puffed up in massive coats, marching rhythmically and carefully. Right foot. Left foot.

They were too far away to be heard, though voices seeped through from the floor below. Leah was an expert at blocking out the shouts, though this time she listened in. Her mum was down there, with someone who'd knocked on the front door about fifteen minutes before. Leah couldn't make out the words but it was definitely a woman. It sounded like they were having a conversation at a normal volume, which was a rarity in the house.

Leah strained to hear but couldn't pick up anything specific. Meanwhile, the search line on the field continued their parade.

The knock on the bedroom door made Leah jump. Her mother never announced her arrival with such politeness, so it definitely wasn't her – and, when Leah crossed and opened it, there was a woman she'd never seen before. She was wearing a smart suit, her hair in a tight bun, as she smiled with her eyes.

'Leah, is it?' she asked.

'Yeah...'

'My name's Shirley and I work with the police. I was wondering if we could have a chat?'

Leah wanted to say no, mainly because she had done plenty of talking the day before. She wanted to be left by herself.

Probably sensing the reluctance, Shirley continued. 'I'm what's called a liaison officer. I'll be popping in every day or so to make sure you and your mum are doing OK after everything that's happened.'

'Oh.'

'Is it all right if I come in?'

It didn't feel as if Leah had much choice, so she stepped to the side, allowing Shirley into her bedroom.

Leah perched on the edge of her bed, as the other woman crossed to the window and leant on the frame. Aside from the bed, there wasn't anything in the way of somewhere to sit.

'Did you sleep much last night?' Shirley asked.

Unlike the officer from the day before at Vicky's house, there was no pad, no notes.

'Sort of,' Leah replied. She still wasn't sure she wanted this conversation.

'How's your mum?'

Leah only realised she had glanced towards the now closed door when Shirley added: 'She can't hear anything you say. This is between us.'

Leah felt the officer searching for eye contact, though Leah couldn't face it. She *really* wanted to be by herself.

'She's OK,' Leah replied.

It didn't sound believable, even to Leah, who'd said the words.

'She asked me to have a conversation with you,' Shirley said. 'I don't think she knows how to tell you that your dad isn't in prison any longer.'

Leah's room was largely bare, though there was a small pile of books in the corner, on the floor. She had never been quite sure where they'd come from. Neither of her parents seemed the sort to actually *buy* a book, and yet it felt as if they'd always been in the room. She'd been staring at the stack but couldn't avoid Shirley's pull any longer.

'What do you mean?' Leah asked, finally turning.

'He was released about a week ago,' Shirley said. 'He's currently staying in something called a halfway house. It's a place where people go after leaving prison, before they return to their local area.'

The room was cold now, the biting breeze appearing from nowhere. 'Is he... coming here?' Leah asked with a stutter.

Shirley's hesitancy was impossible to miss. 'I don't know,' she said, before a very pregnant pause. 'Do you *want* him to come home?'

Leah twisted back towards her books. There were nine of them, and every cover had the corner cut off. She wasn't sure why.

It was an important question, and Leah knew she should say she wanted him home. Her mum would be upset if Leah said anything different. Not just upset: furious.

'I suppose,' Leah said, quietly at first, then louder second time.

Shirley was nodding and it felt as if there was a follow-up question that didn't quite come. As soon as she stood straighter and checked outside the window, Leah knew the opportunity was gone.

'I have a few other things to tell you,' Shirley said. 'People are out searching for your friends today. Obviously we're still hoping they've gone on an adventure and this will be figured out.'

Leah couldn't hide her grimace at the word 'adventure'. She wasn't a five-year-old, for God's sake.

'Hopefully they'll be back for Christmas,' Shirley added clumsily. 'Are you looking forward to Christmas?'

'I guess,' Leah replied. What else was she supposed to say?

Shirley had a final check out the window and then pushed herself up. She took a step towards the door but, before she reached there, she dug into a pocket hidden within her jacket. 'Here,' she said, placing a card on the bed. 'My desk number's on there.' She reached into a pocket on the other side of her jacket and pulled out what turned out to be a small pile of fifty-pence pieces. She popped those next to the card. 'Look, I know it's not necessarily easy but, if you ever need me, there's a phone box on the corner.'

She hesitated momentarily and then picked up the card. She flipped it over and pressed on the bedpost to write something else.

'My home number's there, too,' she said, holding it up for Leah to see. 'Call me if ever you need something, day or night. Even if it's three in the morning, call me at home.'

This time, she pushed the card into Leah's hand, lingering for a fraction of a second as their fingers touched.

'Any time,' she repeated.

Leah stared at the number. Shirley had incredibly neat handwriting, with each digit like something printed in a book.

'Is there anything else you'd like to tell me?' Shirley asked.

Leah turned the card over, reading the typed text: 'Shirley Atkins', and 'Police Liaison Officer', before a phone number was listed.

She shook her head.

'Anything at all?' Shirley asked.

'No,' Leah replied.

ELEVEN

NOW

FRIDAY

A dustbin lorry fizzed along the street, surging through a very late amber light, before disappearing around a bend with a skitter of small stones. Leah waited at the crossing as a man strode around her, hefting his briefcase higher as he bounded onto the road a few seconds before the green man flashed. Leah waited until following.

When she reached the other side, Leah headed towards the glass-fronted building on the corner. She remembered when it used to be a grubby newsagent, partly occupied by older kids buying cigarettes for anyone younger who was happy to pay a premium. If not ciggies, then porno mags. It felt like yesterday but would have been twenty years ago.

Longer.

Either way, the glimmering curved glass that had replaced it wasn't the sort of thing that usually appeared in a town riddled with potholes and moss growing through the pavements.

Leah had driven or walked past the rebuilt office many times, especially as her own workplace was eight or nine doors down. 'Merrivale and King Solicitors' was imprinted into the glass in fancy white type, though Leah could never see that particular last name without thinking of Victoria Merrivale.

Vicky.

The door was heavier than Leah thought, and she had to put her shoulder into it as she pressed inside. As soon as it closed behind her, she was blasted by the cool conditioned air that fired from the vents above.

The girl on reception was young, with a high ponytail that stretched her skin even tauter. She peered over non-existent glasses and grimaced a smile.

'Can I help you?' she asked, with a tone that was more 'I think you're in the wrong building.'

'I was hoping to talk to Esther,' Leah said. The Merrivale from the sign.

'Do you have an appointment?' the girl asked, in the way a person might when they already knew the answer was 'no'.

Leah ignored the passive aggression. 'Can you tell her it's Leah Pearce?'

The receptionist's eyes widened a fraction, which was difficult given the vice-like ponytail. The fake smile wrapped its way into something broadly genuine. 'Let me see what I can do.'

She pushed her chair back and stood, before disappearing through a door that was part of the wall behind.

Leah hovered alone in the reception, turning to take in the rest of the area. There was a series of potted plants around the edges, plus a line of certificates on the back wall that appeared to list the various legal qualifications of both Merrivale and King.

It was a few minutes until the hidden door popped open and the receptionist reappeared. She was all smiles now, her voice a little higher than it had been. 'Do you want to come this way?' she asked.

Leah followed her around the back of the desk, through the door, and along an empty white corridor.

'Are you OK with stairs?' the woman asked.

'What do you mean?' Leah replied.

'It's one floor up but the lift can be a bit slow. Up to you if you want to wait...?'

The woman was somewhere in her early twenties, still at the age when everyone over about thirty seemed like they were one fall away from an old people's home.

'I can do stairs,' Leah replied.

The receptionist led Leah up a set of steps into a corridor identical to the one they'd left. She pointed to a door on which there was a tidy plaque reading 'Esther Merrivale'. Then, presumably in case Leah might dislocate a knuckle at the rickety old age of thirty-nine, knocked for her, before opening the door.

'In there,' she said.

Leah headed into what turned out to be the office directly above reception. A curved temple of glass sloped around the front, giving a panoramic view of the stream on the far side of the park.

Esther had been sitting behind a desk but she sprang up and crossed the room, hand outstretched.

She had come a long way from that hungover teenager twenty-four years before.

'Leah, my word,' she said. 'How long has it been?'

They shook hands and then stood to take in the view. It was only a storey up, giving a view of the same park which Leah cut through if she was running late for work. From the ground level, it seemed like a mud-pit, cluttered with discarded cigarette ends, and the laughing-gas canisters that kids apparently used to get high nowadays. From the elevated angle, town suddenly seemed, well... *nice*.

'Not bad is it?' Esther added. Her first question had gone unanswered.

'I always thought the stream was a bit grubby,' Leah said. 'It looks really good from here.'

Esther didn't reply, not really, though her proud smile said some of it. Leah wasn't telling her anything she didn't know.

A silent awkwardness sat between them, until Esther ushered Leah into a seat so comfortable that it was half chair, half hug. The sort that swallows a person, before charming them into a blissful slumber. Leah was so taken by its cosiness that she almost forgot why she had visited Esther's office unannounced.

'How can I help you?' Esther asked, as she settled into her own seat on the other side of a desk.

'Have you heard they're making a documentary?' Leah asked.

'It was on the front page of the paper yesterday,' Esther replied. 'A couple of people sent me the link as well. I think everyone knows.'

'Right...' It wasn't *exactly* the response Leah had expected. Less speculation, more fact. Probably unsurprising, given Esther's profession. Also, Leah knew Esther had given Owen the keys to her father's house.

'They talked to me yesterday,' Leah said, stumbling a fraction. 'It was a bit, um... not what I thought.'

There might have been a hint of a frown on Esther's face, though – if there was – it disappeared the moment Leah thought she'd seen it. Esther didn't seem the sort to give much away.

'What did you think it would be?' Esther asked.

'I don't know. It was just they'd spoken to my ex-husband and nobody had told me that was happening. They took a couple of things out of context.'

'Like what?'

Leah had known she was going to have to tell the truth but it still felt awkward. 'I told Mark, my ex, about a dream I had a few years ago, where I saw the girls being carried out of the room. He told Owen and they acted like it was something real.'

This time, there was a definite frown on Esther's face.

Leah didn't want a follow-up question, so pressed on. 'Owen said you'd given him the keys to the house, so I was wondering if you're talking to them at some point?'

'Maybe,' Esther said. She was biting the corner of her mouth, before seemingly deciding what she was going to say. 'Owen emailed about eighteen months ago, saying he was thinking about doing something for the twenty-fifth anniversary. I didn't know his name but then it turns out he's Jasmine's brother, and that his film was up for a BAFTA. Not bad for a kid from this town, huh?'

Leah didn't disagree.

'Anyway, he knew about my job and asked what I thought about him possibly making a film about Vicky and the others.'

'What did you say?'

A shrug: 'I told him to go for it. Said I'd help wherever I could. I put him in contact with someone who helped him get some archive news footage, plus I know a media lawyer who's going to give the edits a once-over.' She wafted a dismissive hand, as if this was all in a day's work. 'To be honest, he had a lot of bases covered himself. I guess it opens a few doors when you're up for awards.'

There was another awkward pause, mainly because Leah had no idea what to say. She probably wouldn't have come if she'd realised Esther was so involved in the production.

'I figure we all want to know what happened, right?'

Esther was staring through Leah and it felt as if there might be an unspoken accusation there. Leah wasn't exactly used to it, but neither was it uncommon. People often looked at her quizzically, wondering how one person could sleep through three of their friends disappearing.

'Of course,' Leah said, and it wasn't a lie.

'I dug out a few boxes from Dad's attic,' Esther added. 'Some of Vicky's bits that had been kept. Do you remember how she'd obsess over things and then move on? Her flute was up there, plus all the music books. There was a volleyball, because she wanted to get into that one summer. She was into cults for a while, then *Buffy The Vampire Slayer*. She wanted to be a vet. There was stuff for all that up there, plus more.'

She tailed off and, though Leah had long forgotten about most of it, those memories were suddenly back. Vicky really did fall in and out of interest with things. 'She did judo for a while,' Leah said – which made Esther smile.

'I'd forgotten that. She told me she'd throw me down the stairs if I went into her room!'

It didn't sound like a happy memory but Esther clearly thought so.

'She was into drama for a while,' Leah added. 'She dragged us all along for about a month and then it was her who didn't want to go any more.'

'That's right! She wanted to be Kate Winslet.'

Esther rocked on her chair, which seemed very unlike the demure, unfazed legal professional of minutes before. After so many years, for a moment, the two girls were bonded.

Then Leah had to spoil it. 'How is your dad?' she asked. 'Owen said something about a nursing home?'

The cloud that crossed Esther's features appeared from nowhere and the room suddenly felt dark. 'He's in a hospice,' she said.

'What?'

'They moved him about a week ago. Doctors say he's got up to six weeks.'

Leah blinked. Stared. 'To live?'

It was a stupid question but out before she could take it back.

Esther nodded as she bit her lip. 'Lung cancer. It's been coming. He never could quite give up smoking. To be honest, I don't think he wanted to.' There was a pause and then she forced a sad smile. 'He was never quite the same.'

No. He wouldn't have been.

The chair that had once been so comfortable now dug into Leah's back. She couldn't quite remember why she'd come. Perhaps she'd been hoping for some sort of comradeship? Someone who might be concerned about what Owen was doing with his documentary? Instead, she'd found the person who'd helped set it all up.

As if remembering the question from minutes before, Esther clicked back to her persona. 'I'm probably talking to Owen next week,' she said. 'It depends on our schedules. I gave him Dad's keys and they said something about sending a drone up today or tomorrow, if it stays dry.'

There was another silence, this one even clumsier than the others. That moment of kinship over Vicky's interests was gone.

'I have to get to work,' Leah said, pushing herself up from the chair. 'I suppose I just... wanted to make sure you were OK with everything.'

'Why wouldn't I be?'

Leah wasn't sure how to answer that.

'I just hope they find something,' Esther said, as she stood herself. 'Twenty-five years and all that. It's too long, isn't it?'

Somehow, without quite noticing how they'd got there, Esther had guided Leah towards her office door. It had happened in a blink.

Esther opened the door but stood in it, blocking the way. 'I should've said sorry.' The sentiment had also appeared from nowhere.

Leah almost said 'what for?', but she knew.

'Back then,' Esther added and her persona had changed again. Was this because she was a lawyer? A switch from keeping her cards close, to matey friendship, to earnest apologies? 'For what I said. I knew I shouldn't have done but it was a hard time for all of us.'

Esther stepped to the side, apology complete, allowing Leah to move around her into the corridor.

'It's all right,' Leah replied, although it felt automatic, and definitely not sincere. Perhaps it was forgiven but she would never forget.

'Look after yourself,' Esther said – and, as Leah headed for the stairs, there was something about the knowing tone that almost made her stop. Not a phrase offered as comfort or advice, something closer to a threat.

TWELVE

THIRTEEN DAYS AFTER THE SLEEPOVER

FRIDAY 31 DECEMBER 1999

Leah hadn't wanted to go to the town's new year's celebration. Her mum wasn't going, though she rarely left the house anyway. It was the final day of the century and people had only been talking about two things.

There was the Millennium Bug – Y2K – and how every computer was going to crash, sending the world into a frenzied panic.

Then, more locally, there was the three missing girls.

Leah hadn't been out much since the sleepover, especially as the schools had broken up. It had still felt impossible to miss it all.

Shirley had kept her word by visiting every couple of days. There had been the early upbeat updates about searches and hope, though those had slowly given way to the same old questions about whether the girls had a secret meeting place.

Even though Leah hadn't left the house *much*, it had been impossible to completely stay inside and be around her mum all day and evening. She doubted her mother knew she'd left the house a little after eleven on New Year's Eve. Even if she had, it wasn't as if she'd contact anyone like the police to report another missing girl.

Leah headed towards the town centre and what had been promised as a 'bonfire to bring in the new millennium'. There was something immeasurably crap about a place where the year's highlight was starting a big fire. A town not good enough to make anything, so it burnt stuff instead.

Despite that, Leah, Jazz, Victoria and Harriet had planned to celebrate the new year by watching the blaze, along with the rest of the town. Without them, Leah was by herself.

The night was sharp and, because she couldn't find her gloves, Leah was clenching her fists inside the sleeves of her coat. Her hood was up as she tried to avoid the stares and, worse, questions of anyone who might see her.

Leah easily slipped through the crowd on the park. There were couples huddling for warmth, groups of teenagers a bit older than her hiding bottles of cider in their coats and swigging when nobody was looking. Leah passed some younger children, who were ringed by a set of parents in some sort of staging area, close to the pitch and putt.

The pile of pallets and sticks seemed to grow as Leah neared. Some bloke in a suit was on a stage to the side, though his amplified voice was too echoey to make out. He was holding a giant stick, which probably meant he was going to be the one to start the fire on the stroke of midnight. Leah had seen something on one of the posters about fireworks as well, which felt like it might be more worthwhile than the big fire.

Not that Leah particularly cared about any of it. If the others had been here, the four of them would have been sitting towards the back somewhere, making sarcastic comments about the various people massing around the lame-oh fire.

Sarcasm wasn't much fun when there was only one person.

Leah found a spot not far from the playground. The swings

had been vandalised months before and only the frame remained. Some lad had climbed to the top and was sitting on the horizontal bar, swinging his legs as his mates threw crisps at him.

The man next to the fire with the loudhailer boomed something incompressible as Leah stood with her arms folded, waiting for the fireworks to start.

'Lee...?'

It sounded like a question and, when Leah turned, Esther was standing a handful of paces away, next to a pair of lads and three other girls.

At some point, Leah's hood had come down, although she didn't remember it happening. The six older teenagers eyed her curiously; Vicky's sister front and centre.

'Hi,' Leah said. She'd never been friends with Esther and only really knew her as Vicky's older sister. They had existed in the same space and, aside from those minutes in the living room that Sunday morning, had never had anything close to a conversation.

'What are you doing here?' Esther asked. It was only a few words, though it felt like more. There was something in her voice that Leah couldn't decipher.

'I dunno,' Leah said, because she didn't.

'Have you heard about her dad?' Esther said, talking to the lad at her side. He had a gormless look to him, like an inbred puppy asked to recite Pythagoras.

'Didn't he break that guy's jaw?' he said.

'And his nose,' Esther added. 'Put him in hospital and went to prison.' A beat passed. 'And her mum's a nutter.'

Leah peered along the line of hardened faces of the older teenagers. The escalation had come from nowhere.

'You know what happened, don't you?' Esther added.

'No.'

'Yes you do.'

There was a momentary stand-off as Leah tried not to shrink. Did Esther *really* think Leah knew more than she'd said? Leah had heard the police officers whispering it but nobody had outright said it.

'You should go,' one of the other girls said, harshly.

'Yeah,' Esther sneered. 'Really go. You should get out of town and not come back.'

Leah had taken a step away without meaning to.

'Go on,' Esther urged. 'Get out of here.'

So Leah did.

THIRTEEN

NOW

Leah was sitting at her desk, partially hidden behind the computer screen. Regardless of that, she could feel the sideways glances, not to mention the sheer number of colleagues who were walking past her desk to offer contemplative half-smiles while on the way to the kitchen, or the toilet. They didn't *have* to pass her desk, but they were wondering if she might say something about Owen's documentary.

The previous day's news story, plus all those Facebook shares, had changed everything. It was the same every time there was an anniversary, where Leah would end up second-guessing the intentions of others.

Leah wasn't sure why she'd visited Esther. They'd had very little in the way of interaction since New Year's Eve twenty-four years before. Not long after that, Esther had disappeared off to university and then, years later, she'd reappeared as a solicitor. Then she'd moved into that glass cathedral thing and had turned into something of a local celebrity. Her firm would sponsor various local events, else there'd be an article with her speaking out over some local issue about which she felt strongly. She was sort of omnipotent in local life, simply by way of being successful in a town in which that was viewed with suspicion.

Until the apology in her office, Esther as a bully was something that had essentially been erased. The dolt of a boyfriend had been ditched before university, as had the other hanger-onners, and a new Esther was born.

Except Leah hadn't forgotten.

At least there'd been some sort of apology, albeit two-and-a-half decades late.

As Leah sat at her desk, kind of working but not really, she wondered if she'd overreacted with Owen the day before. She kept circling back to the same thing: it was the surprise that shook her, not necessarily the questions. The fact she'd had a dream about what happened wasn't necessarily a surprise, it was more that Mark the Arsehole had splurged her secrets. If she was in Owen's position, she might have done the same thing.

But if she *had* overreacted, the problem was that she'd done it on camera. She couldn't quite remember what she'd said, but it probably hadn't looked, or sounded, good.

She skimmed through the emails on her phone. The one about 'what you did' had gone unanswered from the night before, largely because Leah had no idea what to reply. What, *precisely*, did it mean? *What* had she done? The emailer must either be guessing, or inventing their own theories.

Leah scrolled to the final one she'd received from Owen, suggesting a day and time they could meet for the interview. She actually *had* agreed to do it. Her 'sounds good' was right there, even though it had never once sounded good. That was one more thing she couldn't hold against him.

Leah considered emailing to ask if he'd leave out the part where she'd stumbled and eventually walked out on the interview. She started her message with a cheery 'Hi!' that was deleted almost as quickly as it was written. Leah didn't get much further, as she wondered if bringing up that awkwardness would inevitably make it even *more* awkward. If asking him to leave something out would ensure it went in.

Maybe she should ask for a second go at the interview? The fact she couldn't remember agreeing to the first, even though it was right there in her emails, was an irony not lost on her. She hadn't wanted to do any interviews and was now thinking about doing two.

Leah deleted the fourth version of 'Hi', which no longer had the exclamation mark. If she was going to email Owen, she needed a longer run-up at it. Was there a word halfway between 'hi' and 'hello'? Something that said 'Remember me? I'm not a psycho, but...'?

As her vision started to go hazy from the staring, Leah pushed herself up from her desk. At some point, she'd have to do some actual work, but not quite yet.

She yawned and headed around the office, thinly returning the smiles of her gossip-starved colleagues, though ignoring their hopeful raised eyebrows.

The kitchen was empty, though riddled with its usual smell of instant coffee. Those giant tubs of Nescafé had an odour that clung to walls like damp in a squat.

Leah filled the kettle and set it boiling, before hunting through the cupboards for the packet of leftover digestives that had been floating around a day or two before. She was never quite sure who bought the biscuits, only that they existed in an existential way. Any inquiries into from where they appeared might stop them showing up in various cupboards.

There were no digestives, only a few crumbs from what might have been a Jaffa Cake.

While the kettle bubbled, Leah treated herself to a satisfying lean against the wall, plus – hey, why not? – a good ol'-fashioned yawn. And another for good luck.

As her watering eyes cleared, Leah realised Naomi had

appeared in the cramped kitchen. Even though they were colleagues, the nature of working in community support meant many hours were spent outside the office. Naomi was one of Leah's younger co-workers, part of the generation who could text at breath-taking pace, regardless of how long their finger-nails might be.

'I was just seeing how you were doing,' Naomi said.

Leah batted away another yawn before it could envelope her. 'O... K...?' Leah replied, although it accidentally sounded like a question. She didn't think Naomi had ever asked how she was, nor vice versa.

'I saw the camera crew last night,' Naomi said. 'They were filming people walking in the centre of town. Lots of people were trying to talk to them.'

'Right.'

The kettle was starting to reach the vinegar stroke but Naomi talked over it. 'Do you reckon they'll find out what happened to your friends?'

'I'm not sure if it's that sort of film,' Leah replied. The successful attempt to stop herself yawning had given her an unintentional straight face.

Naomi stared for a moment or three, hoping for something juicier. When nothing further came, except the excited sputter of the kettle, she continued: 'My sister was in the year above you at school,' she said. 'My dad was part of the search party. He kept a load of the cuttings. I think he still has them. He wouldn't let me stay over at my friends' while I was at school.'

She smiled hopefully, though Leah wasn't sure how to reply. She'd heard similar things before and it always felt as if the person wanted some sort of apology for the stolen joy of youth. There was a time in which it used to annoy her but she'd come to see it was how the town coped.

Not that Leah had any idea of what to say. She returned the smile and then reached for the kettle. 'Want one?' she asked.

'I don't like hot drinks.'

Leah let that one go. Another curiosity of youth. She poured hot water into a mug that had 'World's Best Dad' on the side, and then dunked a Yorkshire Tea teabag into it.

'Can I ask you something?' Naomi said.

Leah kept back the 'I'd rather you didn't'. This was going to be about TikTok, something like that.

Naomi didn't wait for a reply. 'Can you meet a friend of mine?' she asked. 'She reckons she knows what happened to your friends.'

Leah had been committing the cardinal sin of poking the teabag with a spoon and was so surprised, that she splashed boiling water over the counter. She mopped it up with a tea towel and then turned to her colleague.

'Your friend... what?'

'She's a psychic. She's really good and helped me loads before I got married. Helped me pick the venue.'

Leah had somehow missed that Naomi was married and wondered when that had happened. She seemed far too young for all that. What was she? Twenty-two? Twenty-three?

'She helped you pick the venue?' Leah asked, though that was low down on her growing list of questions.

'She's incredibly spiritual and said she felt an aura. She predicted the pandemic, you know?'

Leah *really* forced herself not to roll her eyes. She scooped out the teabag with the dunking spoon, plopped it into the bin, and then splashed some milk into the mug. What with the spoon and late addition of milk, her drink was practically a crime scene.

She tried to reply kindly, a parent telling a toddler that, no, they couldn't visit the moon that evening. 'I'm kind of busy at the moment,' Leah said. 'I've got loads going on.'

Naomi didn't take the hint. 'She won't charge you. I was talking to her about it last night. She says she's going to visit the film crew anyway. Offer her assistance, that sort of thing. I said I knew you and I thought maybe you could talk to her first...? You never know what might come out.'

Leah almost asked about the sort of assistance that was going to be offered to Owen, before deciding she would rather not know. If she wasn't careful, she'd end up doing a second interview, on camera, as this alleged pandemic-predictor asked if anyone knew a person whose name began with a letter of the alphabet.

'I should get back,' Leah said, nodding past Naomi towards the main part of the office.

'I'll tell her you'll think about it,' Naomi added hopefully.

Leah wanted to say that the thinking had been completed, though it didn't feel worth it.

'Sounds good,' she said instead.

She hurried past the other woman, trying not to spill her frothy tea, while simultaneously avoiding any sort of eye contact and the potential interrogation that would go with it. *Yes, I did see the paper. Yes, it is twenty-five years next year. Yes, it is a long time.*

Leah sank behind her monitor and picked up her phone. She opened the email from the night before and typed without thinking.

What did I do?

As soon as it was sent, Leah wondered why she hadn't replied the night before. She knew someone was messing with her, and, despite telling herself she wouldn't get involved, she wanted to know.

The reply was back almost before Leah had put down her phone.

Big Asda. Recycling bins, near the opticians. 4 p.m.

FOURTEEN

Leah knew the spot to which the emailer was referring. It was around six months before that Zac had completed a reluctant clear-out of clothes that no longer fitted. She'd hauled off the pair of black bin bags to the recycling bins while doing the weekly big shop.

The email still read like a threat of sorts, except it was impossible not to be curious. Was the sender going to reveal themselves? What could they possibly have to say?

Knowing she had nobody work-related to visit that day, and that she couldn't concentrate on the paperwork, Leah ditched her grim-looking tea, and headed out. She didn't specifically have work hours and, as long as the job got done in the end, nobody minded too much. She could certainly get away with a bit of a skive.

Autumnal leaves were flittering on the breeze as Leah walked past Esther's theatre of glass and took her car from the parking area, before heading out of town in the opposite direction to where she lived. There were a few hours before her big date at the big Asda, and there was one person in whom she might be able to confide.

The semi-detached house sat on a quiet cul-de-sac that backed onto a wealth of rolling fields. It was the sort of place an estate agent would describe as 'desirable', which largely translated to: 'There aren't many screaming children around these parts.'

Leah knocked on the door and waited for the woman to open it. Shirley might have been twenty-odd years older than when Leah had first met her in her teenage bedroom – but she still stood trim and tall in the same way.

'Lee,' she said, with surprise. 'I wasn't expecting you.'

'How's retirement treating you?' Leah asked.

Shirley pushed her front door wider and stepped to the side. 'Boring. I hate it. There's some talk of them calling in a bunch of old-timers like me to work on cold cases but I've not heard anything back.' She grinned, and didn't appear to realise there was one particular case colder than the others. 'You coming in?' she asked.

Leah headed into the house and then, after Shirley closed the door, followed the other woman through to a conservatory at the back. It wasn't a particularly warm day, but there was a sizzle to the air underneath the glass.

Shirley ushered Leah into a wicker reclining thing. It looked like a cosy cross between a beanbag and a chair, but felt like getting a workover from a drunk acupuncturist. Shirley fussed, offering an array of potential drinks and snacks, before finally settling in a chair identical to the one in which Leah was wriggling.

'How's the husband?' Leah asked.

'He's taken up cycling and I hardly ever see him during the day. He gets up and goes out with a group of them. They head out to some pub in the middle of nowhere, have a pint and pie, then get back at about four every day.'

Leah thought on that. 'If you take out all the cycling, that sounds like a good day.'

Shirley laughed.

'What's *your* retirement hobby going to be?' Leah asked. 'Knitting?'

That got a side-eyed sigh. 'I'm thinking of ripping out the bathroom and putting in a new one myself. I've been watching YouTube videos about it.'

'Don't you need a bit more training than that?'

Another grin: 'What's the worst that can happen?'

'You flood the house?'

'You say "flood", I say "downstairs pool".'

Leah laughed now. She wasn't quite sure when she and Shirley had slipped from liaison officer and teenager into this sort of relationship.

'I did wonder if you might come by,' Shirley said. She was serious now. 'After the paper and all that. It's always good to see you.'

Leah smiled softly, unsure what to say.

'How's Zac?' Shirley asked.

'Good. He's in all the top sets at school. They've got mock exams this year, then full GCSEs next year.'

Shirley let out a long breath. 'Whew. He's that old already? I remember when he was born.'

It really had flown by. That was the thing with children. A blink and they were teenagers, halfway out the door on their way into adulthood.

Leah did have a reason for coming, though she didn't get to it because there was something distant in Shirley's face. 'What's wrong?' Leah asked.

Shirley pursed her lips. 'I was thinking about calling you anyway to ask if you'd come round. Or if I could come to yours.'

The odd thing was that Leah had felt a pull towards her former liaison officer in the last day or so. It might have been because of Owen, and being back in Vicky's house, but maybe there was something more. There'd always been some degree of synergy between them, despite the age imbalance. A teenage Leah hadn't had too many adults in her life whom she trusted.

Plus Leah believed in fate.

Shirley was fiddling with the ring on her finger, twiddling it one way, then the other. 'I've got something to tell you,' she said. 'There's a chance that, with this film being made, it's going to come out. I don't want you to find out from someone other than me.'

'What do you mean?' Leah asked.

Shirley gulped and there was a moment, a frozen fraction of a second, in which it felt as if it might really be bad. That whatever she said was going to change Leah's life, and not for the better.

It couldn't be that big, could it...?

'It's just... after the sleepover it was Christmas and then new year. Right after that, your dad came back to your house and, I've never said this before, but we failed you.' Another sigh. 'I failed you, but not just me. The police, social services, probably the council as well. We all looked at each other and nobody took responsibility.'

A lump had appeared in Leah's throat that was so large she could barely swallow. This exact thing was her job now. She would visit those in need and try to ensure people *didn't* slip through the cracks. That the fragile alliance between social services, the council and the police didn't break entirely. That everybody didn't assume somebody else was doing their job.

'Is that what you wanted to tell me?' Leah managed. She wasn't quite sure how she croaked the words past the lump.

Shirley shook her head and sighed once more. She was staring at the floor. 'No. The reason we took your mum, the reason she ended up in that hospital, is because she said she was going to kill you. It was only a few weeks after the sleepover. That's why she was locked up. It wasn't only for her protection.' A pause. 'It was for yours.'

The windows of the conservatory were closing in, the roof plummeting. Leah realised she was hugging her arms across her front.

'I thought it was because she'd hurt herself...?'

Shirley was studiously avoiding eye contact and even Leah recognised the reversed roles from when they had first met.

'She did,' Shirley said. 'But that wasn't the only reason. It wasn't even the *main* reason. There was the fight with your father and then he took off. Your neighbours called the police, which is why we'd shown up. She told three different officers she was going to kill you. That's why she was sectioned.'

Leah couldn't speak. It felt untrue, except she knew with absolute certainty that it was. How had so much time passed without anyone saying? She had been upstairs the entire time it was happening. She'd heard the shouting and the fight, the slammed doors and then, a little later, the arrival of the police. It was barely three weeks after her friends had disappeared. A week after she'd seen Esther at the New Year's Eve bonfire.

'Why did she say that?' Leah asked, although she knew.

'I wasn't there,' Shirley said. 'I read the reports but it didn't say.'

Leah thought on that. 'She never hit me, not once.' A pause, as her stomach knotted itself.

That wasn't news to Shirley, although it was now the other woman who appeared lost for words.

Leah wanted to give reasons. 'I don't think Mum meant it when she said that,' she explained, and she wanted to believe it.

Shirley didn't reply, not to that. 'That's why you weren't allowed to go back and live with her properly. I know you did when you were a bit older and it was your choice, but not right after. We all kept it from you, including me, but I think this film crew have a source in the police. They might know about what she said. If it comes out, I didn't want you to find out from someone else.'

Leah didn't know how or why such information could end up in the documentary. What happened to her friends, and her mother, were separate incidents – even if they had happened weeks apart.

'I should've told you a long time ago. I guess it never felt right.' Shirley waited a moment and looked up, waiting for Leah to catch her eye. 'I'm sorry.'

Leah nodded, unsure how she felt. If she was annoyed at anyone, it wasn't Shirley.

'Does Deborah know?' Leah asked.

That got a nod. 'She and Nick were happy to take you in anyway.' It felt like she'd finished but she added a quick and clarifying: 'That's not why they did.'

Leah wanted that to be true. Harriet's parents had been so kind and accommodating. A handful of weeks after their own daughter had disappeared, they had opened their doors to the teenage girl who'd been left. Now, so many years on, Leah had found out it was because her real mum had threatened to kill her. Or, maybe, not entirely because. It was hard to know without asking, and maybe she didn't want to know.

'They look after Zac when he finishes school,' Leah said. 'Deborah mainly. He doesn't really need looking after any more but he's been going over for so long that it's his routine now. They love him, like, um... regular grandparents.'

That lump was back in her throat.

Maybe it didn't matter if they'd only taken her in because of that death threat? Even if that was the catalyst, they had still given her that safe space. They had loved her. *Did* love her.

'I'm so sorry it took this long to tell you,' Shirley said.

Leah thought on it for a moment. 'The wrong parent died,' she said. It wasn't the first time she'd thought it, though it was the first time she'd said it. 'It wasn't Mum's fault. She always had moments like that after Dad came home.'

That instance in her bedroom, when Leah had told Shirley

it was OK if her dad came home had hung over so much of her life. Why hadn't she said it definitely *wasn't* fine? She thought about it a lot.

A moment passed between the two women, more than that. Fleeting decades compressed into seconds. They both knew how different Leah's life could have been if not for that lie. Or if Shirley had seen through it.

'Your dad was, er... our main suspect for a while,' Shirley said. 'I think you know that already. Suspect's probably the wrong word.'

Leah hadn't quite been listening. There had been a lot to take in.

'He disappeared from his halfway house the night your friends went missing. We never did find out where he went.'

Leah had heard that before, though hadn't thought too much about it. When it came to her father, especially after the night of the big fight with her mum, Leah tried to ignore much of it.

'Was there ever anything to say he was near Vicky's house?' she asked.

'Not as such. A few sightings of men who could've been him but, in all honesty, they could've been anyone. There was no CCTV back then.'

Leah was nodding, unsure what else to do.

Shirley wasn't done: 'With everything he did later, it's hard to wonder.'

It wasn't true, Leah knew that much. Her dad couldn't be anything to do with her friends' disappearance. Someone would've put together the pieces a long while before.

'Do you still think he might've been there?' Leah asked anyway.

'No... I don't know. I suppose I've been wondering if this film might get some answers for us all.'

It was still hard for Leah to know what to make of any of it. Hard to get past the talk of her mother's threats to kill her.

'Are the crew talking to you?' Leah asked.

'I'm not sure yet. I'm retired, so I suppose there's no issues with having to go through the police. I did get an email from Owen-somebody. I was after some assurances and waiting for him to come back to me.'

'They spoke to Mark,' Leah said.

'Your Mark? Why?'

'They paid him and he told them about a dream I had, where I saw someone taking the girls out of the room.' Leah barely left a space before swiftly adding: 'I didn't *really* see that. It was a dream, years later. I only told him. I didn't think he'd pass it on to anyone.'

Shirley pushed herself up in the seat, the protective liaison officer kicking back in. 'Huh... well maybe I'll have a proper *chat* with this Owen-something...'

She said 'chat' in the way an ultimate fighter might say 'arm break'.

'Don't,' Leah said, with something close to a smile.

Shirley smiled back, the potential arm-breaking off the cards. 'Is tomorrow your mum's...?'

It was only then that Leah remembered why she'd driven over in the first place. She was on the brink of leaving without ever getting to it.

'Yes,' she replied. 'Can you come with me?'

'Of course.'

Leah looked at the clock on the wall. It was half-three and she needed to get going. She pushed herself up and cricked her back.

'That chair's awful,' she said.

Shirley was also on her feet now. 'I know. I've been trying to get rid of them.' A pause and then: 'I'll see you at the cemetery tomorrow.'

FIFTEEN

Leah was sitting in her car, not waiting *at* the recycling bins, but in sight of them. The back end of the Asda car park, away from the petrol station, was almost always deserted. Leah could park in among the regular shoppers' cars, while still having a clear view. If the emailer knew which car she drove, it would be easy to spot her, but Leah would deal with that if and when she needed to.

It was three fifty-seven and Leah's phoned buzzed with a WhatsApp message from Ben, saying that Josh and Zac were safely back at his after school.

Leah got a similar message each day, usually from Deborah to say her son was safe. It was a part of life now, as those around her did their best to prevent her worrying.

She replied to Ben's message with a 'Thanks, have a good night', added a supplementary kiss by mistake, then deleted it in time before pressing send. She was too used to messaging Deborah.

It was three fifty-eight and Leah re-read the email from earlier.

Big Asda. Recycling bins, near the opticians. 4 p.m.

That's where she was, with two minutes to go.

There had been a large power imbalance in her emails with the mystery person. They seemed to know something she didn't, perhaps many things. It also felt as if they were toying with her, although that was hard to know for sure.

She waited. Silence – and then a buzz as an email arrived. For a moment, Leah thought it would be more from her anonymous 'friend'. Instead, it was from the school, titled 'Important note about Monday'.

For an educational institution, someone at the school should learn the definition of the word 'important'. Everything they sent was labelled with language like 'urgent', 'important', or 'critical'. Then it would turn out to be about a minor change to the school's lunch menu.

Leah ignored the email and re-read the one about the recycling bins. Despite her feigned-ignorance reply to the 'what you did' email, Leah had a tiny inkling what it could be. The thing was, only one person knew – and it was impossible for that person to be emailing her. As impossible as it could be.

Leah hammered out a quick message to Deborah, asking how the day's filming had gone. The reply came back a minute later.

Good! Tell you when I see you!

Three fifty-nine.

There was nobody by the recycling area, not even a sign of anybody heading *towards* there. A line of trees separated the recycling area from the road, casting shadows across the row of bottle banks and clothes bins. Someone had got stuck in one of the large metal clothes drop-offs a couple of years before, while trying to see if there was anything worthwhile inside. They'd been in there for almost twenty hours until someone had heard the banging and calling.

Four o'clock.

Leah had been watching the recycling area for almost fifteen minutes and not a soul had been near it. The closest building was a small opticians attached to the supermarket. A poster outside advertised three for two glasses, though Leah hadn't seen anyone head into that place either.

One minute past four.

Someone in a grumbling Volkswagen that appeared to be crossed with a lawnmower did a loop of the parking bays, slowing as they neared the bottle bank. A shadow in the driver's seat angled themselves from side to side, as if searching for something, or someone. For a moment, Leah thought the car was going to stop – but then the driver accelerated back towards the main supermarket.

Still nobody.

Two minutes past four. Three.

Leah got out of her car and stood, turning in a circle to see if there was anything, or anyone, she'd missed. She shivered, feeling watched, even though the only person she could see was a woman on the far side, wrestling a trolley with a dodgy wheel across the car park.

She twisted back towards the recycling bins and then set off towards them. Still nobody in sight, yet that feeling of eyes being on her wouldn't shift.

When Leah reached the row of bottle banks and clothes drop-offs, she braced herself, half-expecting someone to leap out. They'd have been hiding the entire time, waiting for her to approach.

No one.

Leah walked in a small circle, giving herself a chance to check behind the recycling containers. There really was nobody there, and Leah rechecked the email to make sure she was in the right place. There was only one Asda in town, so it couldn't be anywhere else.

She was about to head back to her car when she spotted the canvas bag for life laid flat on the crumbling tarmac. It was bright and new, something that looked like it had been bought recently, as opposed to a bag that had been rattling around someone's car boot for a few years.

Except it wasn't an area for new things. A soggy pair of leggings was sitting in the shadows next to one of the bins, while a scattering of broken glass was almost hidden by the growing shadows of the bottle bank.

Leah stepped across to the bag and stood over it, scanning the car park for movement. Someone was making a mess of reversing into a spot and was up to their fourth attempt of trying to get it straight. The driver was paying no attention to Leah.

She crouched and picked up the bag. It had looked empty but the gentle heft made it immediately obvious something was inside. Nothing too heavy.

Leah checked her deserted surroundings once more, and then opened the bag handles wide to look inside.

Sitting at the bottom was a transparent sandwich bag, the Ziploc clamped closed. It was easy enough to see inside, though Leah couldn't quite believe what she was seeing.

It was a knife.

A very familiar knife.

SIXTEEN

SEVEN DAYS BEFORE THE SLEEPOVER

SATURDAY 11 DECEMBER 1999

Leah was sitting on the floor of Vicky's bedroom, flipping through the pages of a magazine to which she wasn't really paying attention. She had never quite got into the sort of publications girls their age were supposed to be reading. Most of it was clothes they should be wearing, or women they should try to look like. It was hard to care about any of that when she would sit in her own bedroom, listening to the chaos of her parents below. It all felt so trivial.

Leah's stomach grumbled and it was so loud that Vicky looked down to her curiously. Vicky was on her bed, using a pile of pillows and cushions to prop herself into a position that was almost sitting. She also wasn't into the sort of magazines teenagers were supposed to read, but for completely different reasons.

'Do you want to read this?' Vicky asked. She offered what looked like a photocopied pamphlet to a somewhat bemused Leah.

'What is it?' Leah asked.

'I got it in the post. Have a look.'

That hadn't answered the question but Leah took the wedge of stapled-together A4 pages. 'Things They Don't Want You To Know' was printed on the front in a simplistic font, along with some sort of triangle shape.

'You have to mail stamps to this place in Bournemouth, and they send it to you,' Vicky said, as if it was a completely normal method of purchasing goods. 'I saw it advertised in the *Fortean Times*.'

Leah wasn't entirely sure what that was, although Vicky had mentioned it a couple of times. She went through phases of being intensely interested in something, then dropping it a few weeks later. Leah, Jazz and Harriet had long accepted it as one of their friend's quirks and were content enough to let her be, even if one of her recent curiosities was apparently conspiracy theories.

The quality of the magazine was dubious to say the least. Multiple rounds of photocopying left the once black ink a faded grey. Apart from the minimalist cover, there was little in the way of pictures inside. There were a few drawings from a person who was either a toddler or someone using their weak hand. There were no columns, with the words running the full width of the A4 pages. It was like something Leah might print for a school project, but more ramshackle.

The second page had the headline 'What really happened in Dunblane', followed by four pages of type. After that was 'What it's like to live in a suicide cult?', and then 'Who's funding Blair's Britain?'

Even for Vicky, it was... niche.

'Dad says I shouldn't be reading that stuff,' Vicky said dismissively.

'Why *are* you reading it?'

'It's amazing the things they don't want you to know.'

'Who's *they*?'

Vicky thought for a moment. 'Y'know, governments, rich people. You should read that cult thing.'

Leah continued to scan through the pages. There was an article titled 'Revealed! What's underneath Downing Street', which, from what Leah could tell was a series of tunnels. Another piece laid out 'How to survive the Y2K bug', which appeared to be finding a shed and storing lots of canned food.

It was vaguely interesting in the sense that it seemed utterly mad. Still, no harm done. Vicky would have lost interest within a few weeks.

'Dad says everyone can stay over on Saturday,' Vicky said. She was doodling something on a pad as she spoke. 'He's at some football thing, so we'll have the whole house.'

'Who's everyone?'

'You, me, Jazz.' A pause. 'Maybe Harriet.'

'Why only "maybe"?'

A shrug. 'Dunno. She's a bit up herself, isn't she?'

This was a side of Vicky that Leah had seen a handful of times. As with her rapidly shifting interests, it was like she occasionally got bored of her friends and would create drama for the sake of it. Leah had a persisting, niggling, thought that, one day, Vicky would have had enough of her. That she would move on to new friends, in the way she moved on to new hobbies.

'It'll be better if Harriet and Jazz *both* come,' Leah said.

Vicky curled a lip and then shrugged. 'Whatever. You're allowed over, right?'

Leah mumbled a yes. She had no intention of asking her mum as there was no point. Her mother wouldn't notice if she was in or out of the house come Saturday, and, even if she did give permission, wouldn't remember by the time things came around.

'Dad says he'll get in some frozen pizzas, 'cos we spent too much on delivery last time.'

The idea of pizza meant Leah was looking forward to it already.

She turned the page to an article headlined: 'How the charts are rigged'. This at least sounded interesting, although, from a brief skim, the secret seemed to be that the songs which sold more ended up higher in the chart. That didn't seem like much of a rigging.

'Dad's been really weird recently,' Vicky said. 'Weirder than usual. He keeps going on about moles destroying the garden.'

'Moles?'

'Y'know, those giant rat things that dig underneath stuff. He keeps finding these holes in the lawn and then says stuff like, "Just wait 'til I get my hands on one."'

'How's he going to get his hands on one?'

'No idea, that's part of the weirdness. He was sitting outside in the dark last Sunday. I asked what he was doing and he said he was waiting for the mole.'

Vicky laughed and Leah joined in. Leah would have happily taken this degree of weirdness from a father. It was better than the rare occasions her dad wasn't in prison, under arrest for something, or who knew where. The quirky pottering of Vicky's father had to be preferable to the raging arguments that bled through Leah's floor.

'Did he get the mole?' Leah asked.

'I doubt it. He was out there with a rake. What was he going to do? Scratch its head?' Vicky grinned and glanced towards her window and the memory beyond. She had been twisting a ring that was on the index finger of her right hand, then removed it and switched it to the ring finger on her left. As she continued twiddling it, she realised Leah was watching. 'Do you want to try it on?' she asked.

Leah wasn't bothered but Vicky had already removed the ring and passed it across. It was thin and gold, slightly greasy with sweat or dirt. A clear jewel was encrusted into the top, light sparkling across its angles. Leah first held it up to get a clearer look, then pushed it effortlessly onto the little finger on her right hand, before moving it onto her ring finger.

'Is this yours?' Leah asked. She had never seen her friend wearing it before.

'It used to be Mum's.' Vicky lowered her voice and peeped at her closed door. 'Dad doesn't know I have it.'

Leah rotated it on her finger, then took it off. The ring was weightier than she'd have thought, given its dainty size. She passed it back to Vicky, who returned it to the ring finger on her left hand.

'Is it a real diamond?' Leah asked.

'Yes, it's her engagement ring. I found it in Dad's top drawer, at the back.'

Leah almost asked why Vicky had been searching in such a place, except she had also gone hunting through her parents' room on the odd occasion. She hadn't found much of anything there, certainly not anything valuable. If her mum had ever owned a diamond ring, which felt unlikely, it would have been sold long before.

But if Vicky was in the mood to talk about secrets, Leah had something to tell her. She waited for a moment, ensuring Vicky's dad wasn't anywhere close enough to hear. He'd been downstairs not long before, and she hadn't heard anyone coming up.

Vicky was still twisting the ring around her finger, while reading a magazine.

'Can I show you something?' Leah asked. She didn't wait for an answer, picking up her small pink bag from the corner. Her door key was inside, along with a five-pound note that her mum didn't know she had. There were a couple of crumpled tissues, plus a hair scrunchie.

Buried under all that was the only item with any real

weight. Leah gripped it and felt a moment of hesitation as she held it up for Vicky to see. The other girl squinted and reached for it. Leah let her take it and said: 'There's a release button where your thumb goes.'

Vicky tapped it – and let out a surprised 'oooh' as the blade of the knife sprang from its handle. She held the weapon a fraction higher, testing the weight, eyeing the needling, sharpened point.

'Why have you got this?' she asked.

Leah watched the light twinkle from the steel. 'Dad...'

Vicky didn't reply at first. She passed the knife from one hand to the other, and then pressed the blade back into its handle. 'Remember when he locked us in the car?' she asked.

Leah did. Of course she did. For a reason she couldn't remember, he had picked them both up from school. That was back when they had a car, before it had been sold or repossessed. As soon as the two of them had got into the vehicle, Leah knew something wasn't right. Her father was silent, gaze fixed ahead, knuckles white from squeezing the steering wheel. Vicky had barely closed the back door when he'd taken off. He was furious at a slower driver; angrier yet at a red light, for which he barely bothered to stop. Leah still remembered that rippling worry as the central locks *clunked* for no reason, other than that he had decided they weren't for leaving.

She and Vicky lived in one direction, but her father had barrelled in the other. The country lanes had become a terrifying blur of leaves and bushes. Leah hadn't been bold enough to say anything from the front seat, even as she sensed Vicky's terror from the back.

Eventually, her dad had circled back towards town, his incomprehensible rage having disappeared as swiftly as it had arrived. He had stopped outside Vicky's house and unlocked the doors as if it had been a regular drive home.

The girls hadn't spoken of it since – and Leah never got into

a car with her father after that. She would walk in the
hammering rain to avoid such a thing, not that he was at home
too often.

That's why Vicky knew that 'Dad' was enough of an explanation for Leah's knife.

'What about the car journey with *your* dad?' Leah replied,
wanting to change the subject. She didn't need to say which one
and the two girls shared a wordless moment of a much happier
memory.

Tom, Vicky's dad, had once driven the girls to the beach for
the day. They'd eaten ice cream and chips, in that order, and
then – on the way home – he'd pulled over to the side of the
road. They momentarily hadn't known why but he'd walked
them around a large metal gate into a large field with wild
flowers as far as they could see.

'It was so bright,' Vicky said – and it had been. A kaleido-
scope of shades and smells, through which the girls had been
allowed to wander unhindered. Their own private paradise,
hidden in plain sight, in the middle of nowhere. Something
Vicky's father had known about and taken them to. Leah had no
idea where it was, other than the vague notion it was on the way
back from the beach.

Vicky passed the knife back and Leah slipped it into her
bag. She had been keeping its existence to herself and suddenly
felt lighter now that somebody else knew.

'Is your dad out of prison?' Vicky asked.

'No – but Mum said he might be soon.'

Vicky thought for a second and then her features hardened.
'I dunno why she lets him hit her. I wouldn't.'

Leah didn't know how to reply. It didn't feel as simple as
her mum *letting* herself be hit. Except, maybe she did know
how to reply. She felt a fire that had appeared from nowhere
and had to stop herself from shouting that her mum didn't *let*
him hit her. It *wasn't* her choice.

But Vicky had moved on, oblivious to what she'd said. 'Do you take it to school?' she asked.

Leah realised she had been digging her nails into her palms. She couldn't quite speak at first, managing to nod, before croaking: 'In my main bag. In the side pocket.'

She flashed back to the school assembly a few months before, that had happened after the Columbine shootings in the US. Everyone had seen the news footage and it was baffling that children would go to school and end up being shot. Leah had never even seen a gun in real life, and she supposed it was the same for most people she knew.

That hadn't stopped the assembly, in which the deputy head had urged all students to report to a teacher if they knew someone was bringing a weapon into school. At that exact moment, the knife had been hidden in her school bag. Now somebody knew she had it. She instantly wished she'd said nothing, assuming trouble would come down the line.

'Where'd you get it?' Vicky asked.

'Market stall in town. I told the guy I was buying it as a present for my brother.'

'You don't have a br—' Vicky interrupted herself with an 'Oh.'

Leah had paid cash, with twenty quid she'd found hidden in her parents' room. Another reason she hadn't been surprised at her friend snooping in her own dad's space. Maybe all children had that urge at some point?

'Between us,' Leah said.

That got a nod, as Vicky went back to twisting the ring on her finger. 'Yeah,' she replied. 'Between us.'

SEVENTEEN

NOW

Leah stared at the knife that she'd taken from the canvas bag for life. It had been a long, long time since she'd last seen it. Last held it.

It had felt so heavy when she was a teenager and used to carry it around in her small pink bag, or the side pocket of her school bag. It was unmistakeably the same, and yet that heft seemed to have disappeared over the years. She could control it with just her thumb and index finger.

Leah tapped the release button, and the blade sprang forward, making her let out a gentle 'oooh' of surprise.

Somebody else had made the same noise a long time ago.

Leah thumbed the blade back into the handle and then reburied the knife in the supermarket bag. She balled up the bag and then looked around, expecting somebody to be in front of her.

There was nobody. She was alone as she had been moments before.

Except someone had emailed her the location and then left the knife for her. They had wanted her to find it.

The last time Leah had seen it was twenty-four years

before. She had taken it to the sleepover in her pink bag, out of habit than anything more. At some point that evening, or the following morning, the bag had gone missing. Leah had only noticed when she got home and realised she didn't have her key. She'd gone back but Vicky's house had been taped off. She'd thought about asking the police if anyone had found her bag – though hadn't wanted to alert them to its presence, in case they found the knife.

The knife, along with the bag, had vanished.

Until now.

Leah hurried back to her car and threw herself inside. She dropped the canvas bag and knife on the passenger seat and took out her phone. Leah loaded the email from 'A Friend' but was trying to reply too quickly. Her fingers were thumbs and she had to correct the email in half a dozen places until it made sense. Send was pressed without a second thought.

How did you know about the knife?

Leah felt so frantic that she half expected an instant reply. She needed it. How could the person know the knife was hers? *How?* She'd only ever told one person. Even if someone had found it much later, even if it had been in her bag, they couldn't have known for sure it was hers.

The answer was obvious, of course, even if it wasn't. Even if it was impossible.

Leah typed out a second email, simpler than the first. Five characters and a question mark.

Vicky?

EIGHTEEN

NOW

Leah had barely slept.

Ben had sent texts through the evening, assuring her that Zac was safe and well, playing games in Josh's room, broadly under his supervision. As much as any fourteen-year-olds were under an adult's supervision. On any other day, any other occasion, Leah would have been worrying despite the texts. Sure, Zac was safe and well *at that exact moment*, but that wasn't overnight.

Ben's final text had come at half-past eleven, saying he was off to bed. He had checked on the boys, who were doing the same. She had thanked him and then spent most of the early hours in bed, staring at the ceiling. She was concerned about Zac not being on the other side of the wall from her – but there was a lot more to be bothered about.

No email had been received after Leah's 'Vicky?' Nothing to say it was, or wasn't. The emailer – 'A Friend' – specifically wanted Leah to stop the documentary. They must have a reason for that and, if – somehow – it was Vicky, who more than her would want things halted? She would have been hiding some-where for twenty-four years.

Except it couldn't be her.

It wasn't just impossible, it was beyond that.

But what could Leah do? There'd been no explicit threats, no real demands – beyond stopping the film. No crime had been committed. Even if she wanted to tell someone, what was there to tell?

Leah was sitting in her car outside the gates of the town cemetery. She pressed her head on the driver's side window and yawned.

Across from her car, a waist-high rocky wall ringed the graveyard, with the field of headstones banking up towards the secondary space beyond. Clumps of flowers in varying states of rot provided dots of colour in among the slabs, while a lone woman in black was hunched over a plot on the furthest side. She crouched slowly, going down in stages, before dropping what looked like a small teddy, and then standing taller once more.

Leah turned from the cemetery and read the email that gave the time and place for where she'd found the knife. Somebody was messing with her.

As she yawned again, a new text arrived from Zac. Despite her worry the night before, he was fine and had messaged her first thing this morning to say so. After that, he had also asked if he could go bowling with some of his friends later.

Now came the somewhat expected follow-up:

Can you give us a lift?

Despite her mood, Leah chuckled at that. Parents would always be good for one thing: free taxi rides.

She replied to say it was fine and then checked the spam email folder, in case something had been nabbed. There was the usual array of competitions she'd somehow won, despite not entering, three EuroMillions payouts due, something about treatment for baldness, plus a genuine email from a supermarket, saying her loyalty points were expiring. It didn't sound like much of a two-way relationship, if rewards could be wiped in such fashion. Not that Leah read past the subject.

There was nothing from the anonymous friend.

Leah jumped at the gentle tap on the passenger window. Shirley's face appeared, offering a soft smile, as Leah realised she had somehow missed her former liaison officer parking next to her. She removed the keys and then got out of the car, before locking it.

'You look tired,' Shirley said, as she watched Leah loop around the vehicle.

'Good morning to you, too,' Leah replied.

Shirley snorted, almost girlishly. She had a satchel looped over her shoulder and crouched a fraction to look into the car. 'Just us?' she asked.

'Zac's at his friend's.'

'Overnight?' There was surprised concern there, which was probably understandable, even as Leah tried to pass it off as no big deal.

'He's had sleepovers before,' Leah replied, even though she wasn't sure why she was lying. 'It's not like he knew her anyway,' she added quickly, nodding towards the cemetery.

Shirley smiled kindly and it felt like she wanted to say something, even though she didn't. 'Is it on the top field?' she asked instead, turning to take in the cemetery.

Leah nodded beyond her and said 'This way,' before heading through the gates.

The two women took the path through the lower plots and then followed the switchbacks up the slope to the higher meadow. The graves were closer together the further they got from the gates, with smaller stones and fewer words on those stones. They passed a plot bare of any writing, but with a bed of children's toys carpeting the space. Further along, there was an area where a stone frog had been placed, instead of a grave.

They kept walking into the shadows towards the trees at the back. The plots were tighter still close to the furthest wall, and there was little in the way of flowers, toys, or other ornaments. Leah hadn't brought anything herself, she never did. Instead, she settled close to a small gravestone, sheltered by an over-hanging tree. The ground was soft, the grass dewy, with a dotted line of animal prints leading towards the wall. Probably a fox, something like that.

Leah's mother's gravestone was a small mossy square, with a simple 'BRENDA PEARCE' engraved in the centre. When the time had come to pay, Leah didn't have enough to add the dates she'd been alive. There had been some talk of an instalment plan, but Leah knew she wouldn't be visiting too often, and neither would anyone else. It's not as if her mother would be around to care.

'Are you OK?' Shirley asked, and Leah had a creasing shiver of déjà vu. It felt as if she might have asked the same thing the year before.

'I still think about the train driver sometimes,' Leah said quietly, which was something of an understatement. Every time she saw a train – in real life, in photos, on television, anywhere – she would think of the poor sod who was driving when her mum had jumped in front. Had he seen her face in that final microsecond? Had they locked eyes? Was there any way he could have tried to stop? Did he still think about it? She knew what it was like to dream about something many years after it happened.

'It wasn't your fault,' Shirley said softly – and that hair-raising déjà vu was back. It seemed like something else she had said before. 'It would be called mental health issues now,'

Shirley added. 'She'd get a proper diagnosis, there would be a name for it.'

Leah didn't know how true that was, certainly the diagnosis part. There were always stories around about mental health issues going untreated. Back then, people thought her mum was a shouty, mad woman who had problems. Perhaps they would still think the same now?

Leah now knew her mother had made threats to kill her, and been sent to a psychiatric hospital largely because of it. Leah had gone to live with Harriet's parents until her birth mother was released later that same year. Weeks after that, she had thrown herself in front of a train.

That had all happened within a year of the sleepover.

'Lee...?'

Leah jolted back to the present. 'What?'

Shirley stretched and took Leah's hand. The older woman's fingers were clammy from the uphill walk. 'I know I've told you before, that none of this is new, but this wasn't your fault. You didn't ask to be born with the parents you had. You didn't ask for your friends to go missing. You didn't ask for your dad to attack your mum more than once. None of this is on you.'

The former liaison officer released Leah's hand and they continued to stand over the grave. Leah swallowed away the lump in her throat. This wasn't the conversation she wanted.

'Do you think they, um... might be out there somewhere?'

Leah didn't look up from her mother's resting place.

Shirley took a few seconds to find the words: 'Your friends?'

'Yes.'

It sounded madder out loud.

'Maybe not all of them,' Leah added, unsure where she was going, even as she spoke the words. 'Maybe just one of them? Vicky, or...'

Shirley shuffled from one foot to the other as Leah wished she had stayed quiet.

'I know the answer you might want,' Shirley replied carefully. 'But it's been a very long time and it's incredibly unlikely. There would have been a sign somewhere. A clue. Anything.'

It felt like Shirley the police officer speaking, not Shirley the friend. It was probably what Leah needed to hear, and, deep down, what she knew to be true.

None of the girls were still out there, not even Vicky.

Except somebody had left that knife for her to find. Someone knew what it meant.

'People don't just disappear,' Leah said.

Shirley took a breath and Leah could feel her searching for the words. 'The thing is, sometimes they do. Not into thin air but lots of people are there and then not. Thousands. Tens of thousands, if you look wider. Probably hundreds of thousands if we're talking worldwide. It's always been like that. We feel safe if we tell ourselves it doesn't happen, but it does.'

Leah knew it was true. It felt as if every human had their own podcast these days, and that at least half of those were about missing people. Leah thought it would only be a matter of time until someone made one about her missing friends, then she remembered a film was being made instead.

Shirley shuffled the satchel from her shoulder until she was holding it in both hands. 'I know this isn't the right place but maybe, with what you were saying, it's the right time. I didn't know you were going to bring it up. I was going to do this later.'

The older woman lifted the flap of the bag and unzipped an inner compartment, before taking out a cardboard wallet, which she passed across. A number was printed in the top corner, along with 'Merrivale'.

Vicky's last name.

'What is it?'

'You didn't get this from me,' Shirley said. 'I've been told very unofficially by one of my former colleagues that the film-maker, Owen, has a copy. That's the only reason I was able to get this. It didn't feel right that he knows something you don't.'

Leah opened the cover and saw the name 'Victoria Merrivale' at the top. She could read on, except Shirley was still talking.

'If you ever want rid of it, burn it,' she said. 'This copy shouldn't exist but you should look on page three.'

Leah flipped the printed pages and read the first few lines. 'There was a sighting of Vicky...?'

NINETEEN

Shirley turned from the grave, back towards the front of the cemetery. 'I need to get out of here,' she said. 'Let's walk.'

Leah's mum had had her five minutes – ten if the walk was counted – and that was enough.

It was the older woman who took the lead on the journey away from the resting place of Leah's mother. Leah closed the cardboard wallet but clasped it tightly as she slotted in at Shirley's side.

They were on the switchbacks in between the fields, but away from the graves, when Shirley next spoke. 'I couldn't have you finding out from someone else, let alone when the film comes out.'

As they passed a bench, Shirley slowed and then nodded towards it. Leah wasn't going to argue and they ended up sitting together, staring across the lower part of the cemetery.

On the furthest side, a man in a vest had started digging a plot.

'It was not long after the twentieth anniversary,' Shirley said. 'They'd put out those pictures where they'd aged the girls, trying to say what they'd look like as adults.'

'I remember.'

It had happened more than once, with each version of Leah's friends looking more ridiculous than the last.

'We had a call from someone who was certain they were working with Victoria' – Leah let out a low gasp – 'but the Victoria from those images. The one where they guessed what she'd look like. And that stuff *is* a guess. When I told you there hadn't been any sightings of *Victoria*, that's true.'

Leah had the folder open again and was flipping to the end. 'It says "No further action"...?'

Shirley nodded. 'It's why I never brought it up, or told you. One of my colleagues visited the office. It was only fifteen miles away, so down the road. We did it unofficially, no uniforms, that sort of thing. We didn't want to give the impression of seriousness when it wasn't.'

'But you still checked?'

'Not me personally, but yes. We visited the office and we spoke to the person who claimed they were working with Victoria. We also spoke to "Victoria" herself.'

Something brushed the back of Leah's neck.

'From what I was told, the person involved really *did* look like the E-fit, to the point that it could have been a slightly grainy photo of her. She hadn't seen the news story, or the photo, but, when it was shown to her, she assumed they'd used a picture of her. It says in there she was quite upset by it.'

Leah flicked through the pages, wondering if there were photos. Shirley seemed to have read her mind.

'This was all unofficial,' she said. 'It wouldn't have been appropriate to ask her for a photo. The only reason the file exists is because one of our bosses wanted something in black and white. The fact it's been photocopied at least twice is something else that definitely shouldn't have happened. If your filmmaker hadn't been given a copy, you wouldn't have this one.'

Leah continued looking through the pages. It read like a

retelling of two informal interviews for which no notes had been taken. She really wanted to find the old E-fit and compare it to the woman from the office. Her name had been blacked out, so Leah couldn't simply type it into a search engine and see what came out.

'How do you know it wasn't Vicky?'

'Because she said she wasn't her.'

Leah was suddenly invested, utterly convinced this mystery office worker was somehow, miraculously, her old friend. It was this person who wanted Owen's documentary stopped, and who'd left the knife for Leah to find. Things finally made sense!

'Those aged E-fits are unreliable at best,' Shirley said. 'There are apps now. Try it on an old photo of yourself and I guarantee you the result will look nothing like you. The technology four years ago wasn't even as good as that.'

'But you just took her word that she wasn't Vicky?'

Shirley shook her head. She was staring into the distance, watching the man dig the grave. A mound of dirt was in a large barrow at his side and he had stopped momentarily to wipe his brow. 'I always assumed there was some sort of commercial digger,' Shirley said. 'I suppose it has to be done by a person, otherwise the wheels or tracks would destroy the rest of the land.' She stopped, sighed. 'We didn't only take her word for it, no. She has a driving licence, passport, birth certificate. Everything you'd expect. It's all listed in there.'

Leah had closed the folder but gripped it hard. 'You can fake those things...?'

She said it like a question, unsure if a person actually could. It sounded like the sort of thing that happened in sloppily conceived crime novels.

'She went out of her way to prove she *wasn't* Vicky,' Shirley said. 'She was as stunned by the resemblance as anyone else. She showed us her documents, even though there was no obligation, and we hadn't asked.'

Leah thought for a moment. Perhaps this mystery woman was *too* keen to clear her name – except Shirley had read her mind again.

'She'll never be able to win if your starting point is that she's Victoria. If she shows proof it isn't her, she's too eager; if she doesn't, she has something to hide.'

Leah had momentarily forgotten that Shirley had known her for more than two decades, and had spent almost all that time working for the police. She knew her stuff, and she knew Leah.

'Why wasn't there a proper investigation?' Leah asked, tapping the folder. 'Why only this?'

'What was there to investigate? No crimes had happened. Believe it or not, disappearing isn't a crime. People are allowed to walk out on their lives and go somewhere else, not that I'm saying that's what happened.'

Leah wished she knew more about it. She had never known that disappearing wasn't any sort of crime by itself – except of course it wasn't. People could leave abusive partners without telegraphing their move. Was it the same with children? Probably not, though a long time had passed.

If only her mother had left, and taken Leah with her.

Across the cemetery, an older woman had stopped to talk to the gravedigger. He was leaning the spade against his collarbone as he smiled kindly to her. Leah could imagine the small talk: something about hard work on a warm day, that sort of thing. She found her mind drifting, wondering if it was a full-time job, with him visiting different cemeteries on different days. Week after week of shovelling.

'What if it was her?' Leah asked.

'It wasn't, it *isn't*, but – even if it was – she's allowed her privacy.'

It sounded cold but Shirley was probably right.

'It's only an E-fit,' Shirley added. 'It's not like somebody saw a teenager *at the time* who looked like any of them. This was a woman who looked like someone's guess of what a girl *might* look like. And it was twenty years after the event. Even with that, it only came about because one of her colleagues was paying attention to the news. The only reason I'm giving you this is because it could come up with the film. The director will know everything you now do.'

'Does he know the woman's name?'

'I don't know but I doubt it. Leaking a file is one thing; doing it without redacting is the sort of thing people lose jobs and pensions over.'

Shirley reached back into her satchel and removed a much thicker file. The first had contained ten or eleven pages, the new one had hundreds.

'I don't have a job to lose,' she said.

Leah wasn't certain what Shirley was holding, though she had an idea. 'What about a pension?' she asked.

'I wouldn't do this for anyone else.'

Shirley passed across the larger file. There was no writing on the cover and, for a reason of which she wasn't quite sure, Leah didn't open it.

'Will you get in trouble?' she asked.

'It's a copy and everything's digital now. Don't ask how I got it but there will only be issues if someone finds out you have it.'

Leah tapped the cover and then opened it. The first page confirmed what she'd suspected. The file was the copy of the one from twenty-four years before, about the disappearance of her three friends. Leah closed the cover and turned away. It felt like too much. Too big a favour. Too big a risk.

'Why now?' she asked.

'Because if our film director friend has a copy of the supplementary file, which I know he does, I'd be almost certain he has this, too.'

That was something else that felt true. Leah didn't know

much about Owen, and should probably have done a bit more research on him. Their interview made it seem as if he really did his homework.

'How do you know he has a source in the police?' Leah asked.

'Because I have sources, too.' It was spoken with a finality that no more information would be coming.

Leah wasn't sure she wanted to read the file's contents and, if it hadn't been for the emails and the knife, she would have handed it back. So much time had passed and what could possibly be inside that she didn't already know?

She considered telling Shirley about the knife and the emails – but there was so much context to it all. They'd known one another for almost twenty-four years and Leah had never once mentioned she used to carry a knife because she was scared of her father. Nor that she'd lost it at around the time her friends went missing.

And, now, even with the emails, there weren't explicit threats. She wasn't scared of who it could be, it was more curiosity. How could she bring it all up?

Along with Deborah, Shirley was one of the two people who'd helped turn Leah into the adult she was. She didn't want to say something that might tarnish the other woman's opinion of her.

On the other side of the cemetery, the gravedigger was back to work, his hole ankle-deep. He had a long way to go.

'Are you OK?' Shirley asked.

Leah tapped the file and stared into the distance. 'I think so,' she replied, knowing she wasn't. Her past could never be escaped.

'If you find anything you're unsure about, you can always call,' Shirley said. 'Maybe don't write it in a text, though.'

Leah almost asked why, but then realised Shirley knew how much access her former police colleagues would have to digital information. If they wanted to get hold of someone's messages, they probably could.

Suddenly, the file felt heavier than the weight of its pages.

'What do you think happened to them?' Leah asked. The same question she'd been asking herself, and others, for the majority of her life.

Shirley didn't answer, not really. She reached over and touched Leah's knee, then rubbed her arm. 'I don't know, love.'

TWENTY

Ben opened his front door and held it wide for Leah to head inside. He was in loose shorts and a vest, a narrow line of sweat creasing his brow.

'Just got back from a run,' he said, seeing bemusement in her face.

That was the difference between fight club and run club. The first rule of run club was tell everyone.

'Do you want to come in?' he asked. 'I don't think the boys are ready yet.'

Leah had never been into Ben and Josh's house before. There was a meticulous tidiness about the hall, with none of the abandoned shoes, or coats that wouldn't stay on pegs. Those things littered Leah's place, and her kitchen wasn't much better. The worktops were cluttered with a juicer, slow cooker and toastie maker, none of which she used. Ben's kitchen was as spotless as the hall and the only thing out of place was the towel that he plucked from the back of a chair to wipe his brow.

'I barely saw them all night,' he said, nodding upstairs as he leant against the counter.

'It's the same when they come to mine,' Leah replied.

Whenever Josh was round, the boys spent most of the time in Zac's room, presumably playing games.

'I asked what they wanted for food, and ended up ordering in a pizza.'

Some things never changed, Leah thought.

Josh put down the towel and asked Leah if she wanted anything to drink. She hadn't planned on staying but wasn't sure how to say that. She thought the boys would be ready to go but they weren't even downstairs.

Leah told Ben she was fine, even as he supped something green from a protein shaker.

'Have you seen the WhatsApp group this morning?' he asked.

'I muted it when it started buzzing yesterday,' Leah said.

She often did that with the group for parents of children in Zac's class. There was usually some sort of drama, almost always involving the same handful of people. Those who forgot it was non-uniform day invariably also ended up with parking tickets for stopping on zigzags outside the school, or never knew about training days. The last time Leah had muted the group was when there'd been a teachers' strike a month or so before. That had sent a split right through the middle when it came to parents' attitudes.

'Did you get the email to say they're filming at the school on Monday?'

Leah frowned, because she hadn't seen that email. Then she remembered it had arrived as she'd been sitting in her car near the recycling bins at the supermarket. She'd ignored it, because everything the school sent was always labelled as 'important'. She didn't want Ben to think of her as one of *those* parents, whose life was a calamity, with everything shared through that group.

'I saw something about it,' she replied, as casually as she could. It was only as she spoke that she realised, properly, what he'd said. They were *filming* at the school on Monday, which could only mean Owen was going to be there. They would be filming for the documentary.

If Ben noticed her lie, then he didn't let on. 'You're probably better off muting it,' he said. 'Half the group are saying everyone should move on, the other half seem excited by it all.' A pause. 'I think they kind of like the attention.'

That would definitely be true.

'Remember Carly? She was going on about how her daughter deserves to be part of the filming, because she wants to go to drama school. It's all been kicking off.' He took a breath and then: 'I think a lot of people are waiting to see what you'll say.'

That would definitely be true. The drama merchants would want to know on which side Leah fell, and then decide their opinion. As if she didn't have enough going on.

'It's the anniversary of my mum's death today,' Leah said, not entirely sure why she'd said it.

Ben had been drinking more of his green juice but started coughing. He patted his chest and then turned around to cover his mouth. 'Sorry about that,' he said. 'And about your mum. I didn't know.'

'No reason you should.'

'Are you OK? Do you want me to take the boys today? I know they're going bowling but I can drop them off...?'

Leah shook her head. 'It's just been a busy few days.'

Ben put down his shaker bottle as there was a series of bumps from upstairs. It sounded like the boys were moving.

'If you ever need an evening off, an afternoon, let me know,' Ben said. 'Zac's always welcome here. Or if you just want a cup of tea and someone to chat with...?'

There was a sound of footsteps on stairs as Leah wondered if he'd just asked her out. It sort of sounded like it but she didn't get a chance to question things as a pair of teenage boys yawned their way into the kitchen.

Even though she'd known he was fine, that he was upstairs, Leah still felt that pang of relief that Zac was in front of her. He did look like he'd slept less than she had.

She asked if he'd had a good night and got a mumbled 'yeah'.

The two grown-ups exchanged a knowing look, and then the boys were heading out to the car, Leah trailing behind. Zac was in the front seat, Josh behind as Zac huffed an embarrassed '*Mum...*' when Leah asked if they were both wearing seat belts. They were each mysteriously quiet when asked who they were meeting at the bowling alley, which meant girls would be involved. Zac had never had a proper girlfriend, although much of that was likely down to the way he went silent and looked at his feet whenever he was near anyone of the opposite sex.

Leah told the boys she would wait in the upstairs part of the alley and they could come get her whenever they were ready to go. She didn't say she was going to spend her time reading the file Shirley had given her. She wasn't sure what she'd find within the pages, if anything, but it should at least prepare her for anything more that could come up in Owen's film. If she was *really* lucky, there might be a clue to the person who had been emailing her.

When Leah had been Zac's age, before what had happened, her parents had little impact on her life with her friends. Vicky, Jazz and Harriet never visited Leah's house, but Leah's parents didn't stop her going out. If they noticed, they didn't care.

Maybe because of that, Leah had never been one of those parents desperate to cling onto their youth by making themselves a central part of their child's social life. Leah saw it a lot: dads who couldn't simply drop off their kids at Laser Quest, but who had to take part; mums who wanted to be their child's best friend, rather than a parent.

She gave Zac thirty quid and then let him head into the alley with a minute's head start. By the time she got inside, she spotted her son near the area to collect shoes, alongside seven or eight other teenagers. Shirley's file was in a ratty bag for life and Leah carried it past the arcade area, taking the stairs into the café. The menu served everything from lukewarm hotdogs to crisps and a bored young woman looked up from her phone to ask if Leah wanted anything. She then charged a borderline criminal pound for a can of Diet Coke. Someone needed to make a documentary about this level of robbery.

Leah took a seat close to the window, giving her a view across the alley. Zac was still with his group and hadn't moved from the area with the shoes. She cracked open the drink and put her bag on the table, giving her a barrier, behind which she opened Shirley's file.

The first impressions of the document was how dull it was. Leah struggled with the legalese and disjointedness of the opening few pages. Before starting it, Leah had thought she would read the whole document – but it was so overwritten that she found herself flitting and picking between sections.

Early on, it became clear that Vicky's father's explanation of being at the football dinner had been checked and established. Multiple people had confirmed the time he left, as had a taxi driver. According to the record of the cab company, Tom had been dropped off at 12.34, and the driver had watched him go inside.

Whatever happened to Leah's friends had occurred between then and the time Leah had woken up. The police had been up and down the street, checking with every neighbour, none of whom had seen or heard anything particularly untoward. They had spoken to a man who had slept on a bench after drinking too much. He had spent the night at the end of street on which Vicky's house sat, though his recollections were understandably hazy. The only thing he saw of note was a man walking along the street in the early hours, wearing a red and white shirt. The police hadn't identified who that could be, or established if the person existed.

The young woman from behind the counter started wandering around the tables, picking up leftover glasses and plates, so Leah hid the file under the table as the pair swapped slim smiles.

Leah wasn't sure what she'd expected but she was finding the information hard going. When the server had passed, Leah reopened the file and began flipping pages, looking for something other than text. She was almost at the end when she reached the page of composite images. They hadn't been in the file about the office worker who looked like the aged E-fit, but those images were on successive pages in the larger dossier.

The aged version of Jazz looked so, well... real. It was largely because the creator of the image had seemingly kept those bright green eyes with glasses, while aging the rest of her face. There were a few wrinkles, lighter hair, and something of a squarer jaw – but the potential older version of Jazz really did feel like it could be her.

It was the same for Harriet, with her narrow face, pinched nose and numerous ear piercings. The artist had kept those, as if that was the most important part of the girl's personality. Maybe it was? Or would be? A guess that the piercings would still be there was as valid as anyone insisting they wouldn't be. Leah wondered whether Deborah would have seen the image four years ago. She knew she would have done. How must that feel for a mother, whose daughter had been gone for so long?

The final image was Vicky. Back as teenagers, her appearance changed almost as often as her interests. She would have long straight hair past her backside, then decide to have it cut as short as the school would allow. Sometimes, her clothes would be so baggy, they would barely stay on; other times short and tight. Else she'd wear a football shirt, even though she didn't play, and didn't like, sport.

It would be impossible to predict how someone like that would age over twenty years and, when Leah turned the page, she was almost disappointed. The older versions of Jazz and Harriet felt plausible, maybe even possible. Vicky's alternate self was... *dull*. It was a plain face, the type of person who'd be instantly forgettable. That was the opposite of the Vicky that Leah knew. She almost felt sorry for the woman in the office who'd been misidentified as Vicky four years before. Her colleague had essentially seen a photo of a very plain woman, and decided she knew just the average co-worker it could be.

Leah closed the file and left it sitting on her lap underneath the table. She wasn't sure she'd read the rest, even though she didn't think she could bring herself to get rid of it. Shirley had risked a lot to get it to her, so she couldn't leave it lying around, either. It would have to be hidden somewhere at the house.

As she tried to think of places it could go, Leah finished her drink and pressed back into her seat. She was scanning the floor below, searching for Zac, and wondering whether she should get another drink, when a woman walked through the double doors and stopped in between a pair of tables. She scanned the room, as if hoping to see someone in particular. That someone wasn't Leah, as she turned in a semicircle before removing her phone from her bag and starting to type.

Leah stared at her and then quickly reopened the file on her lap.

The woman glanced up again, peering towards the window, which gave Leah a second or so to compare her face to the one in the file.

She found herself whispering it, unable to believe what was in front of her.

'Vicky...?'

TWENTY-ONE

The woman lifted her phone to her ear and half turned her back. Leah was out of her seat, file in her bag, but the single page with the aged Vicky in hand. She started walking towards the stranger, then clocked herself just in time, and headed towards the counter instead. The girl who had been serving was nowhere to be seen, which gave Leah a chance to hang around the counter and get a closer look at the woman.

Not Vicky.

Or, more to the point, she didn't look like the *guessed* version of Vicky from the composite.

It had only lasted a few seconds but Leah had done the same thing as the office worker. The E-fit was of a person so average-looking that, given the lighting and angle, it could be anyone.

The woman tilted her head and glanced towards Leah; she was still on the phone. There was confused hesitation in her eyes, wondering why Leah had suddenly appeared a few paces from her.

On the final night at her house, the real Vicky's hair came to her shoulders. She had been growing it out after cutting most of it off months before. Vicky wasn't the sort to have a neat centre parting, or to brush it all backwards. She was happy to let it do its thing.

There was none of that in this woman, nor the composite. Leah was searching for something that wasn't there. Owen's interview had spooked her, and the mystery emailer had made things worse. She wasn't only seeing ghosts, she was actively searching for them.

Leah forced a smile that she hoped was non-threatening, turned and leant across the counter to pretend she was looking for the server, and then headed back to her table. She returned the image of the adult Vicky to the rest of the file and buried it in the bag. Leah understood why Shirley had given it to her, especially if Owen had a copy, and yet a large part of her wished she didn't have it. It had only been a few days ago that she'd worried that the documentary meant the reminders and the anniversaries would never end – and now she was extending all that for herself.

She checked her phone, put it down, checked it again. There had been no reply from her emailer, though the class WhatsApp group was up to 140 unread messages. Leah assumed most of those would be about the upcoming documentary filming. That filming would eventually become the documentary, and then there would be reviews and rehashed news articles. Then the podcasters would arrive.

This would be the next two years of her life. Minimum. That meant it would be the next two years of Zac's life, which would take him through his GCSEs.

Leah had been staring through the window towards the bowling lanes. It was a blur of colour and motion, with bright balls fizzing across the shiny surface, crashing into the pins at the other end. On the alley closest to the wall, a ramp was set up, with a pair of crash barriers blocking the ball from heading into the gutter. A boy of five or six rolled a ball down the slide and then watched as it bounced between the bumpers on its way towards the pins.

That had been Leah and Zac at some point in the distant past. He'd had a birthday party in the alley when he'd been six or seven. Certainly at primary school. Those were the days when a party would involve an entire class, so Leah and some of the other parents had booked five adjacent alleys. They had spent a couple of hours supervising the carnage of children screaming with joy, before taking them up to this canteen to ply them with hotdogs, chips and jelly.

It was yesterday but it was ancient history.

Leah scanned the alley, looking for Zac and his friends. A group of boys were on the far side, studiously not sitting too close to one another, before taking it in turns to bowl a ball as fast as possible. When one of them hurtled a ball into the gutter, it bounced up and over the divide, before taking out a pin in the adjacent lane. The boys were a year or three younger than Zac, though he wasn't that sort of boisterous kid – and she couldn't see him anyway.

Other than them, there were families, or parents supervising groups of children across a pair of lanes.

There was no sign of Zac or Josh.

Leah checked her phone, even though she'd only put it down moments before. There was no message from Zac, nor anyone else.

The woman who wasn't Vicky had disappeared and there was still no sign of the young woman who'd been serving.

Leah packed away her things and headed downstairs towards the arcade. The wall of noise was impossible to ignore. A thumping *click-click-click* was coming from the air hockey tables, which fought with the *thump-thump-thump* as a pair of teenagers threw basketballs into their duelling hoops. A young girl was attacking some sort of whack-a-mole thing, and all that fought against the dings, crashes and bumps from the sit-in video game karts, the dance machine, and some sort of drumming game.

It was too much. Leah found herself backing away, while trying to find someone she recognised. Zac and Josh both liked their games but neither of them were in the arcade.

Leah headed across to the bowling lanes, which only confirmed they weren't there either. The last time Leah had seen them, the boys had been close to the shoe exchange, but that area was now empty.

It felt unlikely but Leah looked in the small shopfront, where they sold bowling balls and shoes, though there was nobody in there.

Over by the toilets, a group of girls were hanging around outside, each feverishly tapping on their phones. The boys could be in there, though they'd have been inside for a long time, which felt unlikely. None of the girls were from the group she'd seen collecting shoes with Zac.

Where were they?

Leah headed away from the dim lighting and cloying, thunderous, blend of tinny music, splattered bowling pins, and rumbling arcade machines. The sun was momentarily blinding as she burst onto the pavement outside. People were ambling past, heading towards the shops, cinema or restaurants, as drivers circled, hoping for a fabled spot that meant they didn't have to walk across the car park.

As the greeny stars faded and everything slipped into clearer vision, Leah took out her phone again. She typed a quick 'Where are you?' and sent it to Zac. When there wasn't an instant reply, she hard-pressed his name and tried to call. By the time she'd put the device to her ear, the attempted call had already dropped. As far as she could tell, it hadn't rung.

Where was he?

There'd been other times in the past when Leah had felt this familiar rising terror. When he was four or five, they'd been in that big Asda. Leah had bagged up some apples, turned to put them in the trolley, and Zac had disappeared. There had been those initial few seconds of confusion, then the rationality that he couldn't have gone far. Except she walked up and down the fruit aisle and he was nowhere. He wasn't in the next aisle, or the one past that.

Then the panic had really hit. A woman who worked in the health and beauty section had stopped Leah when she was running along the aisle. Between them, they had found Zac sitting on the floor of the pet aisle, playing with a rubber frisbee that had fallen off the shelf. He'd looked up to his frantic mother, eyes wide, wondering what the big deal was.

Years later, not long after he had started walking to school by himself, he'd simply not come home. Leah had driven to the school and hadn't seen him on the route. The school itself was locked, the car park empty. Leah had messaged the parents of his friends, trying to sound as casual as possible. 'Just checking in to see if Zac's with you?' That sort of thing.

It turned out he was at a judo competition, watching one of his friends. He said he'd told her; she insisted he hadn't.

Both times, Leah had felt her heart race, her thoughts cloud, the anxiety grip. He was gone and not coming back. Except he wasn't and he did.

And now, even though Zac was fourteen, even though he went plenty of places by himself, or with friends, Leah could feel that torment pouring. He hadn't replied to her message and his phone hadn't rung. He was gone and not coming back.

She turned towards the cinema in one direction, then the shops in the other. No sign of Zac.

Ahead, a dad was leading a couple of families as they weaved around parked cars towards the McDonald's in the distance. Zac wasn't there, either.

Gone. Not coming back.

Leah took a few steps forward, and only realised she was on

the road when car tyres screeched. She spun to face a silver vehicle that was barely a couple of paces from her. A woman was in the driver's seat, eyes wide, body arched backwards from the impact of the braking. They looked to one another for a moment, a mix of confusion and relief. Leah couldn't quite understand how she'd ended up in the road.

She held up a hand and turned back towards the pavement outside the bowling alley. It hadn't been a few steps, she had somehow walked into the middle of the road, all without noticing.

As soon as she reached the safety of the pavement, the car revved and shot away. Leah moved towards the wall and reached for it. The rough clay grazed her palm, though she pressed against the surface, holding herself up.

Seconds passed. Maybe more.

Zac had to be somewhere. If he'd disappeared, it wouldn't only be him, there was Josh as well – plus the other kids to whom she hadn't paid much attention. There was a *group* of them.

When she turned, there was someone close. A man. He had seemingly been reaching for her but stepped away with a surprised 'oh'.

'Lee...?' he said, although he clearly knew her. They'd seen each other two days before. 'Are you OK?' he added.

Leah blinked and nodded, trying to make herself seem fine, even though she wasn't. Of all the people she wanted to run into, bottom of the list had to be Owen the film director.

TWENTY-TWO

'I saw you in the road,' Owen said, a straightforward say-what-you-see. He seemed to be struggling for words, which was understandable considering he must have seen how close she was to being run over.

'I, uh... I can't find my son,' Leah said. The words made it sound more real, yet also more overblown. She immediately added: 'He's out with his friends, so he must be around here somewhere.'

The biggest part of Leah knew that was true, except that pesky little voice was whispering from deep within. He was gone and he wasn't coming back. Get used to it.

Owen reached a hesitant hand towards her, probably looking to offer some degree of comfort or understanding, before thinking better of it. The last time she'd seen him, she'd walked out on his interview. She'd spent two days thinking he was out to get her, because that was how it felt. There did seem some degree of concern about him now, though.

'Where did you last see him?' Owen asked.

Leah poked a thumb towards the bowling alley behind

them. 'He was there with his friends. They were supposed to be getting a lane but that was a while ago and he's not there now.'

'Could they have played and left? Gone to get some food?'

Leah hadn't thought of that. She had been upstairs in the café for some time, but wouldn't he have said something? She reached for her phone and unlocked the screen.

'He didn't message,' she said. 'He always texts.'

That was more or less true. After the judo incident, she had relented and let him have a phone. It was with the under-standing that, if plans changed, he would message to say so.

Owen was looking over her, probably scanning the area for teenagers. Within a couple of seconds, it felt as if he'd taken in the entire complex. 'There's not a lot of places people can go around here, unless they're driving. Shall we look together?'

Leah must have said 'yes', because she was suddenly at Owen's side as he strode along the pavement towards the skating rink. He was one of those people who marched into any situation as if they belonged. Before Leah knew what was happening, he had spoken to someone on reception and then they were through to the side of the rink.

It was mainly the young girls who were zooming around with effortless grace. A few boys were hanging onto the side for dear life, desperately trying to maintain an air of nonchalance, while trying not to fall on their arses.

Owen looked to Leah: 'Is he here?'

That got a shake of the head, and then Owen was off again.

They headed past the arcade and through the small café. When there was no sign of Zac or his friends, he took her back outside.

'Does he drink coffee?' Owen asked. They were close to a Caffè Nero and, though Leah didn't think Zac drank any hot drinks, that wasn't to say his friends weren't fans. A baffling number of young people seemed to be hooked on caffeine.

Not that Zac was at the coffee shop, or the KFC at its side.

They crossed the car park and checked the McDonald's, then the frozen yoghurt place a little past. The floor was sticky, the bin overflowing with cardboard tubs, the burr of the soft-serve machine a constant.

No Zac.

Leah checked her phone again, but there was nothing from her son. He'd been gone for around an hour – and it felt incomprehensible that he would have walked off without letting her know.

Owen paused outside the yoghurt place, Leah at his side as young children on sugar highs screamed. 'Do you have any of his friends' numbers?' he asked.

The only friend Zac had been with that she knew for sure was Josh – but Leah didn't have his number. Why would she? She could contact Ben to ask but that felt like more of a last resort. An admission that she'd lost control.

'No,' she said.

Owen was staring into the distance. 'There's a couple of shops and the cinema,' he said.

The shops felt unlikely, considering nobody was going to spend an hour in any single one of them. At some point, she would have seen Zac or Josh walking between them.

That only left the cinema – except what was she to do? Enter every screen and call 'Zac?' to see if he answered? Besides, if he and his friends had changed their minds to go to the cinema, he would have said.

Before she could explain any of that, Owen had set off towards the screens. Leah wanted to tell him it was the wrong idea, but she didn't have a better plan.

Large cardboard standees were dotted around the cinema lobby, while booming trailers played on the overhead screens. A small Costa was in the corner, with a row of arcade machines sandwiched between that and a Ben & Jerry's stand. Caffeine, fat, sugar, and a racing game in which players sat in a driving dock and were thrown from side to side. What could possibly go wrong?

No sign of Zac.

Owen said he'd check the toilets, and the hope that had been in his voice had largely gone. He had headed through the doors before Leah realised he wouldn't know what her son looked like. He could just call his name, of course.

That little voice in her mind continued to hiss that Zac was gone and not coming back. If he wasn't at the bowling alley, the skating rink, any of the restaurants, or the cinema, where could he be? Unless someone was going to walk along the dual carriageway, there was nowhere else to go.

Gone.

Not coming back.

Leah sat on one of the Costa seats, ignoring a 'customers only' gaze from the person behind the counter. She needed a minute. Just a minute. She needed to think.

Where could he be?

She closed her eyes, clamped her eyelids tight. She and fate were good friends and always had been. Leah willed her son to be safe, well, and – preferably – with her.

Then she opened her eyes – and he was.

TWENTY-THREE

'Mum...?'

The light of the cinema lobby danced through the murk of Leah's blurry stare. She pushed herself up and reached for her son, who was actually, properly in front of her. It was as if she had willed him into existence.

'Where've you been?' she managed.

'We decided to watch a film. There was a wait for a bowling lane. I texted you.'

'You didn't.'

Zac reached into his pocket and took out his phone. He unlocked the screen and turned it for her to see, then swiftly tilted it back. 'Oh... I don't have any reception.'

He held the device up higher, as if that might help, then showed Leah the screen. In the corner, where there should be a reception bar, there was nothing.

'I texted you!' he said, and there was concern in his voice, too. He looked up and must have seen the worry in his mother's face. 'I did, Mum. I texted.'

She believed him, not that it mattered too much now. Leah

told him it was all right, because there wasn't much more she could say.

He looked as bothered as she felt. He put his device on airplane mode, then clicked it off. Even Leah heard the series of buzzes.

Moments later, her phone fizzed.

40min wait for bowling. Going to cinema. Be about 2hrs.

'Why are you in the lobby?' Leah asked.

'Needed a wee.' Zac was flicking through his phone screen and then he looked up again: 'Eight missed calls...?!'

Leah hadn't realised it was that many. She suddenly felt a wave of embarrassment and was only saved by Owen's reappearance. He started to say something about checking the screens but stopped himself. 'Is this...?'

'Zac,' Leah told him.

Owen offered his hand and Zac shook it. When the older man said he was making the documentary about the missing girls, that one of them was his sister, Zac glanced to his mum, as if asking permission to be OK with it. Leah gave a barely perceptible nod, not that Owen wanted to make conversation.

'I still need a wee,' he said. 'Then can I go back in?'

Leah told him it was fine.

Zac took a step towards the toilets and then turned back: 'Can we still have a lift back after?' he asked.

'Of course.'

Leah watched him go, and, though there was relief, the mortification hadn't gone anywhere. A stupid phone reception problem had caused all this and, worse, it had been Owen who was around to help.

'Are you OK?' Owen asked.

It was so much of an understatement that she laughed, unsure how else to reply. She was and she wasn't. Her son was safe but she definitely wasn't OK, because this was her life. It had been like that for a long time, and – partly because of Owen himself – it would continue to be so.

Owen nodded past her to the Costa. 'Do you want a coffee?'

'I think caffeine's the last thing I need.'

That got a smile and, perhaps for the first time since she'd met him days before, Owen seemed like a normal guy. Driven, determined, but normal.

He nodded the other way instead. 'Ice cream?'

That got another laugh but a different sort. 'Go on then.'

They waited in line, watching a trio of young children in front of them order various sundaes with added, well, everything. Chocolate and strawberry sauces mixed into a gooey sludge, topped with nuts, sprinkles, whipped cream, cherries, corn flakes, brownie crumbles, crushed Oreos, and more. The youngsters crept across to a row of chairs, precariously balancing their concoctions.

Leah craved something similar, though Owen already likely thought she was a borderline wreck. She copied Owen's underwhelming order of two scoops, and then they retreated to a bench outside the cinema, away from the booming music. Behind them, on the other side of the glass, a nine-foot cardboard standee of Keanu watched on.

As Leah wondered what she should say – if anything – it was Owen who took the lead. 'Sorry about the other day,' he said. 'I know the interview ended up being a bit of an ambush.'

'A bit?' Leah didn't bother to hide the scorn.

Owen let a blob of ice cream slip from his plastic spoon into the tub. 'You're right. I don't know what to say. What you saw isn't the sort of film I'm trying to make.'

He ate a scoop of the ice cream, then sucked on the spoon. It felt like he was thinking.

'I suppose I always thought you knew more,' he said. 'Even as a kid. Maybe it's because I'm a light sleeper. I get woken up by cars going past, or my neighbour's dog. I broke up with a girl because she was a snorer. It's just... how can someone sleep through three people disappearing?'

Leah didn't reply immediately. She suddenly wasn't hungry, if she'd ever been. She swallowed a large ball of ice cream anyway.

'I can actually answer that for you,' she said after a while. 'If you'd asked.'

They were sitting next to each other but Owen turned to angle himself towards her. 'What do you mean?'

'I'm a lightweight,' Leah replied. 'Always have been, and I definitely was at fifteen. We all had a bit of vodka and I could barely stay awake. Vicky kept pouring drinks for people but I was struggling after the first. I ended up tipping a couple of drinks into this big pot plant that used to be in the living room. That's the only reason I was able to stay awake until when we went to sleep. When we did settle down, I was asleep more or less right away. I'm the same now, which is why I basically don't drink.'

Owen had abandoned his ice cream to the space on the bench between them. He'd been nodding as she spoke. 'You should've said.'

'Aren't you supposed to be the filmmaker? Don't you ask the questions?'

She had him there.

Owen sighed and it felt like it was more to himself than her. 'Honestly? It's all a bit of a bluff. When I made my first film, I was winging it. Hoping things came together. It did in the edit, but that wasn't only me. Then the film got nominated for some awards, and placed in a few festivals. Everyone assumes you know what you're doing – and then, because you want to make more films, you play on that. Nobody sees all the stupid questions that got edited out. All the time and money we wasted filming stuff we didn't need. I've spent most of the last year figuring out funding but I'm still that same guy hoping it all works out. I'm not a professional interviewer.' A pause. 'I suppose I am, but I don't know what that means.'

He pressed back into the bench and picked up his soupy ice cream. He swallowed three quick mouthfuls and then plopped the remains into the bin. Leah's empty tub sat on the ground near her feet.

As Owen explained it, everything felt so obvious. She'd seen him as a hotshot creator out to get her. Ultimately, he was trying his hardest to act as if he belonged in a world where people who came from a place like them were rarely welcomed.

From nowhere, Leah felt sorry for him.

'I blew it, didn't I?' he added.

'You kinda did.'

'Do you reckon you could say that stuff about being a light-weight on camera?' Owen was tapping his foot, staring at the floor.

'Maybe.'

It wasn't a 'no', and Leah wasn't sure she wanted it to be.

'Talking to Mark was a low blow,' Leah said. 'I can't believe you paid him.'

'He asked for expenses. I actually set out to ask him about the effect everything had on you as an adult. As well as what happened with Jazz and the others, I'm trying to examine how it changed the community. Then Mark said you'd seen them being carried out and I suppose I wasn't sceptical enough.'

It wasn't quite an apology, though it was an explanation.

Leah's bag was at her side, the weight of the police report sitting at the bottom. She only had it because Shirley thought Owen would also have a copy. But if he wanted something from her...

'I could do a second interview,' Leah said. 'But I want a few things.'

Owen sat up a little straighter. 'Like what?'

'I'm not going to be ambushed again, so I want you to tell me if there's anything else you know about me.'

She knew she was pushing it.

Owen sucked in a breath through his teeth and started to scratch his leg.

'I know you have the police file,' Leah said, which made him stop scratching.

'How'd you know that?'

'You're not the only one with sources.'

He huffed another breath. 'Huh.' A pause and then, from nowhere, it came. 'I know about the fight with you and Jazz.'

TWENTY-FOUR

TWO DAYS BEFORE THE SLEEPOVER

THURSDAY 16 DECEMBER 1999

It was always so dark in December. Leah and her friends walked to school in a barely lifting gloom, then turned around and trudged home in the same. Vicky, Harriet, Jazz and Leah were side by side, taking up the whole pavement as they ambled along the high street. A string of white bulbs zigzagged over-head, criss-crossing towards a lacklustre Christmas tree that sat on the common, close to the town hall. A smattering of shoppers were bustling through the cold, collars up, hats down, breaths spiralling into the sky.

One more day until schools broke up for Christmas. The girls were past the age of bringing in games to play, or videos to watch – but there still wouldn't be much to do on the final Friday.

They reached the end of the high street and Harriet said goodbye, before nipping through the lane that led to her house. They walked the same route every day and she was always the last to join in the morning, first to leave in the afternoon.

The trio headed around the common, with the Christmas

tree at one end, and the beginnings of the giant new year bonfire at the other. They made plans to go, assuming they were allowed to be out that late without their parents. Vicky said her dad would probably take them, and then they'd be able to go off and do their own thing. Nobody asked Leah if she'd be allowed out. She always was.

Vicky was next to depart. Her house was on the furthest side of the park, along one quiet, leafy street, onto another quiet, leafy street. Of the four girls, her house was the biggest, which was probably why she hosted the sleepovers and parties. Not that anyone else was queuing up to visit Leah's home.

Leah and Jazz continued side by side, past the nice houses, towards the terraces on the edge of town, where long lines of red-brick houses weaved into one another. The pair moved past a postbox and then stopped on the corner, outside the paper shop. A sandwich board was outside, with a newspaper headline about the local football team. The entrance was open, as always, with the ice lolly freezer buzzing a little inside the door. Leah had fifty pence in her pocket and, despite the temperature, considered spending 10p on a Mini Milk.

Jazz hadn't spoken since Vicky had broken away to go to her house. This was where she would head along one street, while Leah would walk for another half-mile towards her place. Something wasn't right with Jazz – or it wasn't right when it was only the two of them. Leah had sensed it in previous days but hadn't wanted to say anything.

Leah was about to ask if Jazz wanted an ice lolly as well. She'd pay, except she didn't get to say so.

'Mum says I can't hang around with you any more,' Jazz said. She had stepped away from Leah, leaving a few paces between them. She spoke while looking at the ground.

'What do you mean?' Leah replied.

'She said to be careful around you.'

'Why? I haven't done anything.'

Leah knew the answer, even as she claimed she didn't. Most of the children at school weren't slow about bringing any of it up. Some of the teachers, too. In fact, the only people in her life who kept their thoughts to themselves were her friends. Until now.

This type of thing was something that Leah always assumed would happen. That quiet whispering voice in her own mind always said her friends would abandon her – and now it was happening. She thought it would be Harriet's mum first, but seemingly not.

'Because of your dad,' Jazz said.

'What about my dad?' Leah drew it out, needing to hear the words.

Jazz scuffed a foot on the floor and hoisted her school bag higher. She half turned, towards her house at the other end of the road. 'He's in prison, isn't he?'

'What's that got to do with me?'

Another sigh and, deep down, Leah knew her friend didn't want to be saying any of this. It wasn't her decision.

'She doesn't know you're going to be at Vicky's on Saturday,' Jazz added. 'I told her you weren't.'

'I don't get what any of this has to do with me. I've not seen Dad since Easter.'

Jazz took a small step away. 'I'm just telling you what Mum said.'

'Your mum sounds like an idiot.'

Jazz had moved further away but stopped and turned back. 'What?'

'You heard.'

Something had changed. There was still a chill but a wind had started to fizz between them.

Jazz took a step towards her and, in that second, Leah relished it. She knew what was about to happen, and she wanted it.

'Say it again,' Jazz said. Her eyes were narrow through her glasses, fixed. Her mum had been diagnosed with cancer a year back and had only been given the all-clear a few weeks before.

Leah pushed herself onto tiptoes: 'Your mum is an idiot.'

She spat the words as the fury embraced her. She wanted that, too.

Jazz took another step forward but Leah wasn't going to wait for anyone else to make the first move. She lunged and shoved her friend in the shoulder, all in one movement. Leah had moved so quickly that Jazz was off balance. It hadn't been a hard push, but it was enough to send her spinning back, onto the pavement. She landed in a sitting position, her skirt flaring up momentarily, exposing her bare thighs. Her glasses dropped onto her lap as the other girl grunted in surprise and, possibly pain. Jazz spent a moment straightening her clothes and then pushed herself up, brushing the grit from her palms, and then picking up her bag. She lifted her glasses back onto her face.

'Get that from your dad, did you?'

She smirked, knowing what she was doing and Leah seethed. She only realised her fists were balled when a concerned 'everything all right?' sounded behind. A woman had come out of the paper shop, packet of cigarettes in her hand, and had stopped a few paces from them.

Leah relaxed her fingers and allowed herself to sink lower onto her heels.

'Fine,' Leah hissed towards the woman, who didn't move. She was looking to Jazz.

'We're fine,' Jazz replied. It sounded reluctant, unsure, but was enough for the old hag to head off along the street and give herself lung cancer.

Leah thought about apologising, even though she wouldn't mean it. Sometimes it was better to say sorry, even when you weren't. Jazz had spent close to a year thinking her mother might die, just like Vicky's had, so she was obviously going to feel defensive.

Her mum was still an idiot, though.

'Why don't you run back to mummy, if you listen to her so much,' Leah said.

It was impossible to ignore the fire within. She had three friends, *these* three friends, and some stupid woman was going to spoil it all. Would Harriet's mum say the same? Vicky's dad? What then?

'At least *my* mum cares about me,' Jazz said.

There was more than fire now: the eruption in Leah's belly was volcanic. Her teeth were gritted, both fists balled. 'Say it again,' she dared. If it had been anyone other than one of her three friends, they wouldn't have been given a second chance.

Jazz had already taken a step back and Leah knew she wouldn't dare repeat herself. That step became two, three, ten. Jazz was on the other side of the paper shop, underneath the lamp post that was glowing a disconsolate yellow.

'You're not worth it,' she called, as she continued to back away. Leah was a faster runner and they both knew it. Jazz needed a safe distance and, as soon as she had it, she turned and sprinted for home.

'You better run,' Leah said, to nobody in particular, not meaning it.

The anger went almost as quickly as it had arrived, replaced by something far more familiar. There was a pressure behind Leah's eyes, a lump in her throat. The tears were close and Leah found herself pre-emptively blinking them away.

What was she going to do?

TWENTY-FIVE

NOW

'How can you know that?' Leah asked. 'It was only me and Jazz there.'

Owen shrugged. 'I've got her diary. It was her last entry. She said you pushed her over and that she thought you were going to kick her head in.' A pause. 'That's a direct quote.'

'That's ridiculous.'

Leah's defensiveness was instant and dismissive, but, if she *really* thought about it, perhaps that *was* how she had felt in the moment. She wasn't sure she was capable of kicking someone's head in with the brutality suggested by the phrasing, except she really had wanted to hurt Jazz. That moment outside the corner shop had felt as if her world was imploding. Her life was her trio of friends. There wasn't much enjoyment to be had away from them, certainly when it came to her parents. Without them, what was her life going to be?

The irony, of course, was that she was without them days later anyway.

'It wasn't a fight,' Leah said. 'Not really. Your mum told her to stay away from me because of things my dad had done. It felt so unfair and, yeah, I was angry. Called your mum stupid, something like that. Jazz tried to push me, too. It was the final day of term the next morning and it was like it never happened. I waited outside the shop and Jazz came along, then we walked to where we met Vicky.'

Owen pressed forward, elbows on his knees, thumbs rubbing the bridge of his nose. Leah wondered how long he'd sat on all this. Years. Decades.

'It says "fight" in her diary.'

'Because "fight" means more than one thing. What one person calls a "fight" could easily be called an "argument" by someone else. It's not like we were throwing punches, or kicks.'

'But you pushed her?'

'Because she was trying to push me! It was a stupid moment.' Leah could feel the annoyance starting to flow and then it was there. 'My dad used to beat up my mum. Properly beat her up. I watched him kick her down the stairs, and then had her beg me not to call an ambulance. She broke her arm and used a pillowcase to set it. My dad went to prison for having a real fight with a man at the pub, when he rammed a glass in the other bloke's eye. He's in prison right now for killing someone while drunk driving, when he was already banned for previous drink driving. You're not going to lecture me about arguments or fighting.'

Leah had somehow ended up standing over Owen, without realising she'd got to her feet. She had accidentally stood on the remnants of her Ben & Jerry's and the gloopy ice cream was pooling on the ground. She swore under her breath, then picked up the tub and dumped it in the bin.

The cheek of him to judge her.

She slumped back onto the bench and had to stop herself aiming a kick of frustration at thin air. 'You knew all that about my dad already, didn't you?' she asked.

'Yeah.'

'How much do you know about me?'

Leah wasn't sure she wanted to know the answer.

'It's not just you,' Owen said. 'My sister's been missing for twenty-four years. I've wanted to know the answers my entire life. I went to university and did filmmaking to get to this point. I interned as a runner for six months and lived off noodles and baked beans. So, yeah, I know lots about you – but I know lots about everyone involved.'

It wasn't quite what Leah expected, it was worse. There was an undoubted creepiness, even if a part of her understood it.

'Nothing my dad's done over the years is to do with me,' Leah told him. Owen wasn't the first person she'd had to say it to. She doubted he'd be the last. 'That's what I told Jazz years ago. But, everywhere I go, every time I try to live my own life, there's someone who brings him up.'

Owen thought for a moment: 'I think you brought him up...'

Leah wanted to argue, but it was sort of true. He'd asked about the argument between Leah and Jazz, and that had taken her back to her father – as so many things did.

'It *wasn't* a fight,' Leah said, quieter now. Firmer.

On the far side of the plaza outside the cinema, a group of boys and girls had started an impromptu game of football against the back wall of the Mexican restaurant.

'If it was, why did we walk to school together the next day?' Leah added. 'And home? Why were we sleeping in the same room two days later? Didn't you ever fall out with your mates one minute and then end up kicking a ball with them the next?'

Say what you see.

Owen fidgeted awkwardly. He was straightening his trousers, which felt like a sort of tell for when he wasn't comfortable.

Across the plaza, the ball thumped against a fire door and rebounded sideways as a girl chased after it.

'Football wasn't my thing,' Owen said, though Leah remembered football posters on his younger self's wall.

'But you take the point?'

There was a long silence, probably a full minute as the football game continued.

'Yeah,' he said eventually.

Leah had calmed now. It had been a long time since she'd felt that sort of anger arrive and leave in a blink.

'Have you been holding onto this for twenty-odd years?' Leah asked. 'You found Jazz's diary, saw the word "fight", and convinced yourself this was all my fault?'

Owen was tugging at his trousers again, bunching the material a little above his knee and then pushing it down, before repeating himself.

He didn't need to reply for her to get the answer, although his sorry-sounding: 'She was my big sister...' said a lot.

They sat together for a short while, their silence punctuated by the thump of ball on wall and door. After a few minutes, the fire door clattered open and a man in chef's whites burst out. He pointed an angry finger at one of the boys, then made a grab for the ball. As one of the girls kicked it out of his reach, the man slipped, tried to stop himself, but landed on his arse. The smack echoed around the plaza as the kids ran for the ball, their youthful laughs echoing behind.

By the time the man was back on his feet, the children were around the corner and out of sight. He brushed off his hands and scraped grit from his bum, before spotting Leah and Owen. With that, he held up both palms in a silent 'Kids, huh?' pose, before turning and heading back into the restaurant.

Leah couldn't resist. 'Guess we just witnessed a fight...?'

Owen said nothing, as Leah wondered if she should tell him that somebody wanted his documentary stopped. That whoever it was knew about something that only Vicky knew.

Except...

Leah had thought the incident between her and Jazz was something only the two of them knew. Because she had never kept a diary, it hadn't occurred to her that others might. If Jazz's memory of that afternoon on the corner had ended up being written down, perhaps the knowledge of Leah's knife had been passed to someone else. Vicky could have told Jazz, who might have put it in her diary.

It had been a wild couple of hours in which Leah had gone from not trusting Owen, to feeling sorry for him, and now back to not trusting him.

What else was in Jazz's diary? Who else had he shared it with? There could be so much within its pages that could be taken out of context.

It couldn't be him who'd left the knife for her to find because he wasn't trying to sabotage his own film. But she wondered if Owen knew and, if so, who he'd told.

Could this offer of a second interview be yet another ambush? Not one chance to make her look stupid, but two?

'What else do you know?' Leah asked, and it felt a very open question until she added an admittedly snidey: '...Or *think* you know?'

Owen laughed, though there didn't feel much humour there. This seemed like the sort of conversation they should have had before she ever sat down in front of the cameras.

'I'm trying to keep an open mind,' Owen said, which felt slightly disingenuous considering their first meeting. 'I've got interviews lined up for the next week. We're at the school for a bit of background filming, plus there are a couple of teachers who were around back then, and are still there now. I'm talking to a psychic who insists everyone's dead, then another who reckons they're definitely alive.'

Leah snorted at that, wondering if one of them was Naomi's friend. Probably. The idea of conflicting psychics contradicting one another suddenly gave her a renewed interest in the film.

Owen laughed too, but not for long. 'I spoke to someone in the police, off the record. They said there was a man renting a flat about three minutes' walk from Victoria's house. He was arrested two years later because they found child porn on his computer. There's nothing specifically to link him to what happened but they did ask him about it.'

Leah found herself wondering if this was in the file she hadn't fully read. 'What did he say?'

'That Jazz and the others going missing was nothing to do with him. He was never formally part of an investigation and it was an accident they stumbled across him. He took his computer in for repair and the IT guy called the police. The guy had already been convicted when someone noticed his address history. They interviewed him in prison but it only lasted about two minutes. It's not like there was any evidence.'

That was all news to Leah.

'He's dead now,' Owen added.

'Is he going to be talked about in your film?'

Owen hrmmmed for a moment, not sounding sure. 'Maybe. We were looking at having a section about theories. Some are more plausible than others.'

'What else have you got?'

For a moment, Leah didn't think she'd get a reply.

'There were a group of travellers camped on the edge of town. They moved on the day after the sleepover, on the Sunday.'

The town had always had a bit of a panic whenever it came to travellers settling on the outskirts. It happened at least once a year, with stories of items nicked from gardens, plus large clean-up costs for rubbish left in fields after they'd gone. More recently, that came up against those calling people racist for their complaints. The town's Facebook groups would descend into a series of back-and-forth accusations until the posts were inevitably deleted.

The more things changed...

'Why would travellers take three girls?' Leah asked.

Owen turned away and stared into the distance. There was an obvious answer why someone might want to take three girls – and it had been hinted at many times over the years. Pinning that on a specific group was a big jump – and that r-word would definitely be getting thrown around on Facebook.

Leah wasn't sure what he was saying. Was this another theory, like the man in the flat? Did he think this actually happened?

Owen perhaps expected a reaction that he hadn't got, so he moved on quickly. 'There's a public forum in town tomorrow. If I can, I'm going to answer any questions people have. I know some around here would rather I wasn't doing this. I figured it might help.'

Leah almost asked 'help who?' but she waited for the inevitable.

'Do you think you might come?' he said. It wasn't quite asking her to be there but it was close enough.

Leah rubbed her temples and tried to think of the best way to put it. Up until that moment, she had thought Owen might actually understand. Sure, he'd tried to catch her out for no reason. He had also held a twenty-four-year grudge over a fight that wasn't. Despite that, she really had thought he got it. This question proved he didn't.

'Imagine there being a public event,' Leah started. 'It's in your home town, and anyone can go. There will be people there who know you a bit, maybe know you a lot. Your son could go, if he wants – even though he probably won't. But the parents of his friends will be there. And your neighbours. And the people who serve you in shops, or cafés. There will be people taking photos and putting them online, plus a reporter who'll write about it. And the reason they're there is to stand up and ask questions about the worst thing that happened in your life.'

Leah stopped and turned to face Owen, who was watching a spot somewhere towards the McDonald's on the furthest side of the complex.

'Would you go?' Leah asked.

Owen was quiet but Leah wasn't prepared to let that sit.

'Would you?' she pushed, wanting the answer.

'Probably not,' Owen replied quietly. He waited a moment, perhaps judging the mood, maybe even whether they were a strange pair of friends after the events of the day. 'I think people would be kind if you were there,' he added.

Leah side-eyed him. She lived in the town and he didn't. Besides, it wasn't about who was kind, it was about not wanting every part of her life to be compared back to a night she slept through twenty-four years before.

Owen pinched the material of his trousers again and fidgeted from side to side. He stood and rubbed the back of his thighs. For a moment, Leah wondered what he was doing, then realised her arse was also sore. They'd been sitting on a hard, metal bench for quite a while. She stood and together they shuffled from foot to foot, trying to get some degree of feeling back into their legs.

'I've got one other thing,' Owen said – and from the earnest eye contact, Leah knew it was serious. He didn't wait for a reply. 'Your dad was a suspect, too,' he said.

For a moment, Leah thought it would be something much worse. Leah knew her father had been released from a prison stint around a week before her friends went missing. He was staying in a halfway house somewhere, before returning home. Shirley had already told Leah that her dad had disappeared on the night of the sleepover. If Leah had heard it first from Owen, it might have been more of a shock.

Leah played along. Those conversations with Shirley probably shouldn't have happened – and she definitely shouldn't have the police file. 'How do you mean?' she asked.

Owen ignored the question: 'When was the last time you saw him?'

Leah had to think. 'He got fourteen years for, um...'

'Causing death by dangerous driving, or careless driving, under the influence of drink or drugs.'

Owen shrugged as Leah eyed him. That was the exact phrasing and she wasn't comfortable with how much he knew about her.

'The maximum,' she added, though he likely knew that too. 'I hadn't seen him for a good year before that, and they added some time onto his sentence because of something he did inside. I guess...' She counted on her fingers. 'Fifteen years? Sixteen? I've not visited him in prison.'

There was no way he could have known that part, but it didn't feel as if Owen was listening anyway. He still had the big reveal.

'Why?' Leah asked.

'Because I've got an eyewitness who claims your dad was on the street the night Jazz went missing.'

TWENTY-SIX

It had been a long day.

Zac was in his room, largely oblivious to much of the stress he had accidentally caused his mother. He had taken his left-over cinema popcorn up with him, saying he was going to 'tidy up' his homework. The house was quiet, regardless of what he was doing. Plus he was a floor away, safe.

Leah didn't use her laptop often, only usually if there was an important email to which she needed to reply, when she didn't trust the autocorrect on her phone. One of the other parents had once typed 'gnome work' instead of 'home work' and it was still a running joke on the WhatsApp group. The same group that now had over 250 unread messages.

She clicked the link from Owen's newest email, which sent her off to a cloud storage site. She typed in the password he'd given, which gave her access to a folder marked 'RAW to edit'. There was a film file inside, which Leah double clicked. Moments later, a woman's face filled her screen as a camera zoomed in and out, before settling on a shot that framed her from the chest up.

It all felt very familiar to Leah, who'd sat for her own interview not long before. She wondered if her footage was in a folder, waiting to be cut – or if they'd already isolated the part where she had stormed off.

Leah heard Owen's voice for the preambles of the interview. He asked if the woman was comfortable, the same thing he'd asked Leah. Then they asked her to say her name and address. Leah didn't recognise the woman, though it seemed like she lived diagonally across the road from Vicky's place. There was a chat between the crew off-camera about levels – and then they were off.

The woman said she'd told the police that she saw Leah's dad, Paul Pearce, on the night the girls went missing.

'How did you know him?' Owen asked, out of shot.

The woman straightened herself and there was a momentary wrinkle between her eyes. A person about to explain that two plus two was four. 'Everyone knew him,' she said. 'You'd cross the street to avoid him. He was from one of *those* families.'

Leah glared immediate hatred. 'One of *those* families' was *Leah's* family. She hadn't chosen for it to be, but it was. It wasn't only the legacy of her missing friends that followed her, it was that of her parents.

The woman was still talking: 'He was always fighting and drinking. You'd see him around. Horrible man.'

'What did the police say when you told them?' Owen asked.

'They didn't want to know. They said he was in prison, so it couldn't be him. I assumed they knew what they were on about, then I found out later – *years* later – that he *wasn't* in prison.'

Leah paused the footage and stared. The woman had leaned in slightly and gestured with an open hand towards Owen, incredulous that she'd been dismissed by the police. What's more, Leah believed her.

There was a bump from above and Leah left the footage paused as she crept into the kitchen, wondering if Zac might be on his way down. She didn't want him to see what she was watching, and hovered for a few seconds. When no teenager appeared, she returned to the living room and pressed play.

'How certain are you it was him?' Owen asked.

'A hundred per cent.'

'How can you be so sure?'

'He was wearing that red and white plaid shirt he always wore.'

The hairs on Leah's arms were up, because she could picture the exact top. The woman was right – her dad *did* always wear it. He'd have it on in the mornings, then later, when heading up to bed. It's what he shrugged off when he punched Leah's mum in the face in their living room. He had it on the first time Leah saw him being arrested, when the police came to their door and he tried to escape out the back. When he was on the front page of the local paper after the pub assault that got him jailed the first time, he was wearing the shirt.

It was his thing. The most identifiable item in his life. She couldn't picture him without seeing the grubby red and white shirt.

Leah suddenly remembered something else. She grabbed her bag from the kitchen and took out the copy of the police file Shirley had given her. She'd been reading it in the bowling alley café, but had been bored by the confusing writing. Except there it was: the police had spoken to a man, who had slept on a bench, and said he'd seen a man wearing a red and white shirt. He'd been dismissed because he was drunk, but that was two people talking about someone in a red and white top.

Somehow, despite all the people involved, the police hadn't linked things together. It felt like something that couldn't happen, and certainly *shouldn't* – and yet that's why there were so many true-crime documentaries and podcasts. It was always about how the police had missed something that later seemed obvious.

Owen would have almost certainly seen the link, though he didn't know Leah also had a copy of the police file.

Leah restarted the footage and there was a short break as something happened off-screen. Muffled male voices sounded as the woman twirled a strand of hair. When they reset, she sat up straighter.

'What did you see him doing?' Owen asked.

'Nothing, really,' the woman replied. 'He was walking in the middle of the road.'

'What time was this?'

'Just after one in the morning. I remember specifically, because my husband always used to get up at the same time to go to the toilet. He was making a load of noise, so I got up and looked out the window. That's when I saw Paul.'

Leah shivered at the second mention of her father's name. The first time it had been said, it had been both his names. Paul Pearce almost sounded jaunty, which was the opposite of the real man. Hearing him named as a simple 'Paul' sounded so casual for what was being described.

'Did he see you?' Owen asked.

'I doubt it. I went back to bed right after. I wouldn't have thought anything of it if not for all the police outside the next morning. I assumed he'd assaulted someone again. I don't understand why they kept letting him out of prison. Lock 'em up and throw away the key. That's what I say.'

Leah paused the footage, having seen enough. She didn't like the way the woman had referred to 'those families', but it certainly appeared as if she'd have recognised Leah's father.

Owen's email with the link to the footage had included his phone number, saying she could call if she wanted. Leah hadn't been planning on it, except she had the urge to speak to someone.

He answered after barely a ring, with an eager 'What did you think?'

'Where did you find her?' Leah asked.

'She emailed after seeing that I was going to be filming. She went out of her way to track me down via the contact form on my website. She's been sitting on this for years, but nobody wanted to listen to her.' He waited a beat, then added: 'There's another witness in the police file. They dismissed him, too, because he'd been drinking.'

Leah gave what she hoped was a surprised 'oh', as if she didn't already know.

'Do you remember your dad wearing that red and white top?' Owen asked.

'All the time. I barely remember him in anything else.'

'That's interesting!' Owen couldn't hide the excitement and it felt as if he might be about to ask if she could say that on camera, too.

'Other people would have had a shirt like that,' Leah said, not sure why she was playing it down. 'Plus he didn't know I was staying at Vicky's. I didn't know he was out of prison until after everything.'

It felt as if Owen had already thought about that. 'Could your mum have told him?'

Leah needed a moment to think. She had told her mother she was staying the night at Vicky's, and got little in the way of a response – which was normal. If anything, Leah being out of the house was her mother's preferred scenario. If her dad *had* gone back to the house that night, and by some miracle asked about Leah, there was no question her mum would've told him Leah was staying at a friend's. If she'd remembered.

'Maybe,' Leah said. 'But I doubt she'd have remembered *which* friend – and it's even less likely Dad would've known an address.'

Owen's 'Oh...' had an undercurrent of disappointment. It was understandable that he thought he was onto something.

It wasn't the only reason it all felt unlikely to Leah.

'Dad wasn't into girls,' Leah said. 'Not like that. He was in trouble for violence, and most of that came down to a lack of money. He was always furious about people supposedly owing him cash, or others asking him for what he owed them. It was never anything to do with women, or sex, or girls...' Leah let that hang, wondering if she should add the final part. If they'd been face to face, she wouldn't have been able to say it. 'He never touched me.'

She heard Owen's intake of breath and could imagine him fiddling with his trouser leg. Leah wasn't sure what she was expecting, nor what she wanted. Definitely not sympathy.

There was another bump from above, so Leah told Owen she'd be back and then put him on mute. This time, there were footsteps on the stairs, so Leah headed into the kitchen as Zac arrived with a tired stretch and a hand in front of his mouth. There were days in which most of his communication appeared to happen through yawns.

'Didn't sleep much last night, then?' Leah said.

A creased smile slipped onto his face. She'd already assumed he was up half the night playing games with Josh.

Zac was holding a crumpled popcorn carton, which he dropped into the recycling tub. 'Is there any food?' he asked.

'Loads in the cupboards. Quite a bit in the freezer, too.'

Zac opened the fridge and popped his head inside, then yawned his way back out. 'Can you make me a sandwich?'

'Have your fingers stopped working?'

'You do it better.'

That got a roll of the eyes, though Leah was already heading to the bread bin.

Zac leant on the sink and yawned at his phone as Leah made him a cheese and pickle sandwich. She did get a mumbled 'thanks' as he took the plate and headed for the stairs.

'Don't stay up too late,' Leah said, though she didn't hear a reply.

As soon as his door closed, she hurried back to the living room and picked up her phone. She half expected Owen to have hung up – but he was still there.

He was also ready.

'Your dad had not long got out of prison on the night of the sleepover,' he said. 'I get what you're saying about him being in trouble for violence and money things – but we don't know who he met in there.'

Leah was barely back in her seat. 'What do you mean by that?'

'Perhaps he ended up owing money to somebody in prison...?'

It took Leah a couple of seconds to understand what Owen was hinting at. That her father did something with her friends in order to pay off a debt.

Her dad was an awful human being and yet, somehow, this outlandish idea felt beyond even his capabilities. Leah's five minutes of sandwich making had given Owen too long to expand on his theory. Her dad was a lot of things, almost none of them good, but he was a simple man. He drank, he gambled, he fought. He didn't go in for grand schemes because he wasn't that smart. He certainly didn't think them up.

Even if Owen was somehow right about a motive, there was still no explanation of how one man – one drunk, simple man, just out of prison – could make three girls disappear without anybody noticing.

Leah was in front of her computer screen and switched to her emails. Her 'How did you know about the knife?' that was sent to 'A Friend' had been unanswered since she'd sent it. There was also the one before, with 'To stop them finding out what you did'. The person wasn't giving anything away.

Leah clicked into the email that had sent her to the bottle bank, and typed a new reply.

Why do you want the doc stopped?

The call with Owen was still live, though neither of them had spoken in a couple of minutes. It sounded as if he was clicking a mouse, or typing on a keyboard.

'Are you still there?' Leah asked.

'Just doing a bit of googling. Have you thought any more about a second interview?'

As she was speaking, Leah hammered out another email to 'A Friend' and sent that, too.

I didn't do anything! I don't know anything! Who is this?

'I'm going to need some time to think about it,' Leah said. 'If I talk to you again, we'd have to have a proper conversation about questions and anything that might come up.'

'We can probably figure out something like that,' Owen replied.

'Let me come back to you. I'm going to do a bit of googling myself.'

'You've got my number and email. I am sorry about what happened the last time.'

It sounded as if he might be wanting her to say it was fine, though Leah wasn't ready to give him that satisfaction. She gave a brief 'OK', then said she'd be in contact, before hanging up.

It didn't feel to Leah as if she'd sleep any time soon. She was about to close the laptop and head upstairs anyway – except that's when A Friend's reply finally arrived. As with all the other messages, it wasn't what Leah had wanted, or expected. There weren't any words, only a photo. Or, more to the point, a photo of a photo.

It was a digital image of a Polaroid picture, with Vicky and Leah hugging one another.

Leah stared, and for a moment, she was back in her friend's

living room. Not as it was when Owen had interviewed her, but how it had been when she'd watched *Titanic* and then slept on the floor.

Her pink bag was strapped diagonally across her front as she held aloft a slice of pizza with one hand and hugged Vicky with the other. Vicky was cuddling Leah back, while clasping pizza in her other hand.

Leah didn't fully remember the photo being taken but Vicky was in the strappy purple top she was wearing on the night she disappeared. A photo of her wearing it had ended up in all the newspapers, so it was how she was remembered. Even Leah struggled to see her in any other way.

The two girls were grinning, although Leah noticed the slightly open mouths and the drooping eyelids. They were both tipsy: Vicky much more than Leah. Both looked happy, though, and Leah had to really force herself to remember how she'd been feeling that night.

Was she happy? So long had passed. She didn't think she was.

It was hard not to see how slim she'd once been.

No, not slim. *Starved.*

There was never much in the way of food at home, nor money to buy it. Leah couldn't quite remember how she used to get by. She refused to let on to any of her friends that she wasn't eating at lunchtime and would instead claim she'd had it all at break. Or she'd tell them she was going to the canteen, and then hang around the library for half an hour. There were definitely times in which she stole food, usually from the corner shop close to where she'd shoved Jazz. There was a blind spot near the door, which was where they stored the crisps. If Leah was wearing a coat, she could easily get three packets inside.

Not that crisps were much of a balanced diet.

Leah had been staring into nothing, lost in the memories of that famished girl, before focusing back on the emailed image.

There *had* been a Polaroid camera knocking around that night. How had she forgotten for so long? She hadn't even remembered the next morning. Leah couldn't recall whose it was but they took pictures of each other and then... Leah didn't know. The police hadn't ever mentioned it, though it had to have been in that living room somewhere.

As Leah scrolled lower, she realised there *was* a message within the email but that it was underneath the embedded photo.

Look closer.

Leah nudged the screen upwards until she was again staring at the picture of the picture. It was her and Vicky, two friends holding pizza and each other.

She couldn't see anything other than that.

And then she did.

TWENTY-SEVEN

THE SLEEPOVER

SATURDAY 18 DECEMBER 1999

Leah stopped grinning as Jazz lowered the camera and waited for the photo to slide from the slot at the bottom.

'I think it's a good one,' Jazz said.

Leah bit into the slice of pizza she'd been holding, as she wondered how much she could eat by herself without anyone noticing. She'd already had five slices, with the others maybe having one or two. Leah had mashed two slices into one while alone in the kitchen. She hadn't wanted to be seen, and ended up scoffing them so fast the roof of her mouth felt raw. Not that it stopped her eating more.

Jazz was fanning the photo as Leah waited for Vicky to bite into the pizza slice she was holding. Leah had learned that if one person was eating, then everybody noticed. If it was more than one, then nobody did. As soon as Vicky started to eat, Leah attacked her own. This sixth slice was really playing havoc with her belly, although it might have been the vodka. Hard to know for sure.

'Look,' Jazz said, offering the photo to Vicky.

'This is great,' Vicky said, before passing it onto Leah.

In it, Vicky and Leah had an arm around each other, while holding up pizza with their free hands. They looked so happy, even though that wasn't how Leah felt. More than anything, despite the almost six slices of pizza, her stomach ached.

'Is that your mum's ring?' Harriet asked. She'd been on the other side of the room, fiddling with the VHS player but was now back with them.

Vicky held up her hand, posing with the same ring she'd shown Leah the week before.

'Do you want to try it on?' Vicky asked. She hadn't made the offer to anyone in particular, though both Jazz and Harriet were keen.

Leah finished her pizza and wiped her greasy hands on a tissue as the other girls switched the ring on their fingers, while holding it up to the light. When they were both done, Harriet passed it to Leah, even though she'd shown no interest. Leah put it onto her ring finger anyway.

'How much is it worth?' Jazz asked.

'I don't know for sure but there's one in town that's worth three thousand.'

'Pounds?!' Jazz replied.

'What else?'

They laughed, as Leah passed the ring back to Vicky. Leah hadn't known it was worth so much when she'd seen it the previous weekend. She could barely comprehend so much money. Three *thousand* pounds.

Leah's belly was grumbling and she said she was heading up to the toilet. As she reached the top of the stairs, she realised Vicky was a couple of paces behind.

'Are you all right?' Leah asked, somewhat confused as she thought her friend was about to follow her into the bathroom.

'I'm going to put this back,' Vicky said, showing Leah the ring once more. 'Don't want to lose it.' She headed for her dad's bedroom door, where it would presumably be returned to her father's top drawer.

Leah had opened the bathroom door when she felt a tingle, that sense of being watched. She stopped and turned, realising Vicky was at the other end of the landing, eyeing her.

'Are you going to leave some for the rest of us?' Vicky said. There was a smile on her face but it didn't feel friendly.

'What do you mean?'

'You've basically eaten a whole pizza by yourself. Are you going in there to throw up, or something?'

Leah needed a couple of seconds to realise what was being asked. Did Vicky think Leah was bulimic?

'No...' Leah said.

'Jazz says she's not allowed to be friends with you anymore.'

Leah wasn't sure how to reply. 'What about you?' she managed. 'Will we still be friends?'

Vicky's eyes narrowed a fraction and then she shrugged. 'Probably.'

She spoke cheerily, as if being asked by her dad if she wanted to be picked up from school. Like it was all a big game.

Vicky opened the door to her father's room and disappeared inside.

Leah felt frozen. She'd been with Vicky when she'd had little digs at Jazz or Harriet. It had happened the previous weekend when she had suggested not inviting Harriet. She and Vicky had been friends since primary school. They all had.

Leah entered the bathroom and locked the door. She sat on the toilet, waiting. Moments before, she had really needed to go – but not any longer.

A few seconds later, Vicky closed the door of her dad's bedroom and then Leah heard her friend's footsteps heading down to the living room.

Were they friends? Had they ever been?

How many times could Vicky make those little digs about people and it still be OK?

Leah didn't flush the toilet, not yet. She gently opened the bathroom door and crept silently onto the landing. At home, the floorboards tended to creak louder from the middle. Leah had learned to gently shift around the edges when she wanted to be silent.

This was somebody else's house, but Leah suddenly knew what she was going to do. She carefully flanked the landing until she was outside that bedroom door. Inside, at the back of the top drawer, there would be a ring worth more than Leah could ever imagine.

TWENTY-EIGHT

NOW

Things were quiet at the other end of a different landing as Leah wondered whether Zac had fallen asleep. He seemed tired enough when she'd made him the sandwich.

She waited for a few seconds, considering going to say good-night, but then deciding not to risk waking him. Instead, Leah entered her own bedroom and closed the door quietly. She put the laptop on the bed and stopped to take in the rest of the space.

Even though it was her house, her room, Leah still felt an edgy sense of being watched as she headed for her own top drawer.

The hiding place was such a cliché. Perhaps that was why she had chosen it?

Leah shifted her underwear to the side, reaching for the very back, and the pair of tights she'd held onto most of her life. Not that she ever wore them. They were fuzzy with the remnants of a spider's web and Leah brushed it clear, before unspooling the material.

Hidden in the same balled-up tights it had been for more than twenty years, was Vicky's ring.

Vicky's *mum's* ring.

The lure of £3,000 had proved too strong for Leah's starving fifteen-year-old self, yet she had never sold it. It had sat in her pocket the entire time she'd been talking to the police the next morning, and she only remembered taking it once she got home. After that, Leah wasn't sure what to do with it. Vicky wasn't around – and Leah was hardly going to tell the police. She couldn't return it without letting on she'd taken it.

But nobody knew she'd stolen it. How could they? She had never worn it outside, and not worn it at all in more than twenty years. Instead, it had moved from flat to flat, until she'd settled in her current house. Every now and then, Leah would unspool the tights, check the ring was still there, and then wrap it back up.

Except there, in the Polaroid, with the 'look closer' caption, the stolen ring had sat on Vicky's finger, gleaming from the camera flash.

It was impossible anyone else could know what the ring meant – and yet so much of what had happened in the previous days felt like that. How had her knife reappeared? Where had it been? Aside from Vicky, who even knew she used to carry it around? What had happened to that Polaroid camera on the night of the sleepover?

And now the shame of the stolen ring had been presented back to her.

Leah returned the ring to the tights and buried it at the back of the drawer, before collapsing onto her bed. Someone with a car engine that was far too loud farted their way past the window as Leah stared at the ceiling.

It was impossible not to see how bad things seemed for her. The person emailing knew about the knife Leah used to carry around. They knew about the ring she stole. Owen knew that Leah's father, who'd been in and out of prison his entire life, was possibly on the street that night. It was all adding up to a situation in which a lot of questions would be asked of her.

Leah didn't want any of those questions.

She grabbed the laptop and opened the lid. The accusing image of the Polaroid was still on the screen and Leah clicked to reply.

Can we talk? Can we meet?

She sent the message and spent five minutes repeatedly pressing refresh, hoping a reply would come. Leah didn't know what more to do. The only specific request from the emailer was for her to stop Owen's documentary – although Leah had no idea how to do that.

It was after ten on a Saturday night, past the time in which people could reasonably call unless it was an emergency.

Was this an emergency?

Leah spent a couple of minutes trying to think herself out of the problem, then a couple more again pressing refresh on her emails.

There was only one thing for it. She was going to have to make the call.

TWENTY-NINE

SUNDAY

The walls were unbearably high. They had to be, of course, Leah knew that. Except they were even taller than she had imagined. She'd seen them in the distance while driving and then, after parking, they were there again, hovering over the top of the surrounding houses.

Shadows stretched, eventually enveloping Leah as she walked slowly towards the walls. It was a journey she had never made, and never imagined herself making. She had left Zac at home in his room, not telling him where she was going. There would be too much to explain.

The walls were peppered with signs, saying it was a criminal offence to throw anything over the top, or to fly drones in the vicinity. Anybody caught doing so would be arrested and subject to prosecution. As Leah peered up, she thought someone would have to have quite the arm to hurl something over the walls.

Leah followed the signs towards reception, where there was a buzzer on the outside door. She pressed it and waited until a woman in a dark uniform appeared and stared at her with mild bemusement. They had a short conversation, then the woman got on her radio. As she listened to the person on the other end, she looked Leah up and down, eventually shrugged, then gave a look as if to say she didn't get paid enough for that sort of thing.

A minute later and Leah was in a small room with a uniformed man on the other side of a plexiglass counter.

If getting out of a prison was as difficult as getting into one, then escaping would be out of the question.

This second person in uniform had the same sceptical stare as the first. Leah gave her name and said she was there to visit her dad.

The man snorted with incredulity, as if Leah had announced she could control the weather. 'We don't do visits on Sundays,' he said.

'I know but I think you're expecting me anyway,' Leah said.

The man peered at her again, one eye narrowing. 'What's your name again?'

'Leah Pearce.'

He nodded towards the first woman Leah had met in a silent keep-your-eye-on-her way, then disappeared away from his booth through a further door.

Leah sat on the single school-style chair provided and stared at the floor, even as she felt the prison officer watching her closely.

Leah still couldn't quite believe she was in the prison. Every junction she had passed on the motorway gave her an opportunity to turn around and head home, yet she'd forced herself to push on. The person emailing her knew too much and Leah wasn't sure where else to turn.

There was a clunk of doors and then the uniformed officer who had been behind the counter appeared on Leah's side. There was another man with him, someone taller and wearing a tight jumper instead of the full uniform. He had the weary look of a person a few months from retirement, yet having already checked out in any real way.

'Are you Leah?' he asked.

She stood and offered her hand, as it felt like the thing to do.

The man shook it, initially gripping too tightly and then loosening. 'Graham,' he said, introducing himself. 'Have you got your ID?'

Leah took her driving licence from her bag and handed it over. Graham examined it, showed it to the uniformed guard at his side, and then passed it back.

'Shirley's an old friend of mine,' he said. 'We go way back.' He cleared his throat and then added: 'My colleagues here are going to take you through security and then we can talk on the other side.'

Leah did as she was told. She had to hand in her bag and electronic devices, then there was a pat-down, a security scanner, a second pat-down, some sort of security wand, and – eventually – she was shown through a set of heavy doors into a small area, where Graham was waiting. He was sitting on a lounge chair that was too low, legs splaying too straight and too wide. He looked like a giraffe trying to squat. Something about the way he'd angled himself made it seem as if he wanted Leah to sit, so she did. The matching chair was definitely too low and she flopped the unexpected few centimetres, falling backwards and momentarily unsure if she'd be able to get back up again.

'Awful chairs, aren't they?' Graham said.

Leah mumbled her agreement.

'How do you know Shirley?' he asked.

'She was my liaison officer when I was a kid. We stayed in touch.'

That got a nod, like he already knew. 'We did our training together forty years or so back,' Graham replied. 'She stayed in the police but I ended up applying for a job in the prison service. It was a lot easier to move around back then.'

He caught Leah's eye momentarily before looking away once more. She wasn't sure why he was telling her this.

'How is Shirley?' he added.

'Good,' Leah replied. 'I think she's a bit bored after retirement.'

Graham snorted and it felt as if he knew the sentiment. 'I certainly didn't expect a call from her at eleven o'clock last night. She must think a lot of you...?'

Leah felt herself shrinking, unsure what he wanted her to say.

Graham let it sit a moment and then continued: 'We don't normally do this, and I've already had to fill in too many forms, but you're here now, so...'

It sounded a little like an admonishment, especially as he sighed when he pushed himself up.

'Come on then,' he said.

Leah struggled to her feet and followed Graham along an echoing series of corridors until he led her into a room lined with tables and chairs. Leah had expected something with glass separating inmate from visitor, with a phone handset through which to talk. Instead, it was a lot like the canteen above the bowling alley. There were no dividers, nothing to separate people at all.

'You can sit wherever you want,' Graham said. 'We'll bring him through shortly.'

He hovered, waiting, as Leah picked a table more or less in the centre of the room. It rocked slightly as she leant on it, one leg shorter than the others. The chairs still had that primary-school vibe, although there was a little padding. Without looking too closely, she spotted four separate security cameras watching.

'What did he say when you asked if he'd meet me?' Leah asked.

'He thought it was a joke. Then said he didn't have

anything better to do.' Graham clicked his heels and stood a fraction taller. He towered over a seated Leah. 'I'm not going to be here,' he said. 'But there'll be an officer on either side of the hall. You're free to leave whenever you want and the same is true of him. Just because you start a conversation, it doesn't mean either of you are obliged to maintain it.'

It felt like something Shirley would say, or had asked Graham to make clear. Leah said she understood – and that was it.

Graham said it wouldn't be long, before disappearing out of the room, leaving Leah by herself. She eyed the door, a big part of her wanting to call him back and say she'd changed her mind.

The drive to the prison had been laced with chances to change her mind, and assumptions that she would. Through every part of the walk and the wait, Leah had told herself she would leave before she got this far.

It was almost too late.

There was a clunk and a door opened, through which three prison guards headed in. A couple of them nodded at Leah, though nobody spoke. Two of them waited on one side of the room, as the other crossed to the door on the far side.

She could still change her mind. Tell one of this trio that she wanted to leave, and that would be that.

Her phone had been left at reception and Leah had nothing with which to fiddle. What did people used to do with themselves before technology took over? Leah couldn't remember. There was a big clock on the wall, a second hand silently ticking its way around.

Another door banged open, this one on the side where the single guard had headed. Another guard appeared, the fourth, but there was somebody else behind him. This final man was in loose grey joggers, with a matching sweatshirt. The clothes were massive on his slender frame as he limped his way into the large room, blinking curiously into the light.

It *was* too late.

Leah wasn't sure if she'd recognise him, though that had been wishful thinking. Of course she knew him.

The guard released the man from his handcuffs and escorted him across to the table. Leah wondered if she should stand, though couldn't quite bring herself to do so.

The man was staring at her inquiringly, a silent question being asked as he was prompted to take the seat across from her.

He was hunched and limping, no longer the towering, frightening ghoul she remembered. He'd once been so scary but now... now he was nothing. An old remnant of the person he once was.

'Everything OK?' the guard asked, and it took Leah a moment to realise he was speaking to her.

She managed a croaky 'yes', though her throat was dry.

'Lee...' said the man.

'Dad,' Leah replied, unsure what else to say.

His squirrely narrow face was pockmarked by years of the abuse through which he'd put his body. It was as she'd told Owen – it had been fifteen or so years since she'd last seen him, but he was unquestionably her father.

'It's been a while,' he said.

Leah didn't acknowledge it. This had felt like a good idea the night before but, as the morning had progressed, it had seemed increasingly poorly thought-out.

'I didn't expect to see you,' he added.

'I didn't expect to come.'

'I thought you might be here to wish me a happy birthday?'

He sounded hopeful, except perhaps there was a smidge of ridicule as well. Like he knew there was no chance that's why she was there.

Leah didn't bother to hide it. 'Is that today?' she asked.

'Tuesday. I'm turning seventy.'

The gentle gasp was out before Leah could catch it. Seventy. How on earth had he lasted such a long time?

'I'm hoping to be out next year,' he added.

Leah ignored that. 'I'm not here for a reunion.'

He didn't react to that: 'Why *are* you here?'

'I need to ask you something.'

Leah's dad pressed back into his chair and began twiddling his thumbs. He wasn't cuffed, not that Leah felt threatened. Either everything she'd ever seen on television was nonsense, or, more likely, the prison systems in the UK and the US were very different.

'So you need something?' he replied.

'When my friends went missing that night—'

'Are you still going on about that? How long ago was that now? Ten years? Twenty?'

Leah glared but he was unmoved. She couldn't remember a time in which she loved him. He was simply a presence in her life. Had he ever loved her? She doubted it.

'My friends disappeared,' she said, firmly. 'I was in the room with them. It's not like you forget. It doesn't go away.'

'Not like them, then!'

He laughed at his own joke, as Leah took a breath. If she'd thought about it, she'd have known it was going to be like this. Then again, if she'd thought about it, she'd never have come.

'Did you bring any money for me?' he asked.

'Why would I do that?'

'A birthday present?'

He gave that snidey little grin he always had when he was up to something, or trying to get one over on a person. When Leah had been very young, four or five, he'd shown her how to hide CDs and tapes in the back of her clothes. While he distracted the sales staff, Leah would nick whatever she could. Outside, he'd gleefully receive the stolen goods, ready to sell to his mates in the pub. It was one of the few times Leah ever felt valued by her father. She used to think that snidey little grin was love.

'If we're talking birthday presents, you owe me quite a few,' Leah replied.

'You wouldn't be here if not for me!'

It felt as if he meant it. That he felt he deserved respect and reward for producing a single sperm almost forty years before.

Leah didn't rise to it and, when he realised there was no reaction coming, he crossed his arms. 'What do you want?'

'Were you there when my friends went missing?'

It was as direct as possible, the only way Leah could think to communicate with someone who actively seemed to be trying to annoy her. She wasn't sure what she expected, though she got a smirk.

'What makes you ask that?' he said, arms still folded.

'Were you there?'

He laughed at that. At her. He was never worse than when he had something he knew somebody else wanted, even if that something was knowledge.

'I know you were out of prison by then,' Leah said, trying to keep calm. 'You were supposed to be in a halfway house but you went missing. Then you were back with Mum about a week later.'

Leah's father stared away dreamily. 'They wouldn't even let you smoke in that place.'

'The halfway house?'

'You thought you were gonna be free, then they sent you there and started by giving a list of rules.' He focused in on her. 'You know rules were never really my thing.'

'Seems like they have been for at least fifteen years...'

Leah knew she shouldn't have said it, though it had been too tempting to resist.

Her dad unfolded his arms and scowled momentarily until

he caught himself. He definitely wouldn't want any daughter of his to see she'd riled him.

'Were you there?' Leah asked.

The smirk was back. 'Why are you asking?'

'Because they're making a documentary about what happened. Lots of questions are being asked and I don't know the answer to many of them.'

He chewed the inside of his mouth, weighing it up. Weighing *her* up. Leah doubted he'd changed too much and she suspected he was trying to figure an angle. Wondering if there was a way he could twist this to his benefit.

'Why do you think I was there?' he asked.

'Because there was a sighting of you. More than one, actually.'

He continued chewing his cheek as he nodded slowly. It didn't feel like an admission. 'First I've heard of it,' he said. 'The police have never been around for it – and they couldn't leave me alone for years. Whenever something happened in town, they'd be knocking on the door.'

Leah's hands were under the table and she pinched the webbing between finger and thumb, forcing herself not to respond. The reason the police came over was because he was usually the guilty party.

'Were you there?' she asked, trying again.

The cheek chewing had become lip chewing. He glanced towards the officers on one side of the room and shuffled in his chair. It felt as if he was going to call them over, to say he wanted to leave. She'd never get an answer, which was the way he wanted it. If he held something she wanted, he won.

Leah's dad motioned to stand but then sank back into his seat with a soft plop. 'I'm getting married,' he said.

THIRTY

Leah suddenly found herself coughing. She'd been in the middle of swallowing when her father dropped his bombshell. Something had started to come up as she was busy sending it back down. Leah slapped her chest as the blockage cleared. One of the guards had taken a dozen steps in her direction, though her dad hadn't moved.

'Everything all right?' the guard asked.

Leah waved and managed a 'yeah', though he hovered, not returning to the door.

'I've got a girlfriend,' Leah's dad said, unfussed. 'Mandy. She visits twice a week when she can. Lives about three streets away from where you grew up.'

Leah was still breathing heavily. This was too much news for a Sunday morning, especially after the last few days.

'Are you joking?' she asked.

'She started sending me letters about four years ago. We got engaged a few months back.'

He definitely wasn't joking. Leah's father was many things, including a massive liar, but this was almost certainly a rare truth.

It had only been a year or so back that Leah had half watched a TV show about women who got romantically involved with prisoners. Some of them had outright obsessions with serial killers; others liked the idea of having their own freedom outside, while enjoying the commitment of marriage. Most simply seemed lonely.

Leah's father was grinning now, even though it looked wrong on him. He didn't have a face for smiling. 'You're gonna have a new mum,' he said, and the smirk was back.

'Don't,' Leah hissed.

The smug leer didn't move. 'I thought she might've been in contact with you,' he said. 'I know she was thinking about it. She must live close to you.' A pause. 'You didn't move, did you?'

Leah didn't answer, though she hadn't. If Mandy lived close to where Leah grew up, she'd be within a mile or so of her current place.

'She did say something about having your email address,' he added.

It took a second to land. 'She... has my email address?'

It was unclear how Mandy could have Leah's email address, although it was only her dad claiming it was true and he definitely couldn't be trusted. Besides, there was no way this Mandy could know about Leah's knife, or the stolen ring.

A shrug: 'I don't understand any of that stuff. Never sent an email in my life. You'd have to ask her.' A grin. 'Or email her, I guess.'

Leah didn't join in with the hilarity. She didn't know Mandy, though the other woman clearly had some idea who she was. Leah wasn't exactly famous in her home town, but people of a certain age knew who she was. That's what came from being the one who was left.

'When are you getting married?' Leah asked.

'You after an invite?'

Leah sighed. This was how things had always been. Never a

straight answer, regardless of how innocent the question. She supposed this was what came from a lifetime of evading the police.

'How's the boy?' Leah's father asked. He could only mean Zac, even though they'd never met.

'Don't talk about him,' Leah hissed. 'Don't you dare say his name.'

That got a too-familiar smirk. It was incredible how good her father was at niggling her, though Leah suspected he was like that with everyone. A natural antagonist. A lifelong prick.

'You never answered my question,' Leah said. 'Were you there on the night my friends went missing?'

The smirk was replaced by a weary half-yawn, that felt fake. 'Does it matter what I say? If I tell you "no", you won't believe me. If I say "yes", then so what? It was years ago and I'm done with all that. I just wanna get out and marry my Mandy.'

He rolled his shoulders and stretched high. The bit about getting out and remarrying felt like another thing that might be true.

Leah was exhausted.

This was one of the reasons why she hadn't visited her father in so long. It was testament to the type of person he was that this wasn't even the main reason.

'You're done with all *what*?' Leah asked.

That got a shrug.

'It's a yes or no question,' Leah added, and the annoyance was impossible to hide. 'Were you there on the night my friends went missing?'

He didn't react.

'Do you know what happened to them?'

Leah's father rocked on his seat and then leaned in. He flashed a glance towards the officers, not wanting to push his luck too far, though not wanting to be overheard.

There was a moment, barely a second, in which Leah

thought he was going to say something worthwhile and profound.

He was never going to change, though. 'Can't you be happy for me?' he said. 'I told you I'm getting married and all you want to talk about is the past.'

He had finally got to her.

'Do you want to know why I can't stop thinking about the past?' Leah fumed. 'Maybe it's because I watched you slam Mum's head into the wall until she bled? Or because I saw you push her down the stairs, when she dislocated her shoulder and broke her arm? Perhaps it's when I had to go to school the same day as you were on the front page of the paper for nearly killing a man when you stuck a pint glass in his face?'

Leah gasped for breath. He'd got one over on her, again, and she knew it. No point in stopping now, though.

'I had to listen to kids at school telling me my dad was a criminal. I used to barricade my door at night, in case you tried to come in. I carried a knife because I was scared of you. I found out from a text that you killed a man drunk-driving, and tried to escape, before driving into a stream. All that and you have the *nerve* to want me to be happy for you?'

Leah's father stared directly ahead, through her, not at her. He'd not flinched, nor reacted in any way. She could have been reading the dictionary to him.

She'd not noticed it but two of the officers were within touching distance. It was only then that Leah realised there were tears on her face and that somehow she was standing.

'Are you done?' one of the officers asked.

Leah was breathing heavily, struggling to get the air in. '*We're* done,' she said.

THIRTY-ONE

NINE DAYS AFTER THE SLEEPOVER

MONDAY 27 DECEMBER 1999

Leah had dragged her bed across her bedroom floor until it was resting against the door. She hadn't had to do it in a while but it was the only way she could sleep when her dad was home. With the bed blocking the only door into her room, it meant he wouldn't be able to get in without a struggle. That would give her time to get to the window and drop down onto the roof of the shed. From there, she could jump into the yard and then make a break for it.

It had never happened. He'd never come barging in, yet Leah was old enough to know she should have a plan if he did. Escape was plan A. Plan B was her knife, but she'd not seen that since the night at Vicky's house. That meant she needed a new plan B.

Leah lay on her bed, head near the door, listening to the creaking of a different bed at the other end of the hall. The squeaks quickly gave way to louder thumps and even louder moans. She covered her ears and then buried herself underneath the bedcovers, humming a song to herself as something, anything, to distract from what was going on in her parents' room.

This happened every time her dad returned. He'd disappear for a week without saying a word and her mum would swear she'd never take him back. Then he'd show up unannounced and the pair of them would be in the bedroom humping away at full volume. It didn't matter if he was away for longer than a week, or if it was his decision. It wasn't long before that he'd spent five months behind bars and, on the day he got out, he and Leah's mum were in that room the whole evening.

And here they were again, after yet another release from prison. Nothing ever changed.

Aside from Leah's worry about him coming knocking one night, there was a part of her that wanted him to at least acknowledge her. She hadn't seen him in months, yet he hadn't taken even a second to ask how she was, or look in on her. Oh, no, there wasn't time for that.

Squeak, squeak, squeak, squeak.

Leah wondered if she could fix a creaky bed by herself when there was nobody around. She could probably nick some screws from the design tech department when she went back to school, then figure it out from there. The woodworking teacher always seemed slightly afraid of girls, certainly of being alone with them, so it was easy enough to get into the store cupboard.

'Shut up,' Leah muttered under her breath, not that it made any difference.

She closed her eyes, as she turned herself into a ball underneath the covers. She could unblock the door and leave but where was she going to go? School had broken up, Christmas had gone, and the only thing she knew was coming was the new year's bonfire. Well, that and the end of everything familiar when the Y2K bug hit. Plus, if she went outside, someone would recognise her, and then they'd want to ask about Vicky,

Jazz and Harriet. It was close-run but Leah preferred the noise from the other bedroom to that.

It was eventually over as a door opened and the bathroom door closed. Leah heard her father clearing his nose and then flushing the toilet, before there were footsteps on the landing. She expected to hear them heading downstairs but then there was a creak outside her door. Leah had unwrapped herself from the covers and was kneeling on her bed. She could sense her father on the other side of the door, touching distance, except for the layer of wood between them.

'Lee...?'

Leah was suddenly aware of her heartbeat thundering. She eyed the window.

'Yeah...?'

'Are you going to come downstairs?'

He sounded almost, well... normal. That fierce terror that often undercut everything he said wasn't there, likely because he'd just spent time in the bedroom with Leah's mum.

'OK,' she said, trying not to sound as reluctant as she felt. 'Give me a minute.'

Leah waited a moment as, thankfully, her dad headed downstairs. She quickly dragged the bed away from the door and then put on a pair of shoes before following him down. She never knew if and when she might have to rush into the street to get away from the chaos of the house. Leah had learned the hard way that being bare-footed was a hindrance.

As she headed into the sparse living room, Leah's mum and dad were on the sofa. Her mum had her legs stretched long, across her dad's lap. This is how they'd be for a day or three, how it always was. A lovey-dovey horror show, punctuated by repeated trips to the bedroom. Then there would be a spark and Leah would have to take cover once again. The only way anything would ever change was if her dad did something so awful he went to prison for a decent length of time.

'We thought we should make it up to you for me not being around at Christmas,' Leah's dad said. 'What do you want?'

It felt like a dangerous question. If Leah asked for something, it would feel as if she had a problem with her dad skipping Christmas, as he had many others. Not only that, if she asked for something too small, he'd push for something bigger. But if she asked for something too big, he'd say she was greedy and not worth it. This didn't feel like a question for which there was a correct answer.

'I think I'm all right,' Leah said.

'What do you mean?'

'I've kind of got everything I want.'

It was such an obvious lie – and clearly the wrong thing to have said.

Leah's dad slapped his wife's legs off his lap and pushed himself to the edge of the sofa. 'What? You think your old man's not good enough to get his little girl a Christmas present?'

Leah risked the briefest of glances to her mum, who was staring at the wall.

'No,' Leah said, trying to sound cheerful. 'It's just I don't need anything.'

'Why? Who's been buying you stuff while I've been away?' He turned quickly to Leah's mum, sneering. 'You got some fella on the go?'

'No.'

He turned back to Leah. 'Has she? She had some fancy man coming over, buying you things?'

'No,' Leah replied. She'd taken a small step backwards, hoping her dad hadn't noticed. He was still on the tip of the sofa, knees bent, as if about to launch himself upwards.

'So how come you have everything you need?' he asked.

'I don't know.'

He gave that little smirk he always did. The one that Leah could never quite read. It either meant he was winding her up, and would soon crack to say she shouldn't take everything so seriously. Or, he'd turn to Leah's mum and take out some of his apparently endless frustration.

'You think you're special?' he asked, looking to Leah, though his lips barely moved. It was dangerous when that happened.

'No.'

'You think you're special 'cos your little friends left and everyone wants to talk to you?'

'No. It's just I don't need anything.'

Leah knew he was trying to wind her up but took another minute step backwards. She could probably get into the hallway before her dad, but it would be tough to get the front door open and dash through before he reached her. The back door was too far off, and likely locked anyway. That meant the stairs and her room might be the best option. She thought she was probably quicker going up than he was. Would she be able to block the door quickly enough? Or get to the window? She should have left it open – which would be a lesson for the future. If she made it to the future.

Leah's dad nodded at her mum, who was still staring at the wall. 'You hear this?' he said. 'She doesn't need anything.'

Her mother's eyes flashed across her, not lingering. She didn't speak.

'What? Neither of you can talk now?'

The room sizzled as Leah's father glanced between the two women. His top lip was curled and he was still on the edge of the sofa, a snake ready to spring.

'Do you wanna go back upstairs?' Leah's mum said. She was already unbuttoning her top.

Leah's father continued to look between them and it felt as if things could go either way. A flip of a coin. Heads smashed into walls, tails over the bed.

A second passed. Then another. Leah didn't risk breathing, in case she did it too loudly. She shuffled another half-pace backwards. Leah could definitely beat her dad to the stairs if she went now. No point in even waiting for him to kick off.

'Yeah,' he finally said, as Leah allowed herself to exhale. Her mum stood first as Leah's dad whacked his wife's backside. 'Lead the way,' he said.

THIRTY-TWO

NOW

The house sounded empty as Leah arrived home. She closed the front door and called up to Zac, though there was silence in return.

It wasn't the first time.

Leah headed up and knocked on his door. There was a scuffling from inside and then her son opened the door, headset around his neck.

'Just letting you know I'm home,' Leah told him.

He eyed the bag in her hand: 'Did you, uh...?'

Leah reached in and passed him the supermarket BLT. Some kids were into McDonald's, or KFC, that sort of thing. If he wasn't eating Deborah's cooking, then Zac liked sandwiches. He grinned as he took the packet.

'Everything good?' he asked, and she wondered if he was being polite, or if he saw something within her. The truth was, Leah had gone to the supermarket to mooch around the aisles and try to forget the ordeal of the morning. She knew ahead of time it would be a mistake to visit her father and it had been.

'How's the homework?' she asked, avoiding his question. Perhaps a part of her dad had rubbed off on her.

'Done,' Zac replied, as he pulled at the cardboard tab of the sandwich container.

'What are you up to now?'

A shrug. 'Bit of this.'

Which meant he was probably playing games online, or watching streams of other people playing games. She'd never quite understood the appeal of that part.

'Do you need anything?' Leah asked.

That got a shake of the head.

Every time she read one of the horror stories in the WhatsApp groups, of teenage tantrums, or threats to run away, she was grateful she had a grounded son. He liked his laptop and his games console, he was happy with a small group of friends, he seemingly did his homework – and had never been in any real trouble.

At least one part of her life had a degree of sanity to it.

'I'll leave you then,' Leah said.

Zac retreated into his room and closed the door, as Leah headed downstairs. She plugged in her own laptop and got to work.

It was ridiculously easy to find Mandy.

Leah searched for 'Mandy' and the name of her father's prison – and the top link was an article from the local paper about someone named Mandy Archer trying to encourage people to write to prisoners.

Her full address wasn't listed but there was a street name – and Leah knew it was close to the area in which she grew up.

It had to be the same person.

In the photo from seven years before, Mandy had dyed blonde hair with roots that had almost grown through. She had a huge smile that, even through the screen, felt infectious. The sort of person that Leah felt she'd probably seen around town numerous times. There was certainly something familiar about her. She was probably from around her dad's generation –

which was one thing at least. It would've been so much worse had he found someone Leah's age, or, worse, younger.

It wouldn't be difficult to find out Mandy's exact address and Leah wondered if she should visit. Her dad had been right about one thing. Technically, *technically*, Mandy was going to be Leah's new mum.

It was hard not to shiver at the idea of that. Leah barely had a first mother, let alone a second. She was almost forty. What on earth was going on? She did not need this in her life.

Away from snooping on Mandy, Leah checked her emails again. Her 'can we meet?' had gone unanswered, as with so many of her replies to the anonymous friend. There was nothing from Owen, either.

The stolen ring was upstairs, at the back of her drawer – and had been joined by the knife that had been returned to her twenty-four years after she lost it.

She was a step behind everything that had happened over the past few days.

There had to be a reason why the person emailing Leah wanted the documentary to be stopped, along with a reason for why they couldn't try to stop it themselves. The obvious assumption was that the emailer was worried about something that could be revealed in the course of the documentary being filmed. Something that had remained a secret for more than two decades was in danger of coming out.

Leah knew how that felt... except she wasn't sure what the other person thought she could do about it. The 'To stop them finding out what you did' email felt like a blackmail attempt, as did leading Leah to her knife, and the latest implied threat regarding the stolen ring. Someone trying to force her to do something to stop the documentary, else they'd reveal what they knew.

Or, more to the point, what they *thought* they knew.

The thought still persisted that Leah had only told Vicky

about her knife. Vicky could have told someone else – but who? Could Vicky really still be out there somewhere? It felt unlikely for so many reasons.

Impossible.

That word again. Leah kept coming back to it.

There was only one conclusion – that the person contacting her knew what had happened to Vicky, Jazz and Harriet.

She closed her laptop and found her bag, with the police file still at the bottom. Leah skimmed the first few pages that she'd already read in the café above the bowling alley. The more she read, the more it became clear the police didn't have much of an idea what had happened. It was also understandable why they hadn't clocked the connection of the neighbour naming Leah's father, and the drunk man on the bench bringing up a man in a red and white shirt. Those two things were buried among hundreds of small, largely nonsensical, tips. Someone had called to say he had seen a UFO over the town, another person was convinced Bill Clinton had to be involved. Someone suggested the IRA. Everything had been documented but there was a lot of confusing nonsense.

It was also primitive. In the days before widespread mobiles, the police had pulled the landline phone records from Vicky's house. There had been one outgoing call on the night of the sleepover: which had been made to Jasmine's parents. A note on the file read that Jazz's mum said the call was a regular thing, with her daughter checking in to say she was fine.

It was impossible not to see the parallels to Leah wanting Zac to stay in contact when he'd slept over at Josh's place.

Almost every neighbour to whom the police had spoken said they'd been asleep through the night. Someone thought they'd heard Vicky's dad arriving home from his football dinner in the taxi, but that was confirmed by the driver anyway.

There were character statements, saying that Vicky's father, Tom, was a good neighbour. Nobody appeared to believe anything negative about him, with most of the statements insisting they were in awe of the job he'd done after his wife died. The police had checked the medical records for Vicky's mum, and there was nothing untoward in the way she died.

Tom's statement was perhaps the most telling. He admitted he was tipsy when he got in after the football dinner. He had checked the living room, where all four girls were sleeping, and then headed upstairs to bed. The next thing he knew, Leah was knocking on his door, asking if he knew where the other three were.

That was Leah's recollection, too.

Leah read her own statements, along with the officer's observations that she seemed 'shell-shocked', 'fidgety', and 'tired' – all of which were likely true.

In all, Leah read the file three times across the afternoon, as she went down the rabbit hole chronicling of her life. There was nothing within the pages that she either didn't already know, or couldn't have figured out. There were vague sightings of mystery figures but nothing that could be verified.

The crucial point, the most important factor, was that there had never been a confirmed sighting of any of the girls. That was true on the night of the sleepover, as well as the weeks afterwards.

They really had disappeared.

Leah returned the file to her bag and then started making tea for Zac. She wouldn't need many fingers to count the number of times either of her own parents had ever cooked for her.

Zac was drawn downstairs by the smell of food. It wasn't exactly gourmet but he loved a baked potato with tuna, beans and cheese – and he wolfed his down as Leah picked at hers. Considering his age, and the tales of sullen teens from other parents, they ate together two or three times a week at the kitchen table. True, he was often on his phone, but it was better than nothing.

Zac had almost finished when he looked up from his plate. 'You look tired,' he said.

Shirley had said the same thing the day before – and, if Zac had noticed, it must be true.

'Just busy at work,' Leah said. It was partly true, except she'd barely thought of the office since leaving Fiona's one, two... three (?) days before. Was it three days? It felt like longer.

The afternoon slipped by. Zac headed back upstairs and Leah sat in front of the television, not watching it, thoughts endlessly drifting through time.

It was a little after five that the text from Deborah arrived. Harriet's mother checked in on Leah every Sunday evening. She would ask how the weekend had gone, and if Zac was going to go to her house after school the next day. It had been going on for years, largely since Deborah had got a mobile phone. Her first text had been sent to Leah – 'Does this work?' – and then it had never really ended. Not that Leah wanted it to.

For a day in which she'd learned she was on the brink of getting a technical new mum in Mandy, the truth was that Leah already had one, with Deborah. Ultimately, neither of them were blood relations, but that hadn't mattered when Deborah took in Leah after her own daughter disappeared. It hadn't made a difference in the twenty-odd years since. In the absence of real parents, Deborah had stepped in. Shirley, too. The two women had shaped Leah into the person she was. The mother she was.

Except this Sunday's text wasn't a simple check-in.

The forum's in an hour. Do you want to go? I'll go with you if you want.

Leah had forgotten that Owen was hosting a meeting in

town that evening. He'd also asked if she was going to go. It had barely been a day before that she'd said no, but, since then, she'd been sent the Polaroid of the stolen ring, and she'd met her father.

Things were changing so quickly – and, if she wanted answers, perhaps there was one place to find them.

THIRTY-THREE

Deborah did a loop of the community centre car park, arriving back at the entrance as she and Leah realised there were no spaces. The vehicles that had lined both sides of the road on the approach should've been the clue.

'I can't believe it's so busy,' Deborah said, largely to herself. She headed back onto the road and followed the line of parked cars around the corner, before stopping on a side street.

The two women walked back the way they'd come, slipping in behind another couple who were going in the same direction. It was T-shirt weather: the evening sun warm without being stifling.

'Lot of people,' Deborah said. More say-what-you-see.

It felt like half the town had taken up Owen on his offer of coming to ask questions about the documentary. It was a surprise but it wasn't. Hundreds of people weren't suddenly interested in low-budget filmmaking, but they'd never forgotten the missing trio of girls.

A couple passed Leah and Deborah on the outside, the man striding with purpose as his harried wife tried to keep up. As he walked by, he turned to nod, before clocking it was Leah. His pace dropped instantly, with his wife almost bumping into the back of him.

'Oh,' he said, now keeping pace with Leah. 'I wondered if you'd be here.'

Leah had no idea who he was, though the reaction wasn't a surprise.

She gave a quiet 'hi', slowing her pace and forcing him to choose between stalking her and getting on with whatever he was doing. His choice was made for him as his wife poked him in the ribs and gave a 'stop staring' glare.

As Leah and Deborah slotted back into their own pace, Deborah touched Leah on the wrist. 'You OK, love?' she asked.

'Yeah...'

This was one of the reasons why Leah hadn't wanted to come.

They crossed the road and made their way into the community centre car park, where drivers were still doing loops before heading back out again.

'It's not even like this for the farmers' market,' Deborah said.

Leah smiled but said nothing. That was another of the general points of contention on the town Facebook groups. Residents would complain about all the extra vehicles parking outside their houses, while there would always be someone annoyed about the cost of artisan bread, cheese, and whatever else, compared to the local supermarkets. With so little going on, people had to find something about which to moan. It was better than the posts about chemtrails and Bill Gates.

Into the community centre and it was stifling. Rows of chairs were packed, with many more people lining the edges of the hall. Conversations were being held over the top of conversations, an oppressive wall of voices fighting with scraping chairs and scuffing feet for supremacy.

Leah fanned herself with her hand, though only succeeded

in moving around the already warm air. Lots of people were doing the same.

There was no passage through the middle of the room, so Leah and Deborah followed the milling numbers around the edge.

On the stage, Owen was talking to one of the crew members she recognised from the other day. The man who'd held the boom mic was setting up a regular microphone in the centre of the stage, with a cable trailing to an amplifier. It felt a bit karaoke-at-a-summer-fête. As if some divorcee was about to get up and clear the room by banging out 'Total Eclipse Of The Heart'.

It was impossible for Leah to avoid the stares. Some were brief glances, like a teenage boy noticing cleavage, while pretending not to. Others lingered. There were elbow nudges and barely there nods. *Look who's here.*

More or less everyone Leah could see was either her age, or older. It was locals who'd been around at the time her friends went missing. Adults who'd never been allowed their own sleep-overs when they were young, and who were now parents. Or parents from the time who'd spent years fretting over the safety and whereabouts of their own children. Two or three generations who had never quite got past the mystery.

Hard to blame them, really.

A high-pitched whine burned through the amplifier as everybody winced as one. There was a gentle thump and then 'one-two-three' through the PA system. Owen was on the microphone and said something Leah didn't catch. The hum of the crowd settled into a hushed quiet.

'Thanks for coming,' Owen boomed, before turning to one of his crew.

The other man fiddled with something on the amplifier and, when Owen spoke again, his voice was a little lower.

'I'm Owen Poole,' he added. 'I'm a filmmaker and my sister

was Jasmine, one of the girls who disappeared twenty-four years ago.' He turned to his crew members and introduced them as producers, before pointing to a woman Leah didn't recognise. 'This is Sarah,' he added. 'She works on the paper. I think quite a few of you read her story the other day, so I asked her to come along and help run things. She's going to try to make sure people are heard.'

The final person on stage was somebody Leah did know.

'This is someone else I think a few of you know. Esther Merrivale was the older sister of Vicky. The sleepover happened at her house and she's been helping with a bit of legal advice here and there. She's also been great at introducing us to the right people to help with access around the town.'

Esther was sitting with her knees crossed towards the back of the stage. She stood, nodded, and then sat again, before Owen handed the microphone to Sarah.

Leah wasn't sure what she'd expected a public forum to be. Definitely not her scene. Whatever this was began as more of an interview, with Sarah asking questions and Owen answering. They were sitting in chairs a few paces across from one another, like a late-night talk show host and a guest.

The doors at the back of the hall were open and a gentle breeze bubbled around the rear, where Leah and Deborah were standing. Leah was half hiding behind a pillar, away from the gazes of those who kept turning to see how she was reacting to what was being said.

Owen was saying he didn't want to impose himself or the crew on the town over the coming week or two.

'I don't want this to become some morbid tourist hotspot,' he added, although it was probably a little late for that. An enormous cloud had been hanging over the place for close to a quarter of a century, and his documentary was only going to bring in more people. 'I can't promise I'll find any definitive answers. But I've been speaking to a lot of people who were around at the time, some more directly than others.' He nodded towards Sarah. 'We've had incredible co-operation and support from the local news organisations, with full access to newspaper archives, and old television news broadcasts. The police have been as helpful as they can be, and so has the local school. The reception from the community has been more than I could have hoped for.'

Sarah had largely been offering gentle questions but there was a little more punch to her follow-up. 'If you're not promising answers, what are you hoping to achieve?'

Owen took a second. 'I think we want to make something that brings the community together to a point of understanding. If answers come from that, all the better.'

There was a round of applause that began with a hesitant one or two, which eventually included most of the room. Leah wasn't sure he'd actually said anything of substance. What did a 'point of understanding' actually mean?

Sarah said she was going to open up the forum for questions – and it was as hands started to go up that Leah realised she was being watched. She was still trying to escape notice behind one column, but there was a woman doing the same behind the pillar on the opposite half of the hall. As Leah glanced across to her, the woman shuffled further behind the post with a flash of blonde.

Sarah pointed to a man who'd been sitting halfway back in the row of seats. He stood as the boom mic crew member headed from the stage and passed him a microphone. He was wearing a hoody with 'I Did My Research' printed on the back.

'What do you have to say about the mountain of evidence which indicates this was an alien abduction?' the man asked. 'You do realise we all live at the epicentre of an extra-terrestrial invasion?'

There was a collective groan from the audience as the crew member reached for the microphone.

'I've been probed!' the man insisted, as the mic was pulled from his grasp. 'I can prove it!'

Someone at the back of the room muttered a 'for God's sake, Barry', which got a laugh.

'Do you want to answer that?' Sarah asked at the front.

Owen was unruffled. 'The aim of the documentary is to examine what happened, without ruling anything in or out. If you want to pass along your, um, evidence, we'll happily have a look.'

He didn't address the apparent probing.

A tittering of giggles passed around the room, as Leah glanced sideways, towards where the other woman was peeping at her around the pillar. The woman glanced down, towards what looked like a phone, and then started typing.

This time, Sarah pointed to a middle-aged woman, someone who didn't look like she'd confess to being probed in front of an audience.

'I feel like this is the wrong time to be bringing this all up again,' the woman said, talking to Owen. 'I know she was your sister but we're never going to move on if we're not allowed to put things in the past.' She motioned to hand back the microphone and then changed her mind for long enough to add a quick: 'No offence.'

Unlike most instances of 'no offence' being used, it sounded as if she meant it.

A couple of people clapped and there was a murmur of agreement.

Owen was diplomatic enough, saying he understood concerns but wanted to work with the town, not against.

The following twenty minutes continued in broadly the same manner. It was largely amicable, with audience members offering vague support to, or disagreement against, the documentary. It didn't feel as if there was much consensus. Some agreed that the film shouldn't be happening, and that it was going to bring up bad memories for the town. Others were in favour of anything that could finally bring answers and closure. Like everything in modern life, there was a split almost down the middle. Fifty-two per cent thought the forty-eight per cent were out of their minds, and vice versa. If someone were to bring up wind turbines, it would really kick off.

It felt as if very little had been achieved when the microphone ended up in the hands of a short woman near the front. Leah could barely see her over the crowd, even though the woman was standing.

She sounded nervous as she stammered into the microphone. 'This is a question for Esther,' she said, which surprised everyone, considering every other query had gone to Owen.

The woman didn't wait for an OK.

'I used to live on the same street as you,' she continued. 'Almost opposite. I don't know if you remember me...?'

Esther had uncrossed her knees and leant forward in her chair. She'd been almost forgotten through the forum, and it wasn't clear why she was on stage at all. She gave no indication that she knew the woman.

'Do you know there was an empty house on our street when your sister went missing?' she asked. 'It was opposite my house and had gone up for sale a couple of months before. I thought I saw someone in there the day after your sister went missing. My husband went over and knocked on the door. He said he could hear someone inside but nobody came out.'

Esther was blank, and seemingly had no idea what the woman was talking about. She glanced across to Owen, who was holding one of the microphones.

'Did you tell anyone?' he asked.

The woman turned to him. 'I told the police two or three days later. They didn't know it was empty but I'm not sure what happened after that.'

She beckoned across the crew member, handed him the

microphone, and sat down. There was a ruthless efficiency about her that Leah admired. Most of the others who'd been given a microphone had blathered on until it had been wrestled from them.

Owen had been relaxed on stage but now exchanged a curious, pouted-lip look with Sarah, before nodding to one of his crew members.

'I don't think any of us knew that,' he said. 'If you have time, we would definitely like to talk to you about this away from here. Can we take your details?'

There was a break, as the crowd started muttering to one another. Meanwhile, Owen stepped down from the stage and talked quietly to the woman, while seemingly putting her name and number into his phone. There was a buzz in the room, as if something had actually been achieved. It was hard to know whether that was true, though any revelation of new information after such a long time would feel like something of a victory.

Deborah had been largely quiet throughout the forum, sticking close to Leah and acting as something akin to a shield from the stares and looks. Now she leaned in and whispered, 'Are you all right?' to which Leah said she was. She didn't think much had been resolved this evening, or by her being there. A part of her was glad to have been there, though. There was a degree of comfort in that, regardless on which side the community fell about whether the documentary should be happening, there was an investment. It felt to Leah as if her friends mattered, as if she did. She still doubted there would ever be an answer as to what happened after she fell asleep.

Not long after, Sarah wound down the meeting. She read out an email address for Owen and said anybody could send across information if they had it. Barry in his I Did My Research hoody was feverishly typing something into his phone, which likely meant there would be a barrage of information about aliens heading Owen's way within in the hour.

People started to drift off to their cars. The evening had cooled and, as numbers thinned, the warmth of earlier had been replaced by a soft chill.

Deborah gently touched Leah's elbow and said, 'Shall we go?', except Leah wasn't moving. The woman who'd been hiding behind the pillar had crossed the hall, nervously looking between the floor and Leah herself.

'One minute,' Leah said.

Around them, people continued to head for the doors, as the woman weaved between them. Seconds later and she was in front of Leah.

'Are you Leah?' she asked, though she already knew.

'Yes,' Leah replied.

'I was hoping we could maybe have a word. Not now, necessarily, but, um... I don't really know how to tell you this. It's just—'

'It's nice to meet you, Mandy.'

THIRTY-FOUR

Mandy had been in the middle of a word but stopped open-mouthed. She had barely changed from the photograph attached to the news article written seven years before. Her hair was still bleached, her roots still grown out. 'You know me?'

'I visited Dad today.'

Leah suddenly realised that Deborah was at her side, and that this was news to her. Deborah tensed, though didn't say anything. It wouldn't be her way to question, or criticise.

'You... what?' Mandy replied.

'He told me you're getting married,' Leah said, as she felt the surprise of both women around her. It didn't help that people were still slotting past them towards the exit. 'Shall we go outside?' Leah suggested.

She didn't wait for an answer, as she led Deborah and Mandy through the back doors of the hall, around to the side and the children's playground. It was colder than Leah had realised, with an Arctic breeze whistling around the swings.

'You saw him today?' Mandy asked, unable to hide her surprise. 'They don't do visits on Sundays.'

'It's a long story,' Leah told her, as she folded her arms

across herself. 'I've got to get home to my son. I'm working in town tomorrow but if you're around at lunchtime, we can have a sandwich...?'

Mandy almost dropped her phone with the eagerness to swap numbers. She was all thumbs as she tried to type in Leah's details, so Leah ended up doing it for her.

'I'll text,' Leah said, thinking it was hard to dislike the other woman, even though a part of her wanted to.

Mandy muttered a series of 'thanks' and 'looking forward to it', before hurrying past the play equipment, towards the housing estate on the far side of the field.

Leah took a step towards the direction of the car, Deborah at her side. The car park was almost empty as they crossed it.

'I've not seen him in years,' Leah said quietly.

'You don't have to defend yourself to me. It's none of my business.'

It was true but it wasn't. Deborah had given more than twenty years of her life to Leah.

'I've had a lot going on with this documentary,' Leah explained. 'Loads of stuff has come out and a couple of people said Dad was on the street the night everything happened.'

Deborah missed a step and Leah paused to let her catch up. 'The night Harriet went missing?'

It was interesting, albeit unsurprising, how each party described things from their own point of view. For Owen, it was the night Jazz disappeared. With Deborah, it was Harriet. Esther had talked about Vicky.

'He was released from prison a few days before,' Leah said. 'He was supposed to be in a halfway house, before going home. He disappeared on that Saturday night, so I went to ask him if he was on the street.'

'What did he say?'

'Nothing really. He's not changed. He asked if I'd taken in money for his birthday, then told me he was getting married.'

They were back at the car and waited side by side, next to the driver's door. 'To her?' Deborah asked, nodding back towards the community centre.

'Mandy,' Leah replied.

'Do you know her?'

'Never met her – but I saw a photo. She's, um... distinctive.'

Leah wasn't trying to be unkind, though couldn't think of a better word. Mandy was big and garish, blonde and bright. It would be hard to miss her.

Deborah unlocked the car and the two of them settled inside. They didn't speak for the first minute or so of the journey, though Leah had an idea what Deborah must be thinking. Mandy was going to be Leah's new mother: the role Deborah herself had played for Leah's entire adult life. Leah wasn't sure how to tell her that nothing would change in their relationship. The words were there but they wouldn't quite come out. There was too much to sum up in a tidy little sentence.

To distract herself, Leah took out her phone from her bag. She'd not checked it since they had parked a couple of hours before.

There was an email from A Friend.

Do you see now why this has to be stopped?

Leah stared at the words, trying to scroll lower in case there was more.

'Are you all right?' Deborah must have noticed something about Leah's demeanour from the driver's seat.

Leah told her she was fine as she kept trying to move the screen down. Why were the messages always so short?

The person who'd sent it must have been at the forum, or – at the absolute least – must have known Leah was there.

It was Leah who was now all thumbs and it took her five attempts to clean up a typo-ridden reply.

No. Who are you?

Leah checked the time the email had been sent, and it was around forty-five minutes into the forum. She'd been hiding behind a pillar at that point, though plenty of people had seen her.

She hadn't exactly expected an instant reply, but it was impossible for Leah not to be annoyed. Everything was happening on this other person's timetable – and Leah was sick of being messed around. It was bad enough when it was her own father, let alone this stranger.

You were obviously there. Why don't YOU stop it?

The initial version had the line 'Stop emailing me' at the bottom, though Leah deleted it a moment before pressing send.

A part of her wanted the emails to continue, as long as the person told her who they were. Whoever it was knew things they couldn't possibly know.

Even though Leah had largely silenced the little voice telling her it could only be Vicky, another part wanted it to be true. So many questions would be answered, even if bigger ones were asked.

When Leah looked up, she realised Deborah was turning onto her street. She parked outside Leah's house and sat with the engine idling.

'Thank you for tonight,' Leah said. 'I really appreciate you coming.'

'You're welcome, love.'

'It's just... with Mandy... she's not... I don't—'

'I understand,' Deborah replied – although Leah wished she had a better way of expressing things.

'She's not you,' Leah managed.

Deborah reached across the gearstick and pressed a hand to

Leah's knee. 'Look after yourself,' she said. 'You need some sleep.'

Leah almost laughed at that, or she would have done if she wasn't so tired. That was three people who'd mentioned how sleepy she looked.

'I'll see you tomorrow,' she said, before getting out of the car.

In the house, everything was quiet. Leah headed upstairs and knocked gently on Zac's door. No answer came, so she opened it quietly, to find him asleep on top of the bedcovers, still wearing his regular clothes. His tablet was on the floor at his side, YouTube videos still flickering on the screen. Leah picked up the device and closed the app, then locked the screen. It wasn't the first time he'd seemingly fallen asleep in this manner. Back then, she'd almost told him off – before realising that, when she was his age, it was normal for people to fall asleep in front of the television. Not Leah, of course, there was no TV in her childhood room and the idea of leaving herself vulnerable in the living room was unfathomable.

She watched her son sleep for a minute or so, before catching herself. She thought about waking him and encouraging him to change – but what was the point? Instead, she edged out of his room and closed the door, then crossed the landing to her own room.

Leah lay on her bed, staring at the ceiling. Something about meeting Mandy had thrown her. Her natural instinct was to dislike anybody with whom her father was associated, except Mandy appeared, well... normal. Nice, perhaps? She had been so polite and flustered while trying to introduce herself and it was baffling that a person like that could see something redeeming in Leah's father.

Leah closed her eyes and...

Snap.

Leah gasped as she realised she was on her side. She'd been staring at the ceiling and then... what? She must have fallen asleep. She was still in her clothes and something had woken her. Had it? Was it a dream? Had something fallen?

She rocked herself onto her back and blinked through the gloom. The lights were off but the curtains were open and a gentle white from the street lights shrouded the room.

It was quiet. Leah had been dreaming. She remained on her back and closed her eyes and—

Snap.

The bang echoed through the silent house. A familiar sound, except Leah's muddy thoughts were too cloudy for her to figure out what was happening.

She was sitting, then standing. The carpet bristled her bare feet as she reached the landing, where Zac was standing at the top of the stairs. He startled her for a second, mainly because she'd somehow failed to realise how much bigger than her he was. She would say things like 'You're getting tall', but that hadn't prepared her for seeing his shape through the murk of the night. It also didn't stop the glimmer of confused fear in his face as he turned to look at her. 'Mum...?'

He was fourteen, built like a grown man, but he was still her little boy.

'I think it's the letterbox,' he said – and he was right.

Somebody was at the door, but they weren't knocking the glass, or ringing the bell, they were snapping the letterbox.

It banged again, a third time, and Leah headed past her son, down the stairs. The clang of the letterbox still felt as if it was reverberating around her. Zac was a pace behind, keeping close, as Leah reached the hall and neared the front door.

'Who is it?' she called.

The reply was stumbling and high-pitched, as she realised that the shape of the person on the other side of the door barely reached above the lower part. Half a head was visible in the dimpled glass. A child.

'Cody,' said the voice.

Fiona's son. The boy who'd been doing so well at school, as his mother got her life back on track. That moment in Fiona's kitchen a few days before had sat at the back of Leah's thoughts ever since. Her 'Are you OK with that?' had been met by Fiona's 'She's welcome to him' – except that reply had taken that fraction of a second too long to come.

Leah knew that pause. She'd seen it from her own mother many times over. Sometimes Leah had asked the question, other times social workers, or police officers. It wasn't always the same query, though the hesitation was always the same.

'Where's he gone?' – pause – 'I don't care.'

'What if he's sent to prison?' – pause – 'I hope he is.'

'Why don't you leave him?' – pause – 'I will.'

It was never the truth. Never.

Leah unlocked and pulled open the front door to reveal a shivering nine-year-old boy. He was bare-legged, in rubber-soled daps, plus grey pyjamas with cartoon characters speckled across.

'Dad's home,' he said, which was something Leah already knew.

THIRTY-FIVE

Leah ran. Fiona's house was a few streets away, probably five minutes in a car, but barely that on foot. There were alleys and lanes, little cut-throughs and burrows, about which only the locals knew.

She thought she'd been sprinting but, if she was, it couldn't have been too fast. By the time Leah reached Fiona's place, it was a little after one in the morning, and Zac was only half a dozen steps behind. He was carrying Cody and barely out of breath. How had he got so big? So athletic? He spent all day watching YouTube and playing games.

There was no time to question whether he should've come, because Fiona's front door was wide open and lights were on inside.

Leah burst into the house, and the previously tidy kitchen. The clothes rail had been tipped on its side, sending the rainbow of items across the floor. There were plates and cups smashed on the lino, with the kitchen window open and a chair hanging through it. Everything that had been pinned to the fridge was on the floor, and the door to the freezer was hanging open.

Leah almost backed out to look for Fiona elsewhere, except the tiniest of squeaks led her to the upturned clothes rail, under which a woman was cowering. A clump of dark hair was on the ground at her side.

'Has he gone?' Leah asked.

The only answer was a rapid nod and then: 'Cody?'

Leah whispered a short 'he's safe – and then returned to the hall. Zac had been waiting with Cody, and Leah joined him, closing the kitchen door behind her.

'I need you to take him home,' she said. 'Lock the front door, check the back's locked too – and do not open it to anyone, unless it's me.'

Zac didn't question her. He placed a hand on Cody's shoulder and turned.

'Even if they say it's the police,' Leah added quickly. 'Don't answer it to anybody unless it's me.'

'OK.'

Leah stood in the doorway and watched him go. A fourteen-year-old and a nine-year-old hurrying through the night by themselves was far from ideal but she couldn't have them here.

As they disappeared out of sight into the lane, Leah hurried upstairs and opened every door. She looked in the cupboards, and under the beds. Just because Fiona thought he'd gone, it didn't mean he had.

When she was satisfied the house was empty, Leah returned downstairs and closed the front door, clamping the chain into place. It took her a few attempts to figure out how to lock it, but she got there in the end by lifting up the handle.

Back in the kitchen, Leah lifted the clothes rail away from Fiona, hauled the chair back inside, and then closed the window. As best she could tell, the house was secure.

Leah took a breath, a single second that she needed. This

was why she was drawn to Fiona. She made many visits through a week to vulnerable people, checking to see how their lives were going. And, even though everything had been looking up for Fiona, Leah knew this was how things would finish in the end.

She *knew*.

She crouched a pace away from Fiona. The chunk of hair on the ground had come from a spot a little above Fiona's ear. There was blood across her brow that had started to crust and she was staring blankly at the floor.

'Where does it hurt?' Leah asked.

'My back.'

Leah considered trying to help Fiona to her feet, though that felt like a bad idea if she'd hurt her back.

'Wait there,' Leah said. 'I'll get an ambulance.'

She half expected resistance, though none came.

Leah moved out of the kitchen, closing the door behind and heading into the living room. She peeked through the window, seeing nobody outside, so closed the curtains.

When the call handler answered the 999 call, Leah told her she wanted police and an ambulance. There had been a domestic assault, the victim was conscious but injured, and the assailant was gone. It all felt so familiar. Leah had never quite forgotten what to ask for, nor what to say.

As that was happening, a one-word text appeared from Zac, reading 'safe', which was all she needed.

The handler told Leah to wait with the victim until help arrived, so Leah did precisely that. The kitchen was a bomb site, though she didn't want to move too much because it might be evidence. Instead, Leah sat on the floor at Fiona's side, holding the shell-shocked other woman's hand.

As well as the bloodied scrape above her eye, there was a series of smaller scratches around her chin, and a gash in the side of her hand. Leah asked if she was OK, and the only reply was if Leah could put on the kettle.

She did that, although there was broken crockery in the sink to clear. Leah didn't want the specifics of what had happened, and, in many ways, it didn't matter. The outcome was the same. It looked as if Kevin, Fiona's former partner, Cody's father, had thrown everything in sight.

Leah found an intact mug at the back of one of the cupboards, and an upturned box of teabags on the floor. She found one that hadn't touched the floor and put that in the mug. The milk bottle was near the back door, though the lid had remained on. Leah used that and then placed the drink on the floor at Fiona's side.

'Can I do anything else?' she asked, which got a shake of the head as a reply.

It was only a moment later that spinning blue lights filled the hall. Leah moved into the living room and checked through the window to see a pair of police cars at the front. She went into the hall and, with the chain still attached, opened the door.

The officers knew the routine. There was a man and a woman, and both had their ID cards in hand for Leah to see. As she was opening the door for them, an ambulance slotted in behind the police cars.

The female officer went into the kitchen, as the other one waited in the hall with Leah. She told him that she worked in community support and that Fiona was one of the people whom she visited. Fiona's nine-year-old was safe at her house, a few streets away – but that his father had been at the house that night. There was a history of domestic violence.

Moments later and the paramedics were inside. The officer pointed them through to the kitchen, though it was only a few seconds later when one of them returned to the hall.

'She's asking for you.'

Leah returned to what was now a cramped kitchen full of too many people.

Fiona was on her feet, stooped and wincing. 'Where's Cody?' she asked.

'He's at mine, with Zac. They've locked themselves inside.' She turned to one of the officers, pre-empting the question. 'If you're sending someone over, you'll have to wait outside. I've told him not to open the door to anyone, unless it's me.'

The officer blinked with surprise, but this wasn't Leah's first time.

'There's a restraining order,' she said. 'I've got the details in my file at work but I'm sure you have it as well.' Leah risked a glance to Fiona and that moment of hesitation in their conversation the previous week felt even more devastating.

That was the thing when it came to victims like Leah's mum, like Fiona. Even when they went through all the steps to get a restraining order, what they really wanted was for a person to love them who never had, and never would.

'Do you know where he might have gone?' someone asked.

Leah shook her head and everyone looked to Fiona, who whispered an unconvincing 'no'.

Everyone else looked to everyone else. They all knew what that 'no' meant.

'You need to tell them,' Leah said.

Fiona didn't move.

'It's not about you,' Leah added. 'Or me. Or anyone here. It's for Cody. You need to tell them where Kevin went.'

THIRTY-SIX

Hours passed and Leah had sort of slept. Fiona had taken Leah's bed at the house, sleeping next to Cody. Zac had his own room and Leah had made do with the sofa. It wasn't the first sofa on which she'd slept, although she had thought those days were behind her.

Fiona's house was a crime scene but the police had allowed her back the next morning to get some clothes – and then Leah had driven Cody to school. She went into the office and explained some of what had happened the night before. It was a sad reflection that the deputy head didn't seem surprised. It wasn't her first time, either.

Leah had also been in touch with Zac's school, explaining that he'd had a very late night, helping out in a family emergency. It had been such a hectic night and morning that Leah had barely managed more than a 'thank you' to him for his efforts. If he'd been a grown adult, it would have been impressive, but he was only fourteen. Then she remembered the things she had seen and done by that age. Perhaps it ran in the family? At the school itself, Owen's van had been parked outside, ready for the day's filming and whatever that entailed.

Kevin had been arrested the night before, after Fiona had given the police the address of the flat in which he was living with his girlfriend. Or perhaps *had* been living. It was all a bit complicated, and Leah didn't want to know how or why Fiona had that address.

Fiona hadn't gone to hospital, though the paramedics had patched her up as best they could. They told Leah much of it was superficial, though the reality of that was a missing chunk of hair and a face full of cuts. Fiona grimaced and grunted each time she bent or straightened, though she insisted she was fine.

Leah had seen it before. When her mum had her arm broken and tried to set it with a pillowcase, she had angrily told Leah she was fine, before eventually going to the doctor's surgery three days after. She'd never been able to lift anything properly after that.

The police took photos and statements, and, by mid-morning, Leah got the call that it was OK to head back to Fiona's. They did that together, with Leah's work shift turning into a one-on-one day with Fiona. Her boss was aware this was how things could go, given their field of community support.

It was hard to know where to start when the two of them entered Fiona's house and locked the door. The bulk of the damage had happened in the kitchen, but there were broken bits and pieces up the stairs, plus the bathroom cabinet had been pulled off the wall. Leah found that out when she needed a wee. She'd only been looking for a man during her search the night before, and hadn't taken in the extent of the rest.

The two women ended up in the kitchen together, a pair of bin bags between them, plus rubber washing-up gloves and a soapy bucket. They were ready to start but they weren't. Not really.

'Don't you want to know what happened?' Fiona asked.

'Only if you want to say.'

'But don't you want to *know*?' Fiona was leaning on the sink, fiddling with one of the rubber gloves.

The truth was that Leah *didn't* want to know the specifics. She could guess anyway, plus it wouldn't be something she hadn't seen with her own eyes in the distant past. It wasn't only about her, though – so she told Fiona she wanted to hear – and then it came out.

Kevin had shown up, saying he'd split up with his girlfriend and wanted to get back together. Fiona had told him no but he'd come in anyway, saying it was his house. They had what she described as 'a conversation' in the bedroom, before she asked him to leave. He said he was taking Cody. She said he wasn't – and then...

Leah knew the rest. She'd lived it – except Fiona had a question. 'How did Cody know where to go?' she asked.

There was no point in lying.

'I talked to him about six months ago,' Leah said. 'Walked him to my house and back, so he knew the route. Told him that if he was ever scared that he should run to mine, no matter what the time.'

She'd also told him to make sure there were always shoes next to his bed. Something he could put on quickly. Some tips were there to be learned and then passed on.

Fiona took a large breath as one of her eyes twitched. 'You knew this was going to happen?'

'I knew,' Leah replied – because she had. Cody was her. Fiona was Leah's mum. She knew.

'Why didn't you say something?' Fiona asked.

'I didn't think you'd listen.'

It was the truth, though not what Fiona wanted. She opened her mouth, lip curled, closed it again, thought better of it.

'You should've told me you'd talked to him,' Fiona said – and maybe she was right, but Leah wasn't about to apologise.

She picked up the largest piece of a smashed mug and dropped it into the bin bag. Fiona took the hint and picked out the sponge from the bucket. It wasn't fair that she had to clean this herself, but who else was there? The police didn't run a cleaning service, and neither did paramedics. This was one of the cruelties that piled on cruelty.

They worked together in near silence. Leah filled two bags with broken items, as Fiona scrubbed away the blood and grime. *Her* blood. They were most of the way done when the doorbell sounded. Fiona had been working near the back door but spun towards Leah, eyes wide.

Leah said she'd get it, knowing it couldn't be Kevin because he was in custody. She called to ask who it was, with the reply coming that it was the locksmith. Leah still left on the chain as she opened the door, only releasing it fully when she spotted the locksmith van parked outside the house.

As he started work, Leah saw a woman hovering at the end of the path. She flagged down Leah with a wave and beckoned her over. As Leah reached her side, the woman thrust a shopping bag into her hand.

'There are some spag bols in there,' she said. 'Can you make sure Fiona gets them? For her and Cody. I figured she can warm them up. Save her cooking.' The woman pointed to a property with a black door three doors down. 'I'm at number seventeen. Tell her if she needs anything, she should knock. There's always someone in.'

Leah thanked the woman on Fiona's behalf and, before she could turn to head inside, the woman touched her arm.

'Was it him again?'

'Yeah.'

It was another vision of Leah's former life. Those neighbours who'd call the police, the curtains that would twitch. She'd forgotten there was a woman at the bottom of the road who'd call a young Leah across and give her packets of Mini Cheddars. Someone always knew what was going on.

'Tell her I'm thinking of her,' the woman said, before she turned and hurried away.

Leah watched her go, wondering if she should say something, before heading back into the house. The meals went into the fridge as the cleaning continued. The locksmith finished, and then a police liaison officer arrived. It was a woman around Leah's age, with a face that was somehow youthful and world-weary at the same time. Roll it back twenty years and it could be Shirley. The same town, the same cycle.

It was a fraction after one o'clock when Leah told Fiona she had to leave for a bit. The liaison officer was going to be there until Leah brought Cody home from school in any case, so she wouldn't be alone.

'Is it still OK to stay at yours tonight?' Fiona asked.

'Of course. There's a blow-up mattress in the attic, so I'll ask Zac to get that down. Cody can have that and then there's a roll-out mattress under my bed. We'll figure it out.'

It was Leah going out on a limb, to say the least. Professional and personal boundaries blurring in a way Leah knew wasn't right, though this was too close to her. Cody was that young Leah. What else was she supposed to do?

Fiona thanked her, though it still felt as if there was a reluctance there. Leah had gone behind her back to give Cody an escape route – and she'd do it again. She suspected that smidgeon of mistrust was because Fiona didn't appreciate Leah seeing her situation well enough to know that Kevin would be back sooner or later.

Leah had parked a little along the street and, when she reached her car, she checked her phone for the first time properly that day. She had been so embedded in the lives of Fiona and Cody that everything else had slipped her mind.

An email from A Friend was waiting for her, and had been sent almost three hours before.

It can't be me who stops it. I need your help. Trust me, we both need this.

Leah got into her car and read the email back. It felt different to the others, less of a threat, more of a plea. The word 'need' was in there twice. Why would they *both* need the documentary to be halted? What did this person either know, or think they knew?

Tell me who you are.

Leah hadn't even started the engine when the reply arrived.

I can't.

THIRTY-SEVEN

Mandy was waiting at the caff in a garishly bright red and white dress that almost matched the cracked leather upholstery of the seats. Leah had texted to say she was running late due to a work emergency, which was underplaying it somewhat. She couldn't escape the nurdling thought that she was standing up her future stepmother, the idea of which made her stomach sink.

Not that Mandy minded. There was still that familiarity about her. As soon as Mandy spotted Leah, she was on her feet, arms wide, initially offering a hug, before thinking better of it. She lowered her hands and beamed. 'It's so great to see you! Thanks for coming! Have you been before? What would you like? I'll pay.'

It was an old-school caff, with sticky tables and a permanent smell of fried food welded into the walls. There wasn't a single bench in the booths that didn't have ripped material and, when the till was needed, it banged open with a dangerous wallop. The sort of place that preferred cash, and served tea or instant coffee. None of your mocha-this and frappé-that.

On one of the rare good days, a young Leah would skip school and go to places like this with her mum. If there was money floating around, which didn't happen often, she'd get an iced bun and then vacuum it down in the corner of a booth. She would lick her sticky fingers almost to the bone.

Leah was fairly sure she asked for a tea. She didn't get to add that she'd pay for herself because Mandy had already bounded past her to the counter. Leah slotted into one side of the booth from which Mandy had emerged and then waited until the other woman returned with two teas. There was no point in asking for a set amount of milk. Everyone got the same in a place like this: tea the colour of Cuprinol – which was broadly fine by Leah.

'I got you some toast,' Mandy said. 'It's on its way. Felt rude to just order tea.'

Mandy fidgeted her way back into the booth. She never seemed to stop moving. 'I've been trying to get up the courage to visit you,' she said. 'I've been thinking about it for ages. I didn't know you were going to be there last night. I hope you didn't mind me coming over to say hi.'

'It was fine,' Leah replied. 'But why were you there?'

Mandy sat up straighter and smiled wider at being acknowledged. She seemed the sort to find pleasure in anything.

'Oh, I mean, well... I suppose I remember it all happening. I was in my thirties. It was such a big thing back then. I didn't know your dad back then, of course. I only met him four years ago.'

'I know,' Leah replied, not meaning to be rude, even if it seemingly came out that way.

Mandy's face fell a fraction as she pouted her bottom lip. She had the look of a puppy who'd been trod on.

'Right,' Mandy said, nodding.

'Do you know he was on the street the night my friends went missing?' Leah said.

Mandy had been reaching for her tea but stopped. 'Who?'

'My dad.'

'Was he?'

There was no chance for a follow-up as a waitress arrived with two plates of toast. There were no granary loaves here. No fancy sourdoughs. There was white bread, and, if you were lucky – or if someone had messed up at the cash and carry – there might be brown.

White toast it was, though Leah didn't mind that, either. It was pre-buttered and she suddenly realised she was famished. She couldn't quite remember when she'd last eaten. It hadn't been that day and there was no food at the forum the night before. That meant it must've been the baked potato she'd had with Zac the previous afternoon.

Mandy was nibbling at her toast as Leah lost all manners and wolfed down a triangle of her own.

'I just wanna say that I love your dad,' Mandy said. It felt rehearsed, and probably was. Not that it mattered. 'I'm not trying to replace your mum, or anything like that. I'd never do that.'

It was impossible not to like her. Every word she spoke sounded as if she meant it. If it had been anyone else, Leah would've pointed out that her mum had killed herself after years of mental health issues, largely exacerbated by her father's criminality and abuse. She didn't say any of that. Instead, she put down her toast and offered the other woman a slim smile.

'Thank you,' Leah said.

Mandy continued picking at her toast, not really eating it, more eating around it. The crusts were gone but the rest remained. After getting out the couple of rehearsed lines, she had relaxed into the booth and stopped fidgeting so much.

'I've been married before,' she said. 'Just in case you hear anything around. You know what people are like. My husband died about ten years ago in a car crash.'

Leah resisted the urge to say that her father, the man to

whom Mandy was engaged, had killed a man in a drunken crash fifteen or so years back.

'I could never have kids of my own,' Mandy added. 'I fostered for a bit but that went away when Neil died. Then I started writing to prisoners. There was a piece in the paper asking if people would write in, because it would help with their reading and writing. They were doing all these classes inside, teaching them to write properly, but then there wasn't anyone to write to.'

She looked up, making sure Leah was still listening, which she was.

Mandy tapped her heart with her palm. 'I made friends with a few. I'm not going to try to excuse what any of them did – but everyone should get a second chance, you know? The man at the prison told me I was their top letter writer. He reckoned he'd never seen so many.'

This had clearly been taken as a compliment, though Leah wasn't certain it had been meant as one.

'Then I met your father,' Mandy added. 'We wrote back and forth a lot, talking about all sorts of things. It felt different to all the other people I'd been writing to, like he really understood me.'

She gazed earnestly and, though Leah didn't think it was a lie, she also found it bafflingly unbelievable. Both true and false. She doubted her father had ever understood anyone, including himself.

'I visited him and that was it, I guess,' Mandy said. She paused for a breath and then added a wistful, philosophical: 'You can't choose who you love, can you?'

Leah didn't know what to say. If Mandy had been talking about anyone other than her father, she'd have been delighted for a person who'd clearly found love. Instead, she hid behind a triangle of toast forcing herself not to reply with a sceptical *'Really? Him?'*

'Thank you for listening,' Mandy added, with a gentle bow of the head. She really was so sweet.

'I, uh... I'm not sure what to say,' Leah replied. For her, the carnage of Kevin and the night before, the repeating cycle, was at the front of her mind.

Her father had been in prison for almost the entirety of Leah's adult life. He'd been inside for most of his own. Maybe he'd changed, maybe not. She wasn't sure she cared. A big part of her wanted to tell Mandy to run while she could. The only reason she didn't was because she knew the other woman wouldn't listen.

Besides, maybe, just maybe, Leah didn't mind this new person entering her life. Perhaps everyone needed someone around them who exuded relentless positivity? Who saw the good in everything and, unfortunately, everyone.

Leah finished her toast and tea, wishing she'd asked for something more substantial. It didn't help that the smell of frying sausages and congealing baked beans had filled the caff.

'This might be too soon,' Mandy said, leaning forward, and resting her sleeve in the melted butter on her plate. She noticed a moment later, whispered 'fiddlesticks' under her breath, and then knocked the plate onto the floor while trying to grab a napkin. 'Jeepers,' she added – and Leah couldn't last any longer without laughing. She picked up the plate and had a proper giggle to herself while her back was turned. Leah returned both plates to the counter and grabbed a handful of serviettes.

If Mandy had apologised for her language, then Leah really would have lost it. Instead, the older woman was dabbing at the oily stain on her dress. 'It should come out,' she said to nobody in particular.

When she settled, she tried again: 'This might be too soon, but I was hoping you'd be at the wedding. I'm thinking it will happen after your father gets out. He's promised me he'll keep out of trouble, so we're maybe looking at five or six months.'

There was an excitement in Mandy's eye. 'It won't be a big thing, just a register office and I doubt I'll wear white. I was thinking peach but it can't be too bold, can it? Like a soft peach. A sort of orangey pink. There's a dress in the charity shop I liked but it's a bit small. Only twenty quid. I was thinking I could get it and then, if it's still too small, I've not lost that much.'

Mandy had been speaking faster and faster – and it was so difficult to dislike her. A part of Leah wanted to say yes because she'd asked. This poor, lonely woman wanted a favour. If it involved anyone except Leah's father, she'd have said yes.

But she couldn't.

'I'm sorry—' Leah started, and Mandy cut her off.

'No, it's fine. Of course. I get it. I just thought I'd ask.' Her lips said it was OK, her eyes held only disappointment. 'Look, the offer's there if you ever change your mind. I'm not one of those bridezillas who wants everything my way. Do you watch that show? Some of these women, you know...? I don't know how anyone puts up with them.' Mandy stopped for a moment. 'What was I saying? Oh yeah. Just that I can work things around anything you want.'

That was true and not. Mandy couldn't erase the biggest problem with the ceremony – which was the person she was marrying.

Leah kept the kindly smile on her face, wishing she could come up with a better way to let down the other woman.

'Can I keep your number?' Mandy asked. 'Maybe stay in touch?'

It didn't feel to Leah as if they'd have a lot to talk about, though it felt churlish to say no.

'That sounds good,' Leah replied – and Mandy beamed.

'Great! I can call if it's urgent, or text if not. I've got your email, too, in case it's something longer. I think—'

'Why have you got my email address?'

Mandy stopped mid-word.

Leah had forgotten that her dad had told her Mandy had been searching for an email address.

'Um... it was when I wasn't sure if I could bring myself to talk to you. I was thinking about sending an email to introduce myself. I thought it would give me a bit of space to say who I was.'

'Where did you get my email address?' Leah was firmer second time around.

'I, er...' Mandy glanced away and started to crack her knuckles, seemingly without noticing she was doing it. 'I might get in trouble if I tell you,' she said.

'What do you mean?'

Mandy took a breath. 'It's just... I did know you when you were younger. Not your dad or your mum – you.'

There had been that glimmer of familiarity when Leah had walked into the caff that hadn't quite gone. Some vague recollection that she'd met Mandy before. It was there but not there. A ghost of a memory.

'I wondered if you'd remember me,' Mandy added, speaking quickly again. 'I had dark hair back then.' She spoke hopefully, as if it would nudge Leah's memory. When it was clear it hadn't, she went all in: 'I used to be a supply teacher,' she said.

And then Leah *did* know who she was. 'Mrs Archer,' Leah said.

Mandy clapped her hands. 'That's right. Do you remember?'

Leah did in a sort of, kind of way.

'I took you for Home Ec when your teacher was on maternity,' Mandy said. 'I knew you and all your friends. It feels weird now. That was a year or two before, well, you know...'

Leah did know and, from nowhere, it was uncomfortable.

'Anyway, I don't want to name names,' Mandy added. 'I'm not a teacher any more but I know some people who are – and a friend of a friend found me your email address. I never quite got up the courage to write to you.'

The talk of her friends had taken her out of the moment. Mandy having Leah's email address had shown that there were ways to find out such a thing.

'I have to get back to work,' Leah said, which was truthful enough.

Mandy was suddenly on her feet. 'Oh, right. Of course. Yeah. I should've realised. Sorry to have kept you. My friends say I'm always talking too much. It's really great of you to have come. I'll have to message you. Or email. Ha!'

There was too much to take in. Though, when Mandy offered her hand, Leah shook it. She wasn't ready for much more than that. This was very new.

The last thing Leah heard as she opened the door to leave was an enthusiastic 'I'll be in touch!'

THIRTY-EIGHT

It was an unconventional situation in that Leah picked up Cody, who wasn't her son, from school; while her own child walked himself to a surrogate grandmother's house. There were five years between the boys, which explained the situation, though Leah knew how it could look to outsiders.

Cody's teacher told Leah that he'd been quiet through the day, though he had played football at lunchtime, as he always did. The other teachers had kept an eye on him but there wasn't much more to report.

Leah dropped him with his mum and they made plans for Fiona to come over at around seven. In the meantime, Leah drove to the other side of town, and Deborah's house. Unsurprisingly, she had something of a feast on the go, even though Leah hadn't finished the lasagnes she'd been given the previous week. This day's offering was a lentil stew with roast potatoes. The smell was incredible, even if lentils never sounded appealing.

Zac had already had a portion, even as Deborah scooped more into a tub for him. She packed up more than one and made Leah promise she'd eat something that night. People seemingly weren't only noticing that Leah wasn't sleeping, but that she wasn't eating.

Leah and Zac headed out to the car, ladened with tubs of food to add to the ones already in the freezer. No mention was made of Mandy.

The yawns began as soon as Leah started the car and the blowers started huffing cool air. Zac was the first to go, though Leah wasn't far behind.

She ended up parking around the corner from Deborah's because she wanted a mother-son chat.

'I didn't have a proper chance to say thank you for last night,' Leah told him.

Zac was his typical self. A mix of an awkward teenager and a humble young man. He half shrugged, half mumbled something Leah didn't catch.

'If there are any problems with Fiona and Cody staying at ours, you only have to say. It's your house as much as mine.'

Zac was grinning. 'I told Cody I'd show him how to play FIFA properly. He's not very good at the moment, because he doesn't have it at home.'

Leah knew what most of those words meant. 'Thank you,' she repeated. She almost restarted the engine but there was more. 'I need to tell you about something else. You know some of this but, last night, with Fiona and Cody... I was Cody once. That's what happened with my mum and dad. Your granddad.'

Zac was sitting very still. Too still, really. She rarely saw anger in her son, though there was a flicker of something. 'Did he used to hit your mum?'

'Yes.'

'And you?'

Leah shook her head. 'No... but sometimes the fear of it is worse. Just because he didn't, there was a never a time when I didn't think he might.'

Zac nodded, though she wasn't quite sure he got it. It was so hard to explain what it was like to live with perpetual worry. How, even now, Leah didn't think she ever truly relaxed.

'He's going to be out of prison soon,' Leah added. 'Maybe five or six months? He's getting remarried. I didn't want you finding out from someone else.'

She could feel the cogs turning. 'He's getting married again? Isn't he, like, eighty...?'

'Seventy but... yes. I know it's unconventional.'

'Who's he getting married to?'

'Someone named Mandy. I met her today, just so we had some sort of contact. I don't really know what it's going to be like in the future.'

Zac shuffled in his seat, turning as much as he could to face her. He was biting his lip, understandably bemused. She was talking about people he'd never met.

'Are you going to see him when he comes out?'

Leah was drumming her fingers on the steering wheel, not realising she'd started. 'I don't know,' she said. 'I don't think so.'

'Is he going to come back here to live?'

Somehow, in all the talk of the past day, Leah hadn't thought about that. Was he? Mandy lived locally, so probably. She wasn't sure she could quite face the chance of running into her father while doing a weekly shop. While filling up the car with petrol and glancing across to the nearest pump. Him being in prison had given her a security blanket of knowing where he was at all times. Knowing it was nowhere near her.

'I'm not sure,' Leah replied.

She had been trying to reassure her son but, if anything, it felt as if she'd unsettled the pair of them.

With little more to add, Leah drove them home. Zac went up to his room, saying he was going to get his game set up for Cody. Leah picked at the lentil stew in the kitchen, fighting visions of seeing her dad walk past the window as she was getting her hair cut in town. Or she'd be buying toilet roll, when up would pop her father to say something stupid.

It wasn't a life she wanted.

Fiona knocked on the door not long after seven – and Cody bounced his way into the house. That scared rubber-shoed boy of the night before had been replaced by a cute little button clutching a mini suitcase. There was a stuffed giraffe under his arm and, when told that Zac was waiting upstairs for him, he tore up them two at a time.

'He's never this excited,' Fiona said, as Leah took her through to the living room.

The two women watched television, though not really. There was small talk, though they spent most of their time on their phones. Leah hadn't received any further emails and, though she suspected Mandy might fire off a flurry of texted invitations to various things, that hadn't happened either.

Fiona asked if she could have a drink and Leah told her she was welcome to treat the kitchen as her own.

Cody had to be in bed first, even as his mum let him stay up half an hour later. Leah had put down the air mattress in the spare room, so he had that.

The evening drifted and then Leah and Fiona headed up to the bedroom. Leah would have had the sofa, or even the roll-out bed, though Fiona insisted she should sleep on her own mattress. They agreed to share the bed, it was queen-sized, after all – and so they lay together but not, lights off, neither sleeping.

'I've never shared a bed with anyone other than Kevin,' Fiona whispered through the dark. 'Well maybe when I was about fourteen. There was a school trip and it was cold in this dorm, so me and a girl named Charlotte slept in a single bed together.' A pause. 'Kevin's the only man I've ever been with.'

Leah had suspected that might be the case, though had never asked. It was none of her business and she wasn't sure she wanted to know. Leah wasn't sure she wanted to talk too much about who she herself had and hadn't shared a bed with – plus everyone knew about her teenage sleepovers.

'Can I ask you something?' Fiona began, long after they'd started trying to go to sleep. She didn't wait for Leah to reply. 'You've been so helpful over the last year or so. I know I sort of told you but I haven't really. My mum's going to die any day and I was wondering if you'd come with me tomorrow to visit her? You don't have to come in, or anything. It's just, I don't have anyone else to ask.'

'I can move things around at work,' Leah said, which was probably true. She'd moved plenty around that day – though her boss knew the situation with Fiona.

Leah closed her eyes, though something burned momentarily white. When she opened them, her phone screen was flashing. It was a few minutes to midnight and an email from A Friend had just arrived.

Leah propped herself onto an elbow and clicked to open it.

Look where their van's parked! Their stuff is inside. You could burn it.

There was an attached photo of a navy van that Leah recognised as belonging to Owen and his crew. It looked as if it was a recent image, given the gloomy sky and orangey street lights. Park gates were visible in the background, and Leah knew where it was. Anyone who lived or grew up locally would.

Leah typed out the shortest of replies and then put down her phone.

No.

THIRTY-NINE

Taking some degree of charge of the situation sent Leah into her deepest sleep for a while.

At first, the emailer had tried implied threats, some more explicit than others. When that hadn't forced Leah into trying to do anything about Owen's documentary, instead of following through on whatever those threats were, the person had relied on 'trust me'. And then, in a seemingly crazed moment, they had emailed at nearly midnight, wanting Leah to set fire to a van.

Leah wouldn't have known how to do such a thing, even if she wanted to – which she didn't. In the moment she'd typed out 'No' and sent it, Leah had realised that the emailer had no control over her. Not only that, *they* wanted the documentary stopped, while Leah – after having a few days to think on it – wasn't that bothered. What was Owen going to dig up on her? It had been twenty-four years and, aside from vague insinuations from people who didn't believe Leah could have slept through the night, there had been nothing.

When Leah woke up, Fiona wasn't in the bed and, miraculously, a little over seven hours had passed. She was so used to being awake early that Leah didn't even bother with alarms. Today, the thing that woke her was the vague clinking of cutlery or mugs from below.

Fiona was in the kitchen when Leah arrived downstairs. Cody was sitting at the table, eating a bowl of cereal, as Fiona said she'd made him lunch.

'I hope that's OK?' she added, suddenly worried she'd overstepped.

Leah told her it was fine, and then Fiona asked if she could make anything for Leah.

'Tea? Toast? Cereal?'

It was odd to see another person taking charge in her kitchen, though, after the past couple of days, it was a relief to see Fiona in control of her own life.

There was a shuffling from upstairs, with Zac up and about. Leah had slept in, which meant she was running late, too. She was about to tell Fiona she was heading upstairs to have a shower, when the other woman offered Leah her phone.

'Have you seen this? Someone on Facebook says there was a fire in town last night?'

Leah had already half turned towards the door but froze. 'A fire?'

'Look.'

Leah took Fiona's phone and scrolled through a series of photos that had been posted. The picture-taker had zoomed in too far, producing the sort of quality more usually associated with fake sightings of the Loch Ness Monster.

This wasn't fake.

The van was blurry, though the park gates behind it were unmistakeable. Leah had been sent a much clearer photo the night before of Owen's van in the same place. There were

photos of a fire engine, some smouldering flames and then a
river flowing down the street.

'They reckon the fire brigade got there before it spread,'
Fiona said. 'It was right by the park.'

'Was anyone hurt?' Leah asked, as she handed back the
phone.

'Not that anybody said. The person who put it up said it
was about one o'clock last night.'

Leah checked her own phone and, suddenly, the email she'd
received felt even more desperate.

Look where their van's parked! Their stuff is inside. You could
burn it.

Nothing had been received since Leah's 'no'. Presumably,
the emailer had tried to take things into their own hands.

Leah wondered if she should go to the police, except that
would mean having to explain when she'd started receiving the
emails. It would likely mean having to tell someone about the
knife and the stolen ring. It didn't seem worth bringing the
attention to herself for no particular gain.

She swiped away from the email and locked the screen,
before realising Fiona was watching her.

'They're making a decision on Kevin's bail today,' Fiona
said. 'Someone's going to call when they know what's
happening.'

Leah remembered those days, waiting by the landline with
her mum for a call to say whether Leah's dad had been
remanded. She'd been a lot older when she realised that children weren't supposed to know what bail was, let alone spend
afternoons sitting with their mum waiting to find out if their
own father had been given it.

'You can stay here if you want,' Leah replied. 'After we get
back from the hospice, I mean. If he gets out, he won't know

you're here. There's already a restraining order, plus there'll be a no contact condition to his bail if he's released.'

Fiona nodded along. She knew the system in the same way Leah did.

The two women took their sons to school. This time, Fiona went in to talk to the deputy head about what had been going on. The scrapes and bruises on her face would tell their own story.

Leah had another quiet talk with Zac, who insisted he liked having Cody around the house. He added that it was good to be able to beat somebody at games, instead of losing to his own friends. Leah took it as the half-joke she was certain it was.

She stopped in at her office, leaving Fiona in the car, and she had a quick chat with her boss. Fiona staying at Leah's wasn't anything close to policy but there were no spaces available in the various refuges and, until the bail decision was made about Kevin, it was hard for anyone to argue that Leah should have acted differently. Everyone – including Leah – knew she was too close to the situation. Nobody wanted to say it.

After that, Leah drove Fiona out of town to the hospice. It was twenty minutes through deserted lanes with high hedges and crumbling roads. Fiona said that her mum had pancreatic cancer and had gone through a couple of rounds of chemotherapy, neither of which had worked. It was discovered too late and they'd known for around four months that things were going to end this way.

She spoke matter-of-factly, more or less without emotion, although Leah got it. Four months was a long time to process that a person was going to die. Nobody could be on an emotional tightrope the entire time. It got to the point where relaying the awful details of a parent succumbing to cancer became as simple a story as listing the items bought in a supermarket.

That was until the inevitable actually happened.

'Cody keeps asking to come,' Fiona said, as they neared the hospice. 'Mum doesn't want him to see her like she is.'

'Did they get to say goodbye?' Leah replied.

'Sort of. Before they brought her here, we had a day in the park. Mum couldn't do much, so we had a very slow walk around. We stopped on every bench and Cody would run off and do his thing. He wanted to feed the ducks, so he did that. Then he went to the play area, while we watched. Some older boys pushed him on the roundabout. It was a nice day. Maybe we should've told him that would be his last day with her...?'

That felt like an impossible dilemma.

'At least he'll have happy final memories,' Leah replied.

She pulled through the gates of the hospice and followed the driveway to the parking area. It was a large old house, set in the middle of manicured gardens. A man was on a sit-down mower on the far side of the lawn, carefully trimming green strips. In another corner, there were rows of white chests of drawers close to a hedge. It was only after Leah had parked that she realised they were beehives.

Fiona led Leah up a short set of stone steps into the building, where there was checked black and white tile flooring. The medical stench of bleach was almost overwhelming for Leah, though Fiona barely seemed to notice. The woman on the reception desk knew her by name, and started by asking how Cody was getting on at school. She then noticed the marks on Fiona's face, which were explained away by a trip.

'Kicked off my shoes at the top of the stairs and forgot they were there,' Fiona said, which went unquestioned. Leah's mum used to have a lot of mystery trips into doors and stairs as well.

Fiona called Leah her friend, and the pair of them were shown along a corridor to a T, where passages met.

'You know it from here,' the receptionist said, and then she headed back the way she'd come.

They didn't move.

'I didn't mean to drag you out here for no reason,' Fiona said. 'I'm going to talk to Mum by myself, if that's all right. She's just down there.'

Fiona nodded towards the third door along the corridor. There was a sofa pressed against the walls a little ahead of them.

'I think I was kind of hoping I could talk to someone after I've seen her? There's never anybody around, and then I have to catch the bus back. I really appreciate you coming.'

Leah told her it was fine, and then she settled on the sofa as Fiona headed into her mother's room. She heard a soft 'Hi, Mum' and then the door clicked closed.

There was a distant squeak of a trolley being moved, or perhaps something else scraping on the ground. Leah looked both ways, and it felt as if the line of doors continued forever. A faint echo of footsteps was swallowed by the walls as a whispering, flittering chill crept across the tiled floor.

It was too much. Leah assumed she would sit and wait, perhaps fiddle with her phone for a bit, but she couldn't do it. The sense of melancholy was almost overwhelming. People died behind the doors – and it wasn't that uncommon. Sons and daughters, mums and dads, would sit on this exact sofa, waiting for the worst news they would ever get.

Leah was on her feet. She figured she would make her way back to reception, possibly even the car. Fiona would find her. Except Leah's legs could barely move quickly enough, as if the tiles were a slick of gloopy mud, pulling at her, dragging her towards...

There was an open door on the way back to reception. Leah had walked past it once, though couldn't remember if it had been open back then. She should keep moving, of course she should, except, through the open door, there was a silhouette of a man sitting in an armchair near a big window. The expanse of lawn was beyond him, the beehives past that.

He must have felt her watching him, because he turned –
slowly, and with a groan. Leah started to apologise, except...

She stepped into the room, knowing she shouldn't. 'Is this
all right?' she asked, though no response came. Not a verbal one
anyway. Instead, the man nodded a fraction. Or perhaps he
didn't, and it was the light.

Leah felt as if she was out of her body, watching herself.
She was fully in the room now, a pace or two from the man. He
was almost bald, with only a wisp of white hair crinkled across
the top of his head. His face was red, as if covered with a birth-
mark, although Leah knew it wasn't.

Leah knew him – and he knew her.

Esther had said that her father was in a hospice. Her dad
but Vicky's, too. The man whose bedroom door Leah had
knocked on the morning after the sleepover.

'Tom...' Leah said.

FORTY

There was a time when a teenage Leah had a crush on Tom Merrivale. It felt so inappropriate later but that wasn't his fault. He was the father of Leah's friend but he had those hairy arms, dark eyes and that darker stubbly beard, before anyone thought stubble was cool.

He was nothing like that now. His head had sunken into his shoulders and his skin was blotchy and spotted. The dark eyes were sullen and lifeless and his arms flopped limply at his side. He seemed so weak that Leah doubted he could lift himself up.

'Are you OK?' Leah asked, although she knew it was a question that barely scratched the surface. Not only was he nowhere near 'OK', he clearly hadn't been for a long time.

Tom coughed a little and forced a smile. He knew how ridiculous the question was.

'Should've given up smoking,' he croaked, as he nodded towards a chair that Leah had missed. She eked it out from under the desk and sat across from him. 'How have you been?' he asked slowly. 'And your boy? How old is he now?'

'Zac,' Leah replied. 'He's fourteen and he's doing great.'

Tom tried to lean in, though only succeeded in making

himself croak and splutter. He patted his chest and reached for a glass of water that Leah ended up handing to him. His hand trembled as Leah helped hold it. He slurped, though more of the water ended up in his lap than his mouth. As Leah offered to clean up, he waved her away. It felt as if it happened a lot.

He straightened himself and Leah took in the rest of the room. There was a bed a little bigger than a single, with some sort of medical machine at the side. There was a cubicle with a toilet, seat up, door open – and then, on the other side, a small row of framed photographs underneath a mirror. Once she'd spotted them, Leah felt drawn. The closest one was an image of two girls standing next to each other, not quite touching, in front of a fountain. They had the awkwardness of sisters who didn't quite get on – Esther and Victoria – and the image must have been taken a few months before Vicky disappeared.

It was only as Leah looked closer that she remembered how similar the two girls looked. Same straight hair, same angled pose, same dismissive air. That was how Vicky had been on the landing when she'd asked Leah if she was going to leave any pizza for the rest of them. When she'd shrugged and replied 'probably' after Leah had asked if they were still going to be friends.

Leah wondered if, instead of those E-fits and composites of how the girls would look grown up, perhaps Vicky would simply look like her sister.

'Can I ask you something?' Leah said. The idea was in her head now. 'I suppose I was wondering if you think there's a chance Vicky might be out there somewhere?'

It came out more directly than Leah had intended, or perhaps it was exactly how she meant it. She still hadn't quite got past the idea that only Vicky knew about her knife.

Tom smiled kindly, although it took a second or two for his features to settle. Nothing felt easy for him. 'It's been a long time to think that,' he managed.

'Have you always thought she was gone? Did you ever think she'd be back?'

Tom turned partially, towards the beehives in the distance. It took a while, perhaps a full minute, but it came. 'I always knew she was gone,' he said.

He was facing away from her now. There were bristles of fine white hairs around the back of his neck as his gown hung low.

Leah wondered if this was what it was like for parents of missing children. Did they truly always know what had happened? There were so many stories of parents who insisted their child would return – but did they really believe that? Was it simply hopeful thinking?

There was never going to be another time to ask and, though Leah knew she shouldn't, the pull was too much. It couldn't be an accident Fiona had asked her to come to this hospice. Couldn't be a coincidence that this door, of all doors, was open just as she walked past. Fate existed, didn't it? She already knew that. They were friends.

'What do you think happened that night?' Leah asked.

It felt dangerous. The hairs on the back of Leah's neck were up but maybe it was all of them. Her arms tingled too, her entire body.

Tom coughed again. 'You were all there when I got in,' he said. 'Four of you in the living room.'

It felt like the truth. It always had.

'That's not what I asked,' Leah said.

Maybe she knew? Maybe it had always been there, deep down?

He lowered his head a fraction, as if bowing. Acknowledging the point. 'Nobody ever asked about the glasses,' he said.

'Jazz's glasses?'

That got what might have been a tiny chuckle, and then a shake of the head. Tom shuffled in his seat, moaning almost silently to himself as he turned back to focus on Leah. 'Let me ask you something,' he said. 'Why did you swap drinks with Victoria?'

Leah stared into those recessed eyes and there was still something there. Maybe not a twinkle, but life.

'When?' Leah asked. 'At the sleepover?'

A nod. 'You swapped drinks. Was it you who did it? Did you do it on purpose?'

Leah didn't know where the questions were going. 'I don't know what you mean,' she replied, because she didn't.

Tom's features had crinkled into one another as he focused his stare. And, then, as if it hadn't happened, he pressed back into the chair. 'It's OK,' he said. 'It was a long time ago. No reason for you to remember. But you love your boy, don't you? You'd do anything for him...?'

Leah shivered and it didn't feel like a question, more a statement. She didn't like where things were headed.

There was no time, though. Footsteps sounded in the corridor and Fiona strode past before she stopped and retraced her steps to the doorway. 'Lee...?' she said.

Leah was on her feet. Time to go.

'Glasses,' Tom said quietly, for only Leah to hear.

She pushed the chair back under the counter, pausing at the row of photographs. There wasn't only the one of the teenage sisters, there was another of the girls when they were much younger. When Vicky's mother was alive and when Tom stood behind the three of them, beaming with pride and delight at the beautiful women in his life.

All that while wearing a red and white plaid shirt.

FORTY-ONE

Neither of the women spoke much for the journey back to town. Fiona had probably seen her mum for the final time and needed someone to be there, while not necessarily wanting to talk about it. That was fine with Leah because a needling, horrifying realisation was creeping through her.

She knew what Tom meant by glasses.

Or she thought she did. There was someone else who might know.

Leah pulled in outside Fiona's house and, before the other woman was out of the car, Fiona's phone rang. Leah only heard one half of the conversation – but she knew the basics of what had happened before Fiona told her.

The details were that Kevin had been remanded not only for the assault on Leah but for another on whoever his current partner happened to be. The partner had apparently been at court to deny anything had happened, despite a previous contradictory police report, where she'd told them he had punched her in the face. She had tried to explain away her fractured eye socket as a 'trip'. As Fiona relayed that part, she whispered the word, probably recalling her own description of her injuries in the hospice reception.

Leah didn't dare ask Fiona how she felt about things, fearing the answer.

They said their goodbyes and then Leah drove into town. There was a cordoned area near the park, with a police officer directing traffic into the nearby side street. Past the tape, there were the remains of a burnt-out van.

Leah parked and headed out of her way on foot to loop around the area and get a proper look. From the grainy photos, Leah hadn't realised that the navy van actually had caught fire. The cabin appeared intact, though there were dark scorch marks around the windows, and a blackened stain on the ground. She didn't know much about vehicles but there was obviously a fuel tank. It felt as if fire officers had reached the scene just in time.

Suddenly, keeping quiet about her emails felt more selfish that before. Someone could've died, or been seriously hurt. This wasn't a simple prank.

Glasses.

Leah told herself to stay focused. One thing at a time.

She headed around the park towards the row of shops and offices. Leah assumed this conversation would end up happening in that glass-fronted office, except, as she arrived, Esther was on her way out. It was lunchtime and she was striding with purpose towards the Pret across the street. She was almost past Leah when Esther noticed her.

She stopped dead, and tilted her head. 'Lee...?' she said, sensing something wasn't quite right.

'"He was never quite the same",' Leah said.

Esther craned her neck backwards a fraction. 'Huh? Who was never the same?'

'That's what you said in your office the other day, when you were talking about your dad.'

'Did I?'

It genuinely seemed as if Esther didn't remember. She glanced towards the sandwich shop, wanting to move on.

'I thought you meant he was never the same after Vicky disappeared but it wasn't that, was it?'

Esther's attention was dragged back to Leah. Her mouth was open.

'We were drinking that night,' Leah said. 'All four of us. We had vodka. When I woke up, everyone was gone.'

'I know,' Esther said. 'Everyone knows.'

'But it wasn't only them who were missing. Where were the glasses?'

FORTY-TWO

There it was. Esther's little glance away. That momentary hesitation. It was Leah's mum saying she was glad Leah's dad was gone. It was Fiona pretending not to care where Kevin was. Leah was so good at spotting the lies and yet the biggest one of all had been in front of her the entire time.

'Our glasses were on the floor,' Leah said. 'Maybe the tables. We were fifteen and definitely didn't wash up after ourselves – but they were all gone the next morning. Nobody noticed, including me, because we were all wondering about Jazz, Harriet and Vicky.'

If there was a needle to hide, stick it in a haystack. If there were glasses to conceal, do it when much bigger, more important, things had also been hidden.

It was so obvious.

Esther motioned to take a step past Leah, back towards the office. Leah reached and pulled her back. Gripped her upper arm so tightly that Esther squeaked and yanked herself away.

'I don't have long,' Esther hissed. 'I've got to get back.'

'Did you set fire to that van?' Leah asked, knowing the answer. It had been on the other side of the park, giving Esther a perfect view from her office. She must have seen it while working late. Something like that.

'What van?' Esther replied, hurried, annoyed, clearly lying.

'It's you, isn't it?' Leah said. 'It can only be you. You know what happened.'

It wasn't a question.

Esther took a step away and then another. She bobbed from one foot to the other.

'You know,' Leah tried again, then louder again: 'You know!'

'Shush!'

A woman had been walking past them, though paid little attention as she ambled into the sandwich shop.

Esther looked over her shoulder and then leant in closer. 'I have to get back to work,' she said.

'You have to pretend to go along with the film,' Leah said. 'Owen thinks you're like him, that you've been wondering what happened to your sister all this time. He knows you're a lawyer, so you have to help, or it would look weird. Except you know what happened – and that's why you want everything shut down. Why you want me to do it. You found my bag and my knife and held onto it all these years. You wanted to blackmail me.'

Esther put her hand across Leah's mouth, like a mother shushing a wild three-year-old. She only held it there a fraction of a second but it was such a shock that Leah stopped talking.

'Not here,' Esther hissed, as her eyes blazed. She took a small step away and checked over her shoulder again. 'Not *now*.'

'When?' Leah asked.

Esther scratched her head, tugged at her hair. Except Leah had one question that couldn't wait. She thought she knew the answer but she needed to hear it.

'Is she alive?' Leah asked.

'Who?'

'Vicky?'

Leah expected a 'no', although the past few days had tested her confidence.

'No.'

She breathed out. That was one thing. The impossible wasn't true.

Except Esther wasn't done.

'Of course she's not. She's the one who tried to kill you all.'

FORTY-THREE

It was a bright afternoon, not that anyone would know. The blinds were down in Esther's office, the overhead lights on low. The bright, open office of a successful woman now felt like the cramped prison... albeit with an iMac on an expensive desk, and fancy chairs.

Esther was pacing as Leah hovered near the half chair, half hug. She didn't want to feel comfortable, didn't think she could. Esther stopped behind her desk and gripped the back of her chair. 'How did you figure it out?' she asked.

It almost felt too easy.

'I was at the hospice with a friend earlier,' Leah explained. 'Your dad was just... there. I used to see him in town over the years and we'd nod. I asked if he was all right, which he obviously isn't. He mentioned the glasses. I thought he was talking about Jazz's spectacles – but it wasn't that.' A pause. 'What *did* happen to the glasses?'

Esther had been staring, which gave Leah a glimpse of what she might be like in her working life. It felt like being under a spotlight, where judgement would be instant and decisive. The whole time Leah had been talking, Esther had been weighing up if it was true and, if so, which parts were important.

And it seemingly wasn't the glasses.

'I need to ask you something first,' Esther said. 'Why did you swap drinks with Vicky?'

Leah felt like pacing back and forth herself. Something to get rid of the building energy. 'Your dad asked me the same thing,' she replied.

'Did he? Why were you—' Esther stopped herself and waved a hand. 'Doesn't matter. Why did you swap drinks?'

There was a tap on the door and both women turned to look. The woman with the high ponytail who'd been on reception the other day appeared in the gap. 'Your two o'clock is downstairs.'

Esther checked the clock above the door. 'I'm running late. Tell him I'll be with him as soon as I can. And can you call my four o'clock and cancel.'

'What should I tell her?'

'Anything you want.'

There was a finality in the way Esther spoke. Her way or no way. It wasn't missed by the receptionist, who spun and headed back out of the room. She hadn't mentioned the lack of light.

When Leah turned back, she realised Esther had focused back in on her, the question unanswered.

'I didn't swap drinks,' Leah said, although the fact something so specific had been asked twice left her questioning herself.

Esther wasn't satisfied. 'You'd been drinking, hadn't you? All four of you.'

'Right.'

'Vodka.'

'Vicky said it was OK at your house because your dad thought it was better in a controlled place.'

Esther seemed unbothered by all that. She waved that dismissive hand again. 'But you had Vicky's drink that night.'

It didn't sound like a question, instead it seemed like Esther was trying to force Leah to admit something she was almost certain hadn't happened.

No, not *almost* certain. Something she knew without doubt had not occurred.

'Why do you keep saying that?' Leah replied. 'We didn't swap drinks.'

'You must've done.'

'Why?'

Esther banged the top of the chair in frustration. She spun it around and then flopped into it. Perhaps because she'd sat, Leah copied, leaving them on opposite sides of the desk. Esther gently swung herself back and forth and there was almost something childish about it.

'I practically told you the other day,' Esther said. 'Vicky had her interests. You know what she was like: books, music, volleyball. Nothing ever lasted but she'd be obsessed for really short periods. Then, just before it all happened, she was into those weird magazines, about cults, and hidden societies.'

Leah remembered that time sitting on the floor of Vicky's bedroom, as her friend handed down that photocopied pamphlet.

'There was a "Things They Don't Want You To Know" magazine,' Leah replied.

'Exactly! And others. Dad confiscated them all on the day you had your sleepover.'

'Did he?'

Vicky certainly hadn't said that – but, as usual, Esther had moved on. She shared something in common with her sister. Vicky's interests swayed drastically, but Esther's thoughts did the same.

'Dad was having all these problems with moles in the

garden,' Esther said and, for a moment, it felt as if she was going nowhere.

Leah vaguely remembered Vicky saying something about moles and her dad sitting in the back waiting for them – but they had thought it was the ramblings of a slightly paranoid man. What did that have to do with anything?

Esther caught Leah's eye. 'Strychnine,' she said, and her voice was gentler than before, perhaps more feminine.

One word, and suddenly Leah knew the pieces that Esther had put together. It all made sense. No wonder things had happened the way they had.

'It was legal then,' Esther added. 'Google it. You'll see. You could just buy it. Everything's banned and controlled now but Dad got the poison to deal with the moles. Except Vicky was obsessed with things and, when he properly looked through the magazines he took off her, they were all about cults.'

'What's it like to live in a cult,' Leah said, remembering the article.

A nod. 'That's all she was reading about in the weeks before it happened. Dad asked me to talk to her but I was doing my own thing and didn't get round to it, until it was obviously too late. He wanted her to read normal things – whatever that meant.'

Leah already knew that. Vicky had told her as much when they'd been in her bedroom.

'Poison,' Leah said. It was out there now.

A nod. 'Then he got home and there were four girls out of it in the living room, four empty glasses, and a bottle of his poison in the bin. He knew what Vicky had done straight away. Knew he should've stopped her. What else was he supposed to do?'

Leah didn't want to hear the rest, but she couldn't stop. The biggest mystery of her life was solved. It was as incredible as it was predictable. How had she never considered this as a possibility? Everything was right there.

'Then you rolled over,' Esther said.

'Huh?'

'When Dad saw that poison bottle, he knew what Vicky had done but he assumed she was just sleeping. That she'd killed the rest of you. In that moment you rolled over, he thought he was wrong. That you were all fine and it was a mix-up. *You* were breathing but, when he checked the others, nobody else was. That's why you must have switched drinks with Vicky.'

Leah almost said no, because she knew she hadn't. Except Esther needed it to be true, and there was no point in saying otherwise. For once, this wasn't about Leah.

'I suppose we must've done,' Leah said.

Esther finally relaxed, letting herself be swallowed by the chair.

Tom had said the same, which meant father and daughter must have had the conversation a few times over the years. They would have spent that whole time desperately wanting to ask Leah how she'd come to swap glasses with Vicky, while knowing they couldn't. They needed to be right.

What a secret to live with.

Except then Leah remembered what the headline in the photocopied magazine had *actually* said.

'That article wasn't about living in a cult,' Leah said.

Esther looked up, having been lost in her own thoughts. 'What do you mean?'

'It was about living in a *suicide* cult.'

FORTY-FOUR

The pieces were suddenly in place for both women. A decades-long misunderstanding.

'Your dad moved the bodies to protect Vicky,' Leah said. 'He thought she tried to kill us.'

Esther was staring wide-eyed. She had spent so long assuming glasses were switched that it hadn't occurred to her there might be a suicidal element.

'Well, she did, didn't she?' Esther said. 'Tried to kill you, I mean.'

Leah didn't reply. Didn't trust herself.

Esther was still talking: 'He got home from the football do and found you all. He knew what had happened, because he'd only taken the magazines off her that afternoon. He couldn't have you all found like that. Everyone would know what Vicky had done. You know what it's like, don't you? You have a son. You want to protect him.'

Leah knew, except maybe she didn't.

'There was an empty house a few doors down,' Esther added. 'So Dad carried the three girls and left them there. He was terrified you'd wake up.'

For the first time, Leah wondered if that dream about which she'd told her ex-husband actually *was* a dream. The situation Esther was describing was what Leah had told Mark when she hadn't realised he was a massive arsehole who'd retell it to anyone with fifty quid.

'Dad got rid of the glasses and the poison bottle – then waited for the next morning. You know the rest.'

Leah didn't know *all* the rest – but this was a lot.

'How'd he get into the empty house?' Leah asked.

'He and mum were friends with the couple who used to live there. He had a key in case anything happened while they were on holiday. They must've forgot he had it because, when they moved out, they never asked for it back.'

It really did add up. Tom had been lucky that the neighbour over the road had seen him in that red and white check shirt when he wasn't carrying a child's body to an empty house. They'd assumed it was Leah's dad.

Leah thought on it for a moment. No wonder the man she'd seen outside the pub wearing shorts in winter had seemed broken. He had been. There was a wonder Tom had lasted so long before ending the way he had. The poor man had spent his life seeing his daughter as a killer. The one thing he could do for her was save her memory and reputation by carrying her, and her friends, to a neighbouring house in the dead of night.

He'd given Vicky everything, even though there was no way anyone could ever repay him. Only his other daughter had known.

'I suppose what I don't get,' Esther said, 'is if you're saying it was a suicide thing, how did *you* survive? If Vicky poisoned all of you, not just three of you. We always thought you'd accidentally swapped glasses – but what happened?'

'I didn't drink it,' Leah said. 'Vodka always made me so sleepy, so I tipped mine into the pot plant in your living room.'

The metaphorical light bulb above Esther's head pinged

bright. 'Of course! That's the bit we never understood but it makes sense.' She was nodding rapidly, as if the meaning of life had just been dictated to her.

'Were you there?' Leah asked.

Esther turned away and kicked off her shoes. She had the look of a person who wanted a cigarette, regardless of whether they smoked. 'Not at first. Not that Sunday morning when I got home and you were there. Dad told me a few days after. I think it was too big for him. He had to tell someone.' A pause. 'He'd moved the bodies by then. Buried them properly, so nobody would find them.'

Leah pictured that gravedigger in the cemetery and how hard he'd been working. Digging three graves was no easy task.

'I think he figured the story was better as three missing girls, than the girl who tried to kill her friends,' Esther said. She waited a beat and then corrected herself: 'The girl who killed her friends.'

Leah didn't reply. It didn't feel as if Esther was done.

'I'm not naïve,' Esther added. 'I know it was his poison. His vodka, too. Strychnine is transparent. He'd have been in trouble but I really don't think that's why he did it. What would you rather have? A mystical, ageless daughter who disappeared, or a brutal child killer?'

It was so obvious now why Tom had done what he'd done. With the facts as Esther knew them, it was no wonder things had played out as they had.

'Where did he bury them?' Leah asked.

'Does it matter?'

'It does to me.'

Leah expected pushback, perhaps even anger, but there was a solemn nod instead. 'I'll take you,' Esther said. 'Not today but, y'know...'

That was enough for Leah. The closure that should have come a long time before was almost there.

'You're right about Owen and his doc,' Esther added. 'I could hardly say no to him but it's not like I want any of this coming out. I didn't know how good he was at first but he emails me every day with updates of what he's found.' She smiled, with the merest amount of humour. 'Sounds like your interview was a total disaster.'

'Something like that.'

'I've been trying to steer him away from you. The last thing I wanted was for him to look any closer at the house, but he's like a puppy with a ball.' She laughed this time, though there was less humour. 'He's a real pain in the arse.'

Leah laughed too. Owen was – but only because he was good at his job.

'I found your bag that Sunday morning,' Esther said. 'When we were both in the living room but you went through to the front because Harriet's mum arrived. It was right there, by the sleeping bags, so I picked it up and put it in my coat pocket in the hall. I don't really know why. I didn't know there was a knife in there.'

'What about the camera?'

'That was upstairs, in the bathroom. I assumed one of you must've left it there. There were some photos next to it. I moved all that, too. It didn't feel right for someone else to have it.'

Leah knew what was coming.

'Why did you have the knife?' Esther added.

'Dad,' Leah replied. 'He's—'

'I know who he is.'

'Right.'

There was a moment of understanding between them. Relief from Leah that she hadn't been forced to explain why a fifteen-year-old carried a knife.

'I couldn't think of a way to stop Owen,' Esther said. 'Then I remembered I had your knife and wondered if I might be able to do something with that.'

'Does Owen know about the knife?'

'I don't see how he could. I've never told him.' She waited and then added: 'Owen's obsessed with your dad at the moment. The woman who saw someone in his shirt, plus someone in the police report, plus the empty house from the forum the other night. He's convinced your dad did something and asked if I knew anyone in the prison service who might be able to help get him an interview.'

Given how Leah's own conversation with her dad had gone, she almost wanted to see it. Her dad, the natural antagonist and lifelong prick, would make himself the centre of attention, because that's what he always did.

Unless Mandy really had changed him.

'Not a bad distraction from *your* dad,' Leah said, partially to herself, although Esther appeared to agree. If Owen was chasing a story that wasn't true and couldn't be proved, he would hopefully miss the one in front of him.

'How did you know about the ring?' Leah asked.

Esther had been staring into space when she rotated to focus on Leah. 'What ring?'

Leah stared back, wondering why this was contentious, when Esther had admitted everything else. She found the email on her phone and loaded the image of the Polaroid Esther had sent her.

'That ring,' she said, pointing to Vicky's finger.

Esther eyed Leah's phone and then shuffled the mouse on her desktop. Her monitor sprung to life and she clicked a couple of things before swivelling it for Leah to see. The image was the same as Leah had been sent, but zoomed in on the pink bag that was across her front. With the picture blown up, Leah could see the merest hint of the knife handle poking from the top.

Leah had been so taken with her own regret and shame over stealing Vicky's mum's ring, that it hadn't occurred to her the photo was showing something else. It was meant to be another nudge, reminding Leah that Esther knew about her knife.

The inevitable question came as Esther scrolled sideways on the image until it was honed in on her sister's finger.

'Is that Mum's ring?' Esther asked. 'Why did you think I'd emailed you a picture of that?'

It was an afternoon of admissions, and Leah couldn't quite face this lie on top of the others. On top of the big one.

'I stole your mum's ring,' she said. 'I don't really know why. I've still got it if you want it back. It's like you said with the glasses and my bag. Everyone was so focused on the missing people, they weren't looking at the little things.'

Esther blinked and laughed at the same time. 'I didn't even notice it was gone,' she said. 'All these years, huh? You might as well keep it.'

'I don't think I want it.'

Esther shrugged. 'So throw it away.'

Leah knew she wouldn't do that. Perhaps she'd finally sell it? Or maybe she *would* keep it. Perhaps she liked having it hidden in her drawer more than she would ever admit.

'I know I said sorry the other day,' Esther added. 'But the new year's thing, the bonfire...'

'The bullying?'

Esther looked to the floor, suitably – and probably genuinely – shamed. 'The bullying,' she said. 'Dad had told me the day before what had happened and I had no idea how to handle it. I couldn't have anyone looking at him, or me. I suppose I wanted to deflect attention – and you were there. I regretted it right away but it was already too late.'

Leah didn't outright accept the apology but she did nod her head in recognition of hearing it. It was another thing that now made sense so many years on.

'What do we do about Owen?' Leah asked, and then: 'Did you burn his van?'

That got a slow nod. 'Moment of madness. I'd been working on a case involving arson and it was in my head. The only CCTV on that side of the park faces the other way.' She nodded towards the window. 'I saw his van as I was leaving here and I just thought, "Why not?" I think I'd been working too late. Then Dad's so ill, and I've been thinking about that a lot. I had to sit through that stupid forum all Sunday, listening to idiots talk about aliens. I saw you at the back, hiding behind the pillar, and it just all...' She held up her hands. 'Moment of madness. I don't think there was even anything in the van at the end of it all.'

Leah almost laughed at the idea of this respected, suited woman hurrying across a park to set fire to a van, when she knew cameras were facing the other way. Using tips and tricks she'd picked up from working on a case about arson.

'We don't need to do anything about Owen,' Leah said, making the decision for both of them. 'He's got snippets. I'm sure the film will be interesting but there's no way he can know what actually happened.'

It felt as if Esther was going to say something, that she didn't agree. When she did speak, she'd moved on.

'I'll tell Dad,' she said. 'We're the only people that know. The three of us. I'll tell him that Vicky tried to poison all four of you, not just three. I don't know if it's better if it was a suicide thing, or if she was an outright killer.'

She thought on that for a second.

'She was ill, wasn't she?' Esther added. 'That's the thing. We should've got her help. Not just the magazines. The whole thing with having an interest and then dropping it. More than that. There'd have been so many signs.'

Leah let the other woman talk. She had nothing to add.

'You're not going to tell anyone, are you?' Esther asked, suddenly concerned. 'Now you know what Dad did and why. It was for Vicky. He did it for her. It wasn't about him.'

Leah spoke as truthfully as she ever had. 'I'll never tell a soul.'

Esther sighed with relief, slumping deeper into her chair – and there was something about the way she held herself that had Leah seeing Vicky.

'I wish we'd had this conversation years ago,' Esther said. 'I'd see you now and then and I'd always think about a moment like this. Where we just, y'know, let it all out. This wasn't fair to you.'

That much was true – except Esther didn't get to continue because her phone rang. She checked the screen and, for a second, it looked as if she was going to put it back down.

As soon as she said 'hello', there was something in her voice – and Leah knew who was on the other end. There was a 'That's right', an 'OK', a 'Right', an 'At least that's one thing' and then the final: 'I'll finish up here and come over. Thanks for the call.'

Esther hung up and sighed, then rubbed her eyes.

'That was the hospice,' she said. 'Dad died about twenty minutes ago.'

FORTY-FIVE

FIVE DAYS LATER

Esther parked on the verge and popped the boot, before walking around to the back of the car with Leah. She removed the bag and then locked the car.

'This way,' she said – although Leah already knew. She'd known the moment Esther had taken the turn.

They tucked in close to the high hedge, walking until they reached a wide metal gate that was browny-red with rust. Esther squished herself into the space between the side of the gate and the hedge, easing herself around and into the field beyond. Leah copied, fighting the foliage until the women were on the same side.

'Dad said he wanted to lay them somewhere nice,' Esther said, starting to lead the way. 'He said you were on the way back from somewhere one day and—'

'The beach,' Leah said.

Esther slowed. 'You remember?'

'Of course,' Leah replied – and she did. That day at the beach she'd had with Vicky and her dad, followed by the drive back when they'd found that meadow of wild flowers. He had left them to explore all that colour. One of the best days of Leah's life, and a time in which she realised what it was to have a real father. That day had been such a contrast to the time Leah's own dad had picked up her and Vicky – then locked them in the car.

It had stuck in her mind, but it had clearly been in that of Vicky's dad as well.

'He said you just ran,' Esther added. 'You and Vick, just running around the wild flowers.'

The field wasn't like that at the moment. It wasn't quite the season. The grass was long and damp.

'I used to wonder if this place actually existed,' Leah said, as they walked. 'It was this amazing day and it's not like you pay attention to the route when you're in the back of the car. Your dad just stopped and we were here. I guess we were giddy from the ice cream and the beach and, yeah, we just ran.'

Leah allowed her hand to dangle as she touched the top of a long piece of grass. The memory was so close.

'Dad brought me here a few weeks after it all happened,' Esther said. 'It was January and cold. Everything was frozen but he wanted me to see. He kept saying, "It's not really like this," as if the frost offended him. That he hadn't brought Vicky and the others to this icy wasteland, that it actually meant something.'

There was a croak to Esther's voice, perhaps even a tear. It had been a long few days for both of them.

'It's amazing in the summer,' Leah said, and she gripped Esther's arm as the other woman wobbled.

'I never came back until now,' Esther said. 'I kept looking for it on maps, wondering if there was a satellite picture of the colour. Wanting to know who owned it. It just sort of... exists.'

That was the way Leah saw it, too. A fantasy field that now meant more than she could have ever guessed.

Esther was walking slower now, openly weeping as she

gripped Leah's hand and led her towards the back of the field. An ancient oak towered high, drenching the area in shadow, and Esther continued past that, into the dim sunshine.

'They're here,' Esther said. 'I don't know exactly where. Dad brought me past the tree and said this was the spot. He said it took him four nights to dig three graves.'

There was nothing to mark the spot, other than its position to the tree.

Esther opened her bag for Leah to see. The pile of Vicky's cult interest magazines were inside.

'I wondered if we should burn them,' she said. 'Not right here, but' – she opened her arms indicating the wide open space – 'here.'

Leah didn't ask why Esther had kept everything for such a long time – but then Esther answered anyway.

'I think I always knew I'd have to tell someone one day. I didn't know it'd be you.'

She held up the bag, an exact copy of the one in which Leah had been returned her knife. 'Where d'you reckon?' she asked.

Leah wasn't bothered and it was hard to pretend she was.

In the end, Esther found a spot in the corner of the field, far enough away from the hedge to ensure no fire could spread. She really did know about burning things.

The two women watched as Vicky's old magazines first singed and then caught fire. Despite the dampness of the ground, they lasted barely a minute before curling and crisping into blackened ashes. The flames shrank with the lack of fuel – and then disappeared entirely as Esther stamped them out.

That was that.

The two of them walked back to the area in which the three girls lay somewhere beneath their feet. The leaves on the tree whistled and fluttered their song. Leah wondered if she'd return when the flowers were out. Maybe.

'Are you going to be OK?' Esther asked.

'Dad's getting out of prison within a year,' Leah said. 'He's getting remarried. His soon-to-be wife wants to be friends.'

'A new mum.'

'Don't say that.'

Esther smiled kindly. 'I didn't mean it like that.'

'I know.'

'Do you think we should check in on each other?' Esther asked. 'It's just, this is our secret, isn't it? We know something nobody else knows, or is going to know.'

Leah thought of the women in her life who'd shaped her. Deborah was the main one, of course. Shirley, too. Perhaps there was room for one more, even if there wasn't much between them in age.

'I think I'd like that,' she said.

'Me too,' Esther replied quietly. When it was only them, when they were out of her office, there was a softer tone to her voice.

'Did I tell you Owen's van was empty,' Esther said. 'All his footage is in the cloud and his equipment was in his hotel room. The only damage was to the vehicle.'

'Is that a good thing?'

Esther thought for a moment. 'The good thing is that he told me the police have no leads on who set the fire.'

'Kids,' Leah said.

'Always kids,' Esther replied. 'They get blamed for everything.'

It was true. Kids or Leah's father.

'Do you want me to forward you Owen's emails?' Esther asked. 'He contacts me every day with updates on who he's spoken to, and what he's found. It feels like you and me are in this together now.'

'I don't think I want to know,' Leah said. 'I know the proper truth.'

'I told him you're the biggest victim of everyone,' Esther

said. 'That he should make that clear in his film. You're the innocent one, aren't you? You didn't do anything.'

Leah bit her lip and stared off towards the tree. 'No,' she said. 'I didn't.'

FORTY-SIX

THE SLEEPOVER

SATURDAY 18 DECEMBER 1999

The stolen ring was burning a hole in Leah's pocket as she headed into Vicky's kitchen. An untouched pizza sat on the side, the pepperoni slices curled and juicy, steam still rising. Leah's mouth was watering as she felt the urge to grab a slice and stuff it down. The only reason she didn't was because of the footsteps behind her.

It was Vicky, smiling and bright, as if the moment upstairs hadn't happened. Like she hadn't made the cutting remark about eating too much, or openly speculated on whether Leah was worthwhile as a friend.

Leah was holding a glass of water and used it to tap the vodka bottle that was open on the side. 'Do you want some more?' Leah asked.

Vicky eyed the bottle but ignored the question. 'Do you want to see something?' she asked, moving on without waiting for a reply. 'Remember I said Dad was annoyed about his moles, look at this.'

She opened the cupboard under the sink and knelt,

reaching right to the back, before pulling out a small bottle marked 'strychnine'.

'It's poison,' she said. 'I can't believe he's going to kill all the moles just because he likes the grass. It's ridiculous isn't it? Poor things.'

She returned the poison to the back of the cupboard and then pushed herself up.

'Do you reckon I should say something to him?'

If she'd asked the question an hour before, Leah would've given an honest answer. Now, she wasn't sure. It felt like a test in that, if she gave the wrong answer, Vicky might come to a different conclusion as to whether they should be friends.

Leah couldn't think of a way to tell Vicky that this was all she had. These three people were her life.

'I don't know,' Leah said.

'I think I might tell him tomorrow,' Vicky replied, although the final word took her two attempts and a hiccup. She was tipsy at best, probably a bit drunk. 'You gonna eat that?' Vicky asked, nodding at the pizza. She sounded friendly, and yet the split personality of the cruelty from upstairs gave everything a darker tinge.

'I'm not hungry,' Leah lied.

'Suit yourself.' Vicky picked up the plate and was past Leah, on the way towards the living room when she stopped and eyed the vodka.

'I'll bring in some drinks,' Leah said.

Vicky bit into a slice of the pizza and giggled. There was no reply as she disappeared through to the door.

Leah stood, listening as her trio of friends laughed about something from the living room.

Laughed about something, or laughed about... *her?*

There was Vicky saying that Leah's mum let her dad hit her, as if that was in any way true. The dig about the pizza. The idea that they would 'probably' still be friends. That had all been started by Jazz and her stupid mum, saying they couldn't be friends any longer. And then there was Harriet. Stupid Harriet with her...

...With her mum and dad who actually loved her.

Stupid, lucky Harriet.

It was all going to end, whether Leah wanted it to or not. They'd be back at school in the new year, the new millennium, and Jazz's mum would have banned her from being Leah's friend. Once that happened, Vicky and Harriet would pick a side – and it wouldn't be Leah's

This was their last night together... and if that was the case, it might as well *really* be their last night.

Leah poured three glasses of vodka and topped up her own with water. She'd had one drink and that was plenty enough for her. She was already feeling sleepy from the vodka and pizza.

Leah waited for a moment, eyeing the trio of drinks – and then she opened the cupboard under the sink.

FORTY-SEVEN

The vodka.

Leah remembered now.

She always had, really – but it was at the front of her mind.

The tree waved and whispered in the breeze. It knew Esther's secret but it didn't know Leah's. Nobody did, and nobody ever would.

Leah had watched her mum be punched in the face and then look into a police officer's eyes to insist she had walked into a door. A fifteen-year-old Leah knew lies and she knew secrets. How many other girls her age could claim such a thing?

She had been as surprised as anyone when she had woken up on a Sunday morning to an empty room. Leah had expected three bodies. She figured she'd tell the police that Vicky had made the drinks all night, because it was her vodka. The poison was Vicky's dad's, and why would anyone else know about it? They'd see the bottle in the bin and figure it out.

Leah even had the excuse about tipping her drink into the pot plant ready to go, as if Vicky had tried to poison her as well. The idea was so ingrained that she'd told it to the police officer – and Owen two decades later. In truth, she had only had one drink of vodka all night. Everything else had been water and that one drink really *had* knocked her out.

The key to being a great liar was to surround the fib in truth.

She *was* a lightweight and she *had been* a heavy sleeper. Two truths. One massive lie.

Failing that, Leah would deny and deny and deny – just like her mum. If someone said they'd watched Leah's father get violent, her mum would say it wasn't true. It was a door. It was the stairs. Silly her. Deny, deny, deny.

Leah had tipped her drink into the pot plant because she was a lightweight. Say it, repeat it, say it again – and nobody would be able to claim otherwise. She was ready.

Then she'd woken up and there were no bodies. The rest of the world had lived through a different mystery to Leah. They all wondered where the girls had gone, Leah wanted to know what had happened to three dead bodies.

She'd wavered in recent days, a creeping concern that, somehow – impossibly – Vicky was alive somewhere.

She wasn't, of course.

Leah would always wonder if she really had seen Tom moving the bodies, or if it was actually a dream. The things she'd done had caused him to spend more than two decades *believing* his daughter to be a killer.

After carrying Vicky, Jasmine and Harriet to the empty house, he'd driven them to a field and dug their graves. Leah had seen how hard it was to dig just one. What must it have taken from him – not only then, but in the years since?

He would have lowered his unmoving, unbreathing, daughter into the ground and driven away to live with that forever.

And none of it was true.

Leah was the person responsible. He'd thought he was saving his daughter but, instead, he'd saved somebody else's.

And, perhaps, Leah hadn't been dreaming when she saw

him doing it. What was true was that she should never have opened up to Mark, and wasn't sure why she had. There was love, of course – but it wasn't real, not with him. There hadn't been a lot of love in Leah's life.

Now, back in the field that would again be wild flowers one day, Esther could talk about the secret they shared – but there was only one *actual* secret, and it was Leah's.

'I have to get back,' Esther said, eyeing the gate in the distance. 'Shall we go?'

In the moment, Leah had forgotten the other woman was there.

Leah eyed her feet, and what was below. It was the end of this chapter of her life. Sometimes, she wondered if she regretted doing what she had. They didn't deserve it, did they? It wasn't Jazz's fault that her mum was a bitch. It wasn't Vicky's fault that she flitted between interests and had a nasty streak. Esther speculated that she was ill but Leah didn't think that was true.

And then poor Harriet, who did nothing except have parents who loved her. Wonderful, kind, devoted Deborah. The mother Leah never had.

And then she did.

Leah hadn't planned it that way but then she hadn't arranged to be at the hospice at the same time as Tom's door was open. Leah had fate in her corner. It had given her Deborah's love. It had given her Shirley's. It had led her to Tom.

No, not 'it'. Fate was a she. Leah and fate were friends. They always had been.

Besides, Leah was a good person and good people didn't do bad things. Look at the help Leah had given Fiona and Cody. Look at the son she had raised. A bad person wouldn't do that, would they?

Leah took one final gaze at the old oak tree. She didn't think she'd return to see the wild flowers, after all.

'Let's go,' she said.

KERRY WILKINSON PUBLISHING TEAM

Editorial
Ellen Gleeson

Line edits and copyeditor
Jade Craddock

Proofreader
Tom Feltham

Design
Emma Graves

Production
Hannah Snetsinger
Nadia Michael

Marketing
Alex Crow
Melanie Price
Occy Carr
Ciara Rosney

Publicity
Noelle Holten
Kim Nash
Sarah Hardy
Jess Readett

Distribution
Marina Valles
Stephanie Straub

Audio
Alba Proko
Melissa Tran
Carmelite Studios
Olivia Darnely

Rights and contracts
Peta Nightingale
Richard King
Saidah Graham